Maybe safety wasn't the only thing on Mary's mind.

Despite her bruises, aches, fears and anger, she could not remember ever feeling as turned on as she did now, strapped into a bucket seat beside Ford, sailing down a deserted highway, watching for a murderer in the rearview mirror.

Unreal as that seemed, her wanting him made a weird sort of sense. Ford wanted her. His eyes said it. All those little touches said it. If she gave him a chance, he would follow through.

Any civilized woman would fight it, she told herself. She would concentrate on the other, more imminent danger. The threat of death. That ought to cool her off in a hurry…

Dear Reader,

Welcome—we're sure you'll find that only Silhouette Sensation can provide a truly sensational start to the New Year.

To prove it, Linda Turner brings us *The Man Who Would Be King*—the brand-new, exciting first story in our ROMANCING THE CROWN series. One book a month for twelve months, where the royal family of Montebello are determined to find their missing heir. But the search for the prince is not without danger— or passion! Look out for the second story, *The Princess and the Mercenary*, next month.

Where one series begins, another ends. Popular author Ruth Langan provides us with *His Father's Son*—the final instalment of her highly successful trilogy THE LASSITER LAW. We hope to see more from Ruth soon.

Also this month, there's a mystery that only one drop-dead gorgeous man can help with in popular author Cheryl St. John's *The Truth About Toby*; a detective and his suspect who get up close and personal in *Remember the Night* by Linda Castillo; a less than amused abductee who can't stop lusting after her captor in Lyn Stone's *Beauty and the Badge*; and a possible husband-and-wife reunion in *Keeping Caroline* by Vickie Taylor.

We hope you enjoy them as much as we did.

Happy New Year!

The Editors.

Beauty and the Badge

LYN STONE

SILHOUETTE®
SENSATION™

*First published in Great Britain 2003
Silhouette Books, Eton House, 18-24 Paradise Road,
Richmond, Surrey TW9 1SR*

© Lynda Stone 1999

ISBN 0 373 07952 4

18-0103

*Printed and bound in Spain
by Litografía Rosés S.A., Barcelona*

LYN STONE

loves creating pictures with words. Paints, too. Her love affair with writing and art began at primary school, when she won a prize for her colourful poster for Book Week. She spent the prize money on books, one of which was *Little Women*.

She re-wrote the ending so that Jo marries her childhood sweetheart. That's because Lyn had a childhood sweetheart herself and wanted to marry him when she grew up. She did. And now she is living her 'happily-ever-after' in north Alabama with the same guy. She and Allen have travelled the world, had two children, four grandchildren and experienced some wild adventures along the way.

Whether writing romantic historicals or contemporary fiction, Lyn insists on including elements of humour, mystery and danger. Perhaps because that other book she purchased all those years ago was a *Nancy Drew!*

To Margaret O'Neill Marbury, for encouraging words, attention to detail and suggestions that really work! Thank you for everything.

Chapter 1

Two years out of the jungle definitely refined a man's tastes, Ford Devereaux thought. He recalled much uglier feasts than this mangled package of stale peanut-butter crackers.

He drained his can of warm Coke, memory giving it the flavor of the tablets he had once used to purify swamp water.

This job definitely paid better than chasing around the armpits of the Southern Hemisphere on covert operations. But just for a fraction of a moment, he missed that. Missed the adrenaline rush he used to crave. The danger. The action.

Ford bit down on the last cracker, laughed softly and shook his head. He certainly didn't expect any excitement today, not in tailing a nursery-school teacher around Nashville. The only places she'd been so far were home and work. Boring.

Well, at least now that he was working for a civilian

agency, he could feel reasonably certain he would live to cash his next paycheck.

The tasteful oval sign, barely visible from behind the hedge where he had parked his Jeep, read Cartland's Pre-school Academy. A prestigious day care is what it was, set smack in the middle of one of Music City's more affluent communities. He'd lived in this town for twelve years as a kid, and had never known places like this even existed. His early day-care had consisted of the old lady next door, who'd been obsessed with soap operas. Ford couldn't even remember her name now, only the smell of her cigarettes and the lack of food in her refrigerator.

Ford wondered why his subject, Mary Shaw, worked here. Getting experience for raising a future brood, or as a cover occupation? Judging by the house she lived in and the Jag she drove, she sure didn't need the salary.

The Bureau didn't have much on her yet, but they soon would. By this time tomorrow, they would know everything about her, right down to the kind of toothpaste she used. At the moment, all they knew for certain was that she held a fortune in diamonds in her hot little hands.

The quiet drone of a motor alerted him. Ford watched as a green sedan rolled slowly past the school. When he glimpsed the familiar profile of the driver, Ford snapped upright. *Damien Perry!*

The old adrenaline Ford had missed kicked in, switching every sense he had on alert. To hell with the surveillance, he had to get the Shaw woman out of there *now*.

Parents would be picking up the kids soon and then the teachers would leave. Perry probably would circle the block a few times to check out the terrain, then park and wait until she came outside. When she did, he'd snatch her. Or put a bullet through her head, depending on which he'd been hired to do. From what he knew about Perry, Ford would bet on the bullet.

He had to hurry before Perry got in place. There was no time to plan; he'd just have to wing it. He cranked his Jeep, pulled up the circular drive to the entrance of the nursery school and got out. With one hand, he checked the position of his weapon at the back of his waist while he pushed the door open with the other.

Just inside, a young woman behind the counter—Lucille Gibbons, according to her desk plate—glanced up at him and dimpled. "May I help you, sir?"

Ford started to flash his badge, but thought better of it. No time for explanations. He quickly strode right past her, unlocked the low gate, and noted the colorful signs along the hallway. Mary Shaw's name sign stood out like a bright red flag on the very first door.

"Wait a minute!" the receptionist called, charging around the counter like a defensive end. "I'm sorry, you can't just—"

Ford opened the classroom door, sensing the chunky little Miss Gibbons right on his heels.

Toddlers scooted here and there, dragging tiny chairs into a loose formation around a woman seated cross-legged on a big red cushion. She held a Dr. Seuss book in her hand.

When she looked up at him, Ford took a second to verify her identity since he had never seen her up close in person. Mid-twenties, long dark hair, green eyes, left hand sporting a good-size solitaire. Yep, everything fit.

He couldn't help but notice the heavy lashes, perfect nose, and wide, expressive mouth. She looked...soft, vulnerable. Her file never mentioned those little details. And whoever took those lousy photos of her ought to have his camera smashed.

Again, Ford started to identify himself, but the sputtering receptionist was too close, close enough to hear every word. No point in letting Perry know exactly who had Ms. Shaw. Instead, he drew in a deep breath, moving forward as he spoke. "I can't let you marry him outta spite, honey! Just because we had that one little fuss—"

"What do you mean, coming in here like this?" she demanded.

Ford pushed a path through the curious children, leaned over and grabbed her arms just above the elbows. Off-balanced by her ungainly position on the big pillow, she dropped the book and struggled to get her feet under her.

He pressed his lips against her ear and whispered curtly, "I've got to get you out of here. You're in danger."

Then Ford kissed her soundly on the mouth and she froze, just like he knew she would.

Ford recognized the direction of her right knee and shifted his hips to avoid the blow.

Without pausing, he dipped his shoulder to her middle and clamped the backs of her knees with his arm. When he hefted her up, her breath huffed out, choking off a scream.

Miss Gibbons screeched and took off like a shot for the front desk.

Quickly, Ford tried to wade back through the rowdy little toddlers who clung to his legs. "Hey, want to play a funny game with us?" he shouted to the kids.

A chorus of excited "yeahs" and "uh-huhs" erupted.

"Okay, quick! Everybody sit! Hands over your eyes!"

The children dropped like rocks, still noisy, but at least they were out of the way.

He ignored the Shaw woman's breathless curses and the sharp fists bruising his back. He prayed she didn't go lower and hit on the Glock hidden under his jacket.

Ford hurried out the door of the room, giving his burden a sharp bounce to ensure she stayed winded.

Miss Gibbons was busily punching in numbers on the phone—911, no doubt. Ford passed the desk and smiled. "Mind the kids, Miss Lucy!"

As soon as they'd cleared the front entrance, Ford jerked open the Jeep's door and dumped Mary Shaw in the back. By the time she realized the childproof locks wouldn't let her open the rear doors, he had reached the driver's side.

He hopped in and hit the main lock in case she decided

to come over the seat and try the passenger door. She was raising hell, punching at his head and tugging his hair.

Ford had just turned out of the driveway when he saw Perry's Dodge turn the corner. *Damn!* He'd hoped for a clean getaway.

Ford elbowed the Shaw woman off him while the Jeep shot down the street and took the corner on two wheels. Still she flew at him from between the front seats, shrieking like a wild woman, going for his eyes now. He held her off with one hand, his other one maneuvering the steering wheel as best he could.

"FBI!" he shouted, trying to cut through her panic. "Stop fighting me, damn it! Credentials are in my pocket." It took a moment too long for his message to sink in. Her teeth had already sunk in. Right into the back of his hand. "Ouch!"

She let go before she drew blood and backed off. "FBI?"

"FBI," he repeated with a nod for emphasis, flexing his bruised hand. "Right jacket pocket. Go ahead and verify."

For a second, she just sat there. He stole a glance in the rearview mirror and caught her expression of disbelief.

"Sorry about the roughhousing back there, but believe me, it was necessary. I had to get you out of there in a hurry."

She dug into his pocket for his badge folder while he flew down the residential street, checking every few seconds for Perry's vehicle in the mirrors.

"These could be fake," she remarked after she had examined them. She slapped the folder shut and threw it on the front seat.

He scooped it up and stuck it back into his pocket. Lose that, and his ass was grass. "They're real. You can call and check."

"Then why didn't you use them?" she asked angrily. She was beginning to believe him, though, he could tell.

"I'd have had to explain everything, and persuade you

to come with me. Could have taken all day, and I had to hurry.''

Ford glanced in the mirror just as she cocked her head to one side and traced her top lip with her tongue. Lord, she ought not to do that, he thought, glad that he couldn't afford right now to give her his undivided attention. Brief as it was, that kiss had shaken him up a little too much for comfort.

''Does this have to do with Antonio's murder?''

''Bet on it. Somebody's after you, all of a sudden, and *he* doesn't have a badge.''

''But that was night before last. The police kept my name out of the papers. No one has bothered me.''

Ford grimaced as he swung the Jeep into a narrow alley and zipped through to the one-way that would take them back in the opposite direction.

''Trust me, this guy meant to bother you, big time. And he still does. He's about a block and a half behind us.'' Ford swerved suddenly down another side street. He would have to lower his speed. They were approaching downtown now and the traffic would be heavy.

She scooted down in the seat as if she expected gunfire. ''Can you outrun him?''

''Not a chance.''

She gasped. Great. Now he had scared her to death. Well, if she knew the whole truth, she'd be cowering under the seat, hands over her head and screaming. Perry was a suspected hit man. Maybe the Bureau didn't have enough evidence to put him away, but they had put together a file on him. It listed his connections and contained at least two sharp photos that placed him in the right places at the wrong times. Ford never forgot a face, especially one like Perry's.

''We'll have to ditch the Jeep and lose him on foot.'' Ford cut down Deadrick Street. The state museum was a maze Ford knew pretty well. Molly would be working today and she'd help him out. They could cut through the

place and be gone before Perry found the other exit—unless
Perry already knew where it was, guessed the plan, and
was waiting when they came out. It was unlikely, but entirely possible.

But suppose they didn't exit? Ford formed an even wil-
der plan. The boss would choke, and probably stick him
behind a desk for the next five years, but what the hell. He
had already been a little too creative today to get by without
a reprimand, anyway. Blevins would get off on that. The
man lived to chew butt, and Ford's ex-military behind
seemed to be his favorite.

"Hey, you game for a little cat and mouse, Miss Shaw?"

"Only if I can b-be the cat," she answered. Her half
laugh sounded a little sick.

Ford couldn't see her now, crouched as she was in the
corner of the back seat. The poor kid sounded scared, but
he didn't detect unreasonable panic in her voice. She'd
even tried to make a joke. Had to give her an A for effort.

"We'll shake him in the museum," Ford assured her.

He wheeled into an empty space near the entrance,
slammed on the brakes and hit the master unlock button on
his door. "C'mon, kid, make it snappy!"

She bounded out at a run and beat him to the doorway.
Ford risked a quick look down the street to see if Perry had
made it. Not yet, but he would in a minute.

Ford followed her through the two sets of glass doors
and rushed across the lobby to the info desk where his sister
sat straightening pamphlets. She looked up and grinned.
"Hey, Ford! What are you up to?"

"Look, we got a tail on and can't shake him. I need your
van," he snapped.

"Trade for a baby-sit?"

"Two hours, max. And don't go near my Jeep when you
get off. Catch a cab."

"Gotcha," Molly said. She reached into her pocket and
tossed him her key ring. "Wreck it and I'll kill you. Anybody I should watch out for? You need backup?"

"Nope, just stay cool. Thanks, Moll. Pay you back."

"Sure will. Next Saturday at ten," she called after him.

Ford bulldozed through a group of Japanese tourists crowding the stairs, and led the way down to the exhibits. Other than that bunch, the museum seemed fairly deserted for a Friday.

He yanked Mary Shaw along at a fast walk until he spied the covered supply-wagon backed against a dark wall, part of a Civil War camp scene. The large display consisted of trees, bushes, a tent and several mannequins dressed in gray uniforms. Ford whisked up two of the rolled gray blankets lying near the fake campfire and grabbed a billed kepi from a reclining soldier's head.

"Get inside," Ford ordered, and pushed her toward the wagon. "He'll probably be here in a few minutes. We need to see *him*, but I'd just as soon he didn't see *us*, okay?"

"All right." She climbed the wheel, jumped in and huddled down inside the front corner of the wagon. Ford followed her and crouched down beside her.

"Now listen carefully," he instructed. "I'm going to cover you with this blanket. I want you to peep between the cover and the edge of the wagon, right through here." He pointed out the gap.

"When our 'friend' comes by, take a good look at him. Be quick about it. Some people can sense a stare. Don't move. Don't make a sound. Don't even take a deep breath. I need to know if this is the man you saw shoot Antonio. Wait until he's gone and I uncover you before you move or say anything. Got it?"

She looked up at him, her eyes wide with terror.

"You can do this. I know you can," he whispered, then squeezed her shoulder.

He draped the blanket over her and watched for a few seconds after she began staring out the narrow gap between the wagon's canvas cover and wooden frame. Ford admired the way she took orders and behaved under pressure. Not exactly a bundle of courage, but at least she hadn't gone hysterical.

Ms. Shaw made a very small, silent and motionless lump wedged into the corner of the wagon. Even if someone looked in, they couldn't see her unless they climbed up on the wheel and craned around to see inside.

Ford drew his weapon, donned the cap and wrapped the other blanket around himself. Then he quickly stationed himself against the back of the vehicle where he could face the oval opening.

He could see a portion of the open area Perry would have to cross to pass by the exhibit. If the man approached the wagon with anything at all in his hand, Ford fully intended to take him out.

An older couple ambled into Ford's line of vision, walked over and began studying the exhibit. With the kepi pulled low over his eyes, his body wrapped to the neck in the blanket, Ford stared straight ahead. He counted on passing in the dark shadows for another dummy.

Just then, Perry arrived in the area behind the couple, one hand in his jacket pocket. Ford watched his sharp, squinting gaze dart left, then right, scanning for possible hiding places.

With a loud sniff, the old man turned away from the wagon and pointed to one of the standing figures in the foreground. "Hey, Martha, this un looks like Billy's old history teacher, don't he?"

"Just *like* Mr. Carpenter!" the woman agreed, a little too enthusiastically, gaining them a cursory glance from Perry. He walked up behind the couple and gave the exhibit a once-over, settling on the wagon.

Ford inhaled slowly, then held his breath. He didn't dare raise his weapon to draw a bead on Perry, and he couldn't risk firing with the old people between them in any case. He remained frozen. God help them all if the Shaw woman sneezed.

After what seemed like hours, Perry backed away and

continued his search. The interested duo remained for a while longer, arguing the authenticity of the uniforms, piece by piece.

Ford felt his muscles cramp from the tense inertia. Yep, he'd pulled too many routine assignments since he'd left covert ops. Two years ago, he could have held himself immobile for hours. He was out of shape mentally, if not physically.

He hadn't heard so much as an indrawn breath from Mary Shaw. Hadn't seen the slightest wiggle or shudder. Maybe she had fainted in place.

Finally, Martha and her grizzled companion drifted away. Ford could hear their voices diminish with distance. He glanced down at his watch and then held himself motionless for another ten minutes. There were no further sounds that would indicate other visitors nearby.

"Are you okay?" he whispered to the bundle in the corner.

The top of the blanket moved slightly.

"You did just fine," he said, scarcely breathing the words. He clicked his weapon on safety and carefully crawled into the corner next to her.

She shivered then. It escalated into a racking shudder. Ford embraced her rigid little form, patting her back gently. "We'll need to stay here awhile, until he's had time to give it up. Why don't you relax now? Try to sleep or something."

"Sleep!" she rasped. "Are you crazy?" But she didn't attempt to move away. Instead, she fitted her body even closer to his until he felt wrapped around her.

A great sensation, he admitted to himself, but not one he ought to get used to. Her hands twisted in the fabric of his shirt, reminding him of a kitten burrowing out a comfortable place to curl up and nap. Or hide. He squeezed her shoulder with a firm hand, offering what reassurance he could.

Her smallness and air of fragility moved him somehow,

made something tighten right around where her hands were. Lower, too, but he wouldn't let himself think about that right now.

"Was it him?" Ford asked. "Did he shoot your friend?"

"I—I don't know," she said, "I wanted to tell you before—I never saw his face. But it *must* be him! Why else would he be after me?"

She shook her head and quaked again, but she didn't cry. That surprised Ford. He began stroking the tense muscles on either side of her spine. "That's okay, hon. Just take it easy. We'll wait an hour or so, and then I'll take you someplace safe. I won't let him get to you, I promise." Same thing he'd tell anybody who was this scared, Ford assured himself. Made sense to pour oil on the waters, didn't it?

She nodded against his chest. His admiration for her upped another notch. No tears, no screams and no wild panic. That didn't mean she wouldn't fly to pieces when they reached safety, however. He expected that, and would deal with it. For now, though, Ford just thanked his lucky stars she was holding it together.

Finally, she relaxed against him and he could feel her steady, quiet breathing. Maybe she had fallen asleep after all, a handy escape mechanism Ford wished he could ape about now. Every nerve in his body screamed for action. One by one, he encouraged his muscles to unknot.

A mantra would be good, he thought with a smirk; something to chant over and over until it stuck in his brain. Something meaningful like Keep Your Cool. He felt as hot as hell, stirred up to the max, and knew it wouldn't work. He tried it anyway.

She didn't move and neither did he as the heat built. If she woke up right now, she might think he had an additional weapon stuck in the front of his jeans. It felt like steel and was certainly loaded.

His coarse imaginings did absolutely nothing to ease the situation. The harder he worked to suppress his thoughts, the more attention that took from his watching for Perry, so he let them wander as they would.

Ford held her that way for over an hour, hidden from the halfhearted inspection of a few visitors, until his watch read five forty-five. The museum would be closing shortly. He wondered if they should stay the night.

With nothing else to do, Ford tried to analyze the appeal of the woman in his arms. His physical reaction to her came as no real surprise. She was a looker. Not his type, of course. Not by a long shot.

He never picked fragile women who needed coddling. Give him one who'd been around the block a few times, one who could poke disaster right in the eye and then laugh it off.

The guys he worked with might joke around about his tomcat reputation, but Ford chose his women carefully. No soft, sweet clinging vines for him. Not after Nan.

Experience had taught him there were two kinds of women. His mom and his sister, Molly, were both independent, tough, aggressive. Never leaned on a soul.

His ex-wife had been about as opposite to those two as anybody could ever get. And Nan had been *his* opposite as well, in a hell of a lot more than grit and gender.

The differences had appealed to Ford at first. Her pampered upbringing had been the flip side of his own. As Ford's grandma would have said, Nan had been "gently raised," but Ford had been *"drug up."*

She'd had everything she'd ever asked for. But in her second year of college, her father had gone broke, just lost it all. When the old guy had found out that taxes were as inevitable as death, he'd up and died on purpose.

Nan had scrambled around for somebody to latch on to, but none of her former prospects wanted anything to do with the daughter of a suicide who practiced tax evasion. She'd had to search further afield, and had stumbled on Ford. Biggest mistake of her life, he thought. And of his.

Nan's dependence on him, her bid for constant and undivided attention had fed his ego. But it sure hadn't done a damned thing for his career. He had resigned his commission and left a job he did well, intending to study law the way she wanted. Six years in the military down the tubes, just to make his wife happy.

Couldn't say he hadn't tried. The minute the paperwork came through, however, she had left him anyway. For a damned banker. A very rich banker, at that.

Ford blamed himself for letting Nan change his life that way, but he blamed her, too. Not much in the way of a fifty-fifty settlement, but he hadn't had much else to offer.

It had taken her over a year of marriage and a hasty divorce, but Nan had certainly cured his need to be needed. Now he picked women who didn't demand total commitment and half his soul. A few hours of fun and games were about his limit, and he stuck to that. He didn't want anyone stirring up any protective feelings except those required by the job.

Ford glanced down at the sweet-scented cocoon nestled trustingly against him. No, he could never afford this little butterfly, even if she were available. And innocent.

The night before last, she had witnessed the murder of Antonio, the antiques dealer they'd had under investigation for smuggling stolen jewels out of the country for recutting and sale. The death was related, no doubt about it.

A listening device had picked up the conversation between Mary Shaw and Antonio just prior to the shooting, when Antonio had given her the gems.

Three weeks ago, while delving through the reports, Ford had made a connection between a series of three major jewel heists, this robbery of the Portsmouth gems included. Each of the owners had gotten a recent appraisal on his collection that was subsequently stolen. They all had used the same appraiser, a Nelson McEvan from New York. The man had since disappeared.

The perp who cracked the safe and shot the owner had been apprehended in the Portsmouth case. He couldn't identify the mastermind who had hired him anonymously to steal the gems, but had named Antonio as the man who was to receive the goods. These were not stones anyone could sell on the open market. They'd be instantly recognizable by their size alone.

The team Ford worked with would locate McEvan eventually, but meanwhile, they meant to capture every human link in the chain that led to Amsterdam, where the disposition of the gems was to take place. So, they were following through with this little bag of goodies, the Portsmouth diamonds.

Blevins himself had taken his turn watching the antiques dealer that night. He had seen Mary Shaw enter the shop. But he hadn't seen the murderer. Too busy listening to Mary's conversation with Antonio, Ford supposed. Blevins's ineptness at street work didn't surprise him much. The man was a computer wienie, and a good one, apparently. That was how he'd gotten promoted to senior agent. But being in charge of a task-force team was a real challenge for him. He had let Mary Shaw walk without even having her searched, saying she would lead them straight to the overseas courier. So far, she hadn't done that.

On Blevins's orders, Ford had monitored her every step since then. No way she could have passed those jewels on.

One of their junior agents had questioned her briefly before the police had released her. Blevins, as agent in charge, immediately ordered Ford to watchdog duty.

Now Perry was after her. If he intended to kill her, that was probably to keep her from identifying him as the shooter. If he wanted to grab her alive, that meant he must know she had the gems. Either way, she'd wind up dead if Ford didn't prevent it.

Just what he needed, Ford thought with a smirk—a hard-on for a woman who was either a criminal or stupid enough to help a friend who was. But he had a gut hunch Mary Shaw had been suckered into all this.

Now that she realized this was no lark, she was scared

out of her little mind. Or maybe this delicacy was all an act and she was tough as boot leather.

Whatever the truth turned out to be, Mary Shaw was not a female he could afford to fool around with, even in his fantasies. Trouble was, every time he touched her, every time he looked at her or even thought about her, those fantasies gained a few more details.

Now he wished he had stayed in the jungles of South America where all he had to worry about were rebels and snakes.

Chapter 2

Mary woke with a start. She brushed frantically at the scratchy mask covering half her face.

"Easy there," a deep voice whispered. "You're okay."

She pushed away from the hard, masculine chest where she had rested and sat up. Everything came back in a rush: the preschool, this man, the car chase, hiding here. The *murderer!* Had she fainted? "Where is he?" she whispered.

"Probably outside watching the Jeep."

"How will we get out of here?" she asked, not even caring that she sounded afraid. She was afraid. Damn scared.

"Back way. We'll take my sister's van, like I planned."

Mary nodded, remembering the incident at the front desk and the tall, pretty redhead who acted as though this happened every day. "Molly?"

"Right." He smiled down at Mary and brushed the hair out of her eyes with one long finger. "You ready to go, ma'am?"

Ma'am, indeed. Too late to play the gentleman now, Mr.

Fed, she thought. Not very convincing after the caveman act. But he *had* saved her life.

He helped her untangle herself from the musty blanket and climb out of the wagon. Silently, he clasped her hand in his. It felt as warm and comforting as his voice, though there was nothing soft about this man.

Mary followed him up the stairs and toward an unmarked door. She shuddered as he drew his gun and checked the surrounding area. He kept her directly behind him as they exited the museum and headed for a blue van parked nearby.

"Where are we going?" she asked while she buckled in and he cranked the vehicle. "Agent—Devereaux, is it?"

"'Ford' will do. We'll go to my place until I can arrange to take you to a safe house."

Mary inspected the man who was taking her home with him. Up until this point—though she *had* noticed—she had been too frightened to care much what he looked like.

It was the aura of the man that had really impressed her, even when he had first arrived in her classroom, even as he had carried her out like a war trophy. The man possessed a presence that instantly overpowered, and not just physically.

He tempered his tough aggressiveness with a kind of humor Mary didn't understand. But it did soften his attitude enough that she found him intriguing instead of detestable. He was a rogue. She recognized the type, and it was one she always avoided.

Yet he had made her feel protected, even while someone was stalking her. He exuded an air of capability only certain men possessed, as though he always had everything under absolute control. Mary found that a lot more important than his looks or his manners. Especially in this situation.

But the man's looks were certainly nothing to disregard. She stole another glimpse to reaffirm her impressions. Thirty to thirty-five, she would guess. Strong, very tall, with the build and grace of an athlete. Square jaw with the faint

shadow of a beard. Dark hair, nearly black, which he wore
a bit too long for government work. A real head-turner, she
observed clinically. And he knew it, too.

His deep blue, long-lashed eyes had seemed very warm
and kind until she had returned the look. Then they turned
wary, cool, and looked away. Not interested. Fine, then.
Neither was she.

She wouldn't look again. What did she care if someone
had broken his nose? It was none of her business. He'd
probably asked for it. She'd have done it herself this very
afternoon if she could have reached it.

Mary risked a quick glance. And while she was at it, she
wouldn't think about that perfect mouth with lips that
gently curved down when he was lost in thought. Like now.
Or how it felt against her own when he had kissed her at
the school. She was definitely not interested in his mouth.

All right, so he was handsome, she admitted to herself.
Gorgeous enough to stir lust in a statue. A hotshot, too—
she would bet her last dime on it. A daredevil.

Thank God he *wasn't* interested. After all he had done
for her today, she would hate to have to tell him to get lost.

Mary smoothed her wrinkled slacks over the cramped
muscles of her thighs and sighed. "That man. He's trying
to kill me, isn't he? Because of what he thinks I saw him
do."

She felt him cast her a long look as he stopped for a red
light. "Yes, he is," he answered honestly. She wished he
had lied. Then he added, "But I don't intend to let him."

Mary smiled, still staring down at her hands. She flexed
the finger wearing Jim's ring. "Thank you."

"You're welcome," he said, and chuckled. She liked the
sound, deep-pitched and suggestive. It did something warm
to her insides that no other laugh had ever done. The fact
that he found the situation humorous should make her angry, but instead she found it somehow reassuring.

"Are you always this polite or are you just still scared
to death?" he asked, grinning.

"Yes."

He laughed full out then, as though they hadn't a care in the world. "Both, huh? At least you're honest. I gotta say, you held up pretty well, all things considered."

Something suddenly occurred to her, and Mary turned in her seat to stare at him.

"What?" he demanded, shooting smiling glances at her while he changed gears and maneuvered through the traffic.

"I just now thought about it. Why did we hide in that wagon when you had this van available? We could easily have made it out the back door before we were followed. Was what you subjected me to back there really necessary? Couldn't the police have arrested that man later and arranged a lineup for me to identify him?"

"Hey, where'd your adventurous spirit go, girl?" he asked a little too brightly.

"I am not a *girl!* Now was it *necessary?*" she repeated, more firmly this time.

His lips tightened and he concentrated on the next turn, ignoring her question.

Mary shook her head, more disappointed than she could have imagined that he had proved so reckless with her safety. "You risked my life, Mr. Devereaux. *Our* lives!"

He pulled into a complex of modest condominiums, guided the van into a parking space and shut off the motor. Then he faced her, his expression serious and very professional. "Sometimes, in this business, snap decisions are necessary, Ms. Shaw. What happened frightened you. Naturally, you would have preferred a safer course of action."

"Recognizing my feelings, are you? Think that gets you off the hook?" she fumed. "Well, I happen to believe avoiding danger is a mark of sanity, even if you don't!"

He scoffed. "So now you're saying I'm insane! Is that nice?"

"It was an idiotic thing to do!" she replied, angry enough to punch him. Somewhere in the back of her mind, Mary realized her sudden fury might be a result of the afternoon's harrowing events. Nerves. Had he done the only reasonable thing? Or was she right about him? "You must have some deep-seated need to show off, or else a death wish."

Very slowly, his movements deliberate as if to control his temper, he removed the key from the ignition, opened the door and got out. Mary watched as he rounded the van and opened her door.

"Let's get inside, and you can play doctor all you want."

Mary stiffened at the outrageous suggestion. "I would hate to think that was intended as sexual innuendo, *Agent* Devereaux!"

"I would hate for you to think so, too, Miz Shaw," he drawled. "It could be very embarrassing if you confused your wishful thinking with reality. I was merely anticipating the rest of your half-baked analysis."

"You are…really crude!" she said through gritted teeth, wishing she dared call him what she was really thinking.

"And crazy," he added with a lift of one dark brow. "Let's not forget crazy."

For a long moment they stayed exactly where they were, glaring at each other until he broke the highly charged silence.

"Now why don't we get you inside where you can throw the rest of your little tantrum without the risk of getting shot?"

Mary stalked along beside him, shooting daggers he didn't even bother to notice.

"Here we are," Ford announced as he opened the front door of his condo. They would be safe enough here for the time being, he thought. He had only moved in a week ago and the address wasn't on file at headquarters yet. Nobody knew he had bought the condo because he really hadn't bought it for himself.

He meant to live here only for as long as he was based in Nashville—a couple of months or less—and then move his mother in when he had to go. She would never leave their old neighborhood unless he pretended he needed somebody to live here and look after the place for him.

"Love your decor," she said as she scanned the living room.

Ford looked around, seeing it through her eyes. She would be used to something a hell of a lot fancier, but his place wasn't all that bad. It looked like what it was—temporary bachelor digs.

"At least everything matches, even the cardboard boxes," he quipped. The furniture was mostly new, and he hadn't bought a single thing that wasn't some shade of brown. Guy stuff, and it suited him just fine. "I lean toward early chaos."

She hummed some kind of noncommittal response, then asked, "Do you have a bathroom?"

"Indoor plumbing and everything, would you believe it?" He pointed down the short hallway. "Careful, don't step on the rats. They're pets."

After she disappeared, Ford shucked off his jacket and went to the kitchen. He was examining the contents of the fridge when she returned.

"I sincerely hope you keep something besides samples of evidence in there," she said.

"You want food or penicillin?" he asked, as he emerged with a half carton of eggs. He thanked God there wasn't really any mold or junk on anything. Probably the only thing that saved him was the fact that he had been here less than a week.

He saw that she had combed her hair and washed her face. Even free of makeup and wearing those wrinkled clothes, she still looked classier than any model he had ever seen. Must be in the smooth way she moved or her bone structure. Hard to tell. It was just there, whatever "it" was. Probably inborn, like the silver spoon in her mouth. That continued to bother him. Why would a rich girl get tangled up in a jewel theft? Thrills?

"You cook?" she asked, one haughty little eyebrow arched.

Ford laid the eggs on the counter and reached for the cheese. "I guess you expect eggs Benedict or something."

Both eyebrows flew up in a hopeful expression. "You make eggs Benedict?"

He laughed. "I don't even know what the hell it is, much less how to fix it. You get 'em scrambled."

She shrugged. Ford delved into a lower cabinet for his nonstick frying pan, talking over his shoulder. "Hunger's a good sign you've recovered from our race around town. Since you have, I wonder why you aren't playing Twenty Questions about now."

She made herself right at home, Ford noticed. Reaching up, she dragged down two plastic plates out of the cabinet and began opening all the drawers looking for silverware.

"Someone tried to kill me and you got me out of danger," she said softly. "Now I suppose you will have them caught so that I can get back to my life. What more should I know?"

"That your faith astounds me?" he asked dryly, whipping the eggs with a vengeance. "Put on some coffee, will you?"

He watched her comply, marking the tremble of her hands and the paleness of her face. Much as he was tempted to offer her a little sympathy right now, it would just make her fall apart. When she did that, Ford didn't want it to be on his shift. Since he was such a sucker for tears and lost-kitten looks, he didn't trust himself not to get really involved. Blevins could handle all that after Ford took her in.

"Toast?" he suggested, nodding toward the bread box and toaster as he scraped the eggs around the pan.

She took a deep breath and gave her head a quick shake, unaware that Ford kept her in his peripheral vision. Too bad, he thought. Got herself in a little too deep. That would teach her to choose her playmates more carefully next time.

Mary Shaw didn't strike him as tough enough for this kind of deal. If she had a motive, he couldn't think what it might be. She must have plenty of money. Her clothes were obviously expensive—looked like designer stuff to him. And he'd damned near die for a vintage Jag like hers, left sitting in the back lot at the preschool. Why had she gotten mixed up in all this, and how deeply involved was she?

He doubted she'd do much time for it, if any, given her lack of priors. She would plead ignorance. Maybe she really didn't know where the gems came from. Yeah, right. And maybe she never read the papers or watched the news.

The diamonds weren't on her, he knew that much. Her sweater and pants fitted her too well to conceal them. Wherever she had hidden the things, the guys would find them eventually. She couldn't have gotten rid of them since the murder because Ford had watched her every move. She hadn't been anywhere except home and the school. No drops had been made. Nobody had contacted her in person or by phone. No outgoing mail.

If only Perry hadn't turned up, Ford could have waited her out the way he was supposed to do.

Ford heaped the eggs out onto the plates while reveling in the rich scent of coffee. He loved it. Boy, how he'd suffered being smack in the middle of Colombia that time and unable to get a decent cup of the stuff. Irony at its worst. Staying out of sight and alive had taken precedence then, but only just.

He laid the frying pan in the sink and went back to the refrigerator. Then he plunked a bottle down on the table in front of her. "Want some catsup on your eggs?"

She cringed, looking a little nauseated. Probably all the excitement was catching up with her. Ford shrugged and turned to pour the coffee.

The man was altogether too sure of himself, Mary thought. He was certainly no gentleman. But considering her current problem, sensitivity and politeness ranked way down there on her list of preferred qualities in a man.

His quick thinking had saved her. Surely he hadn't turned right around and risked her life on purpose. Now that she thought about it, he must have had a very good reason for not escaping out that back door of the museum immediately.

Her accusation had riled him, that was all. Had made him too defensive to explain why. He liked to goad her—she knew that much. He did it on purpose.

Well, she didn't have to like the magnificent Neanderthal, but she supposed she really ought to be thankful.

And Devereaux *was* magnificent, all six feet of him. Tanned and muscled, with quick blue eyes that didn't miss a trick, and a smile that stunned. If she were not already engaged to a perfectly wonderful man, she might even consider looking twice.

Even then, she would never do anything but look, however. Ford Devereaux epitomized the kind of man she dodged at all costs—brash, cocky, and just too…physical. Judging by his occupation alone, he was a born risk-taker. Just like her father. That weapon tucked in at the back of his belt made her shiver just looking at it. She hated guns.

Still, he provided safety. True, he had kissed her and later cuddled her in that wagon. And he touched too often, though not in a salacious way. She admitted she found it comforting that he seemed worried about her as a human being, not just as a potential victim under his protection. They probably taught agents to do that, to keep from seeming brusque and impersonal.

FBI rules surely would protect her from any serious advances on his part. And she somehow knew that Ford would protect her from everything else.

The hugs and pats were one thing, but that kiss was quite another. That troubled her. He kissed just the way he drove—expertly, at warp speed, and with a definite destination in mind. She knew now that he had kissed her in pretense, of course. Surely she needn't worry that it would happen again.

It bothered Mary that she could recall the exact texture of his lips, the taste of him, and the look in his eyes when he had released her mouth.

Even stranger than her ability to remember those things so vividly, was the fact that they had totally erased the memories she had of other kisses that certainly should rate more significance—such as Jim's kiss when he had proposed and given her the ring she was wearing.

Mary frantically searched her mind, trying to remember where that event had taken place. Her children might ask one day and she would have forgotten it completely.

She jumped as Ford spoke. But when he did, he seemed to be speaking as much to himself as to her. "Since the surveillance is shot, we might as well get right down to business. If I keep you hidden from Perry, your contact won't be able to find you anyway."

"My 'contact'? What are you talking about?"

He addressed her directly enough then. "You have the right to remain silent. Anything you say may be used against you in a court of law. You have the right to an attorney. If you cannot afford one, one will be appointed—"

Mary stared at him in total disbelief. "My rights? You're reading me my rights?"

"Do you fully understand—"

"You're damned right I understand! What in the world—"

He looked away from her then as he cut in on her question. "Trust me, Mary, you'd be wise to cooperate fully right up front. If you could give us the big guy, the one who set all of this up, that'll get the Bureau off your back and most likely get you full immunity."

"'Immunity'? From what?" she demanded.

"Prosecution," he stated, his voice flat with what

sounded like regret. "Accessory to armed robbery. Maybe murder, since you were actually present at the scene."

Mary issued a wordless gasp, struck dumb by the very idea. *Accessory to murder?*

"Hey, even the guy who drives the getaway car in a felony gets the full treatment," Ford informed her. "Now, do you know who put it all together?"

"No!"

After a moment of silence, he nodded. "Okay, I didn't think that was too likely, but it was worth a—"

"Damn you, why are you doing this to me? *I* reported the murder! Did that occur to you?"

He continued as though she hadn't interrupted him, as though the blood were not pounding in her ears so loudly she could barely hear. "I'll keep Perry from killing you in any case, but you gotta know we're also after the rocks and who you're supposed to give them to. Just turn them over now, give me a name, and we can set you up in witness protection until Perry's caught. You'll probably get off with probation if you do what I say."

"Rocks?" she asked, thoroughly confused.

"The Portsmouth gems." His penetrating gaze unnerved her.

Mary didn't dare look away. Avoidance might make her seem guilty. "Mr. Devereaux—"

"Why aren't we on a first-name basis, I wonder?" he drawled. "We *are* sharing an intimate little meal here, and about to pass diamonds back and forth. Aren't we?"

Mary laid down her fork very carefully before she was tempted to stab him with it. "I do not have these gems you're talking about, and I cannot imagine why you think I do."

He blew out a harsh breath and sat back, fiddling idly with his paper-towel napkin, which still lay beside his plate. She watched him put on his friendly-cop face.

"Mary, look, I'm trying to give you an out here," he said. "If you tell us who your contact is, it'll go a lot better for you, I promise. Try to play this out to the end, and you could do some hard time. Now, give up the gems, for a start.''

''For the last time, I do not have any stolen diamonds!'' Mary declared, slamming her fist down on the table.

His eyes turned icy blue as they fastened on hers. ''The shop was wired. We know Antonio gave them to you.''

''He did no such thing! I don't know what you think you heard, but he did not give me any gems!'' she insisted. Her heart pounded and she felt ill. She knew nothing about the Portsmouth gems other than that they were missing—six very large diamonds stolen from a wealthy businessman somewhere in Virginia. She recalled reading that the owner of the gems had been shot during the robbery. Ford thought someone had killed Antonio over those same diamonds. She leaned toward him, hoping to make him believe. ''Ford, you are *wrong* about this. Please—''

''You have them, Mary. I know you do.'' He looked certain.

She would call his bluff. ''Then shouldn't I call my lawyer?''

He shrugged. ''Sure, if you want to, be my guest. I'd just hoped we could work this out between us here and now. No promises, but maybe we can even keep you out of it altogether.''

The oaf really believed she was a thief. ''I tell you I don't know anything about it! I swear!''

He smiled, not in sympathy, but in challenge. ''I made a tape off the master. Want to hear for yourself?''

Mary watched him get up and amble into his living room, retrieve his jacket and reach into the pocket. He withdrew a small pocket recorder as he sat back down in his chair. ''I want you to listen. Then I expect you to cooperate,'' he said as he punched the rewind button.

The soft whir accompanied his words. ''If you're doing this for kicks, Mary, now's the time to get out of it. If you need the money—which I don't believe for a minute—then you're going to have to find it somewhere else. Everybody involved is going down for it eventually, and I don't want you to go with them, all right? I'm pretty sure I can get you a deal. Your only option is to help. Turn over the goods, point us to whoever's supposed to get the gems next. That's all you have to do.''

Mary shoved her plate away and rested her elbows on the table. This tape would prove her innocence. Once he listened again, he would realize it wasn't her. He knew her voice now and he would know it was someone else. The rewind clicked off and he punched Play.

Dread collected in her stomach as she heard Antonio greeting her, questioning why she came so late to the shop when he'd asked her to come by before closing time. This recording was not going to help her. Not at all.

She heard herself answer. Her apology sounded a bit irritated, hearing it now. Mary felt terrible about that, now that Antonio was dead. She had been too tired to put up with his fawning after a rough day at school, but she'd felt sorry for him and had tried to be nice.

"The reason I called, I want you to handle these for me,'' Antonio was saying. He sounded a bit desperate in retrospect.

"Oh, my, these are genuine, aren't they? And so lovely,'' Mary had replied. She recalled shaking her head vehemently. "I really don't want to be responsible, Antonio.''

"Come on now, Mary,'' he said, cajoling her. "Just do exactly what you did with the others. I'd feel so much better if you take care of this. Please. Think how much they'll bring!''

"Well, all right, but—''

"Hush!'' Antonio's voice interrupted. Silence reigned for a moment, then he whispered, "Into my office. Hide, Mary! Quickly!''

Ford snapped off the recorder. "Heard enough?''

It took Mary a moment to drag her wits back to the

present. The events that had followed were replaying in her mind as accurately as they would have on tape.

Mary had suspected a break-in the moment they heard movement in the storeroom. Rushing to Antonio's office, she had hidden behind the door, peeking through the crack, trying to muffle the sound of the portable phone she'd grabbed from his desk as she dialed the police.

"They argued," she said, unable to dispel the images. "I couldn't understand what they said."

"Neither could we."

"A moment later, he shot Antonio," she whispered. "Just shot him. Little puffing thuds, but I knew what the sounds were. I almost screamed."

Mary heard the sirens in her mind, and then running feet. Her legs had crumpled beneath her. She felt crumpled now, hugging herself, leaning forward over the table.

Agent Devereaux's table, she recalled. A man who thought Antonio had given her stolen gems, and that she still had them.

"He gave me dolls," she said absently.

He scoffed. "C'mon, Mary. You expect me to believe that?"

Mary shook off her remembered terror. "Two *dolls!*"

He smiled sarcastically. "Of course he did."

"Really! They're antiques, eighteenth-century fashion dolls." When she saw he still didn't believe her, she continued explaining, "Look, I'm a doll collector, all right? Antonio just wanted me to set them up in glass display cases. You heard him. Well, I know how it sounded, but I tell you that's all he gave me, I promise. I can show you the dolls. You can check them for hidden diamonds, if you want, but I assure you they contain nothing but what they're supposed to. Antonio would never desecrate antiques like that just to hide something inside. The dolls themselves are extremely rare, due to their small size. Very valuable. They'd bring a fortune at auction."

He pursed his lips and thought about it. Mary could al-

most see him going over the conversation between her and
Antonio.

"Okay, I'm not saying that I buy your story, but suppose
I give you the benefit of the doubt for right now. Some
things he said didn't quite jibe with a transfer of the diamonds. But I will have to check out those dolls. It may be
that you're an unwitting courier."

"Fine." She sat a little straighter. She hated to see any
antique deliberately torn apart, especially dolls. But if Antonio had hidden the gems inside them, the discovery might
exonerate her as his accomplice. Or it might not.

"Where are they?" he asked.

"At the school in my purse," she said with an impatient
glare. "Which I would have now if you hadn't yanked me
away without any warning!"

"Why did you have them in your purse?" he asked,
suspicion even more evident.

Mary threw up her hands in dismay. "I was going by
the bank to put them in my safe-deposit box until I had a
weekend to work on them. They are very valuable items,
not something you leave lying around!"

He snorted. "So you take them to school where they're
subject to a roomful of toddlers?"

"My purse is safely tucked away in my cubby," she
argued.

"Your *cubby?*" He laughed out loud. "Never mind, I
know what that is. I guess they're secure for now, but we'll
have to get them soon."

He got up for more coffee, dumped hers, and refilled her
cup with hot. "Better drink it. You look a little peaked."

Mary didn't eavesdrop when Ford made the call. She
didn't care what he was saying. She would show the agents
what Antonio had given her and they would know she had
nothing to do with those missing diamonds, even if the
stones did happen to be concealed inside.

She gulped the coffee, ignoring the food, which had
grown cold. Her appetite had disappeared completely the

moment Ford Devereaux had become the dispassionate investigator who seemed utterly certain of her guilt.

Mary liked him so much better as the happy-go-lucky daredevil who ate catsup on his eggs.

Chapter 3

Mary hated this whole nightmare. Her mother would have loved it, had she lived. Danger, adventure, intrigue. Better than rock climbing or bungee jumping.

Her father would eat it up, even now. Maybe she should call him, she thought wryly, if she could figure out where in the world his latest fiasco had taken him. He would die for a chance to jump right into the investigation, wear wires and dodge bullets.

But people like herself were meant for car pools and cookie baking. Junior League. Faculty teas and lunch with friends. And her teaching, of course. She craved a normal, ordinary life.

That was her vision of the future and she'd been getting there, too. Until Tarzan, here, had swung in on his vine and scooped her off into the jungle. Yet the predator had already been encroaching on her nice, safe utopia, hadn't he?

Mary shot Ford Devereaux her most piercing look, hoping he would turn around and get the full force of it.

How in the world had she allowed herself to get caught

up in all this? Well, she wouldn't stay caught up in it, that was for certain. This had gone on long enough.

Why should she have to tolerate these accusations? ''Benefit of the doubt,'' indeed. Surely, either the police or the FBI would have had her locked up already if they had anything more than supposition. Even with that tape, they didn't have a case against her. Or did they? Circumstantial evidence might work for them.

Ford Devereaux was fishing. All that cuddling in the wagon, all those gentle pats on the back and words of comfort weren't real. He had used them to butter her up, make her trust him.

Saving her life hadn't been all that heroic, after all, now that she thought about it, because he didn't really care whether she lived or died. As long as she didn't die before he got his hands on the stolen goods. He had only kept her alive so he could find the damned diamonds.

Well, she didn't need him. She knew how to hide herself. Her paper trail would end with a visit to her ATM and a plane ticket. Nobody would find her once she reached another country.

She had visited places no American had ever seen before, and she'd be welcomed there. He wanted her safe, he said? She would find her own safety—from the jerk who was out to kill her and from this one who thought her a felon.

''Where do you think you're going?'' he demanded as she marched past him to the door.

''Fun's over, Agent Devereaux. Either arrest me, take me home, or call a taxi.''

''I'm sorry,'' he said. ''But you can't leave.''

Mary saw that he meant business. He could physically restrain her. She was exhausted, angry, and more than a little frightened, almost as much of going to jail as she was of the man who had chased them. ''Look, I just want to go home.''

''You *are* home. At least for the time being. We're probably safe enough here. I called in with Perry's last location. Described the car. They're looking for him now.''

"Perry? The man who was following us, right?''

"Yeah.''

Mary shivered and began to rub her shoulders to generate some warmth. Despite her bravado of a few moments ago, she worried that she might not live to buy that plane ticket. She couldn't do it without funds or credit cards, anyway. That meant going home or back to the school for her purse.

"And if this Perry does find out where we are? Do you have a plan?''

"We evade and run if we can,'' Ford said as simply as if he were suggesting an alternate TV program. "If not, I might have to shoot him.''

"You'd enjoy that, wouldn't you?'' The thought of another shooting made her stomach quiver.

"Not particularly. You did ask.''

Mary backed up and flopped down on the pillowy leather sofa.

He came over and sank down beside her, linking his hands behind his head. "Sorry if it upsets you, but it could happen.''

He glanced sideways and raked her with a slumberous gaze. "Hey, you'll be fine, doll. Don't wimp out on me now. Okay?''

"Don't call me 'doll.' It's disgustingly chauvinistic.'' He was baiting her again, and Mary wanted to slug him. She'd seen a friend murdered, somebody was trying to kill her, the FBI might haul her in for grand theft or worse, and he was telling her not to wimp out? This idiot definitely had a screw loose.

The weapon he drew from behind his back made her wince. When he began checking it out, Mary felt the blood drain from her head. Quickly she leaned over so that her head was between her knees. "I won't faint!'' she declared. "I refuse to faint.''

"Glad to hear it,'' he said. "Why don't you lie down?

In that position, you might do a forward roll onto the floor."

She turned her head to one side and glared up at him. "Go to hell."

The phone rang.

Mary watched as he picked up and listened, his face darkening with anger as the seconds passed. The voice on the other end sounded clipped and angry, though she couldn't hear the words distinctly.

"I'm not ready to cut her loose yet. Yeah, yeah, I know that. But what if—"

After a few moments of listening, Mary tuned him out. She went over and over the contents of the tape in her mind, trying to decide whether the diamonds could really be concealed in those dolls Antonio gave her.

Suddenly Ford slammed the phone down with an epithet that made Mary cringe.

"Damned bureaucrat!" He pounded his fist on one thigh. "I swear if I didn't need this job—"

He halted his tirade and looked down at her, his eyes softening, clearly showing regret and helplessness. "He says they've located Perry and will be picking him up any minute. I'm supposed to let you go."

She relaxed on the sofa, letting her head rest against the cushiony back and crossing her arms over her chest. "And follow me again? So I can deliver the damned diamonds to somebody?"

He stared at her silently. "You really don't know anything about the gems, do you, Mary." It didn't sound like a question.

She answered anyway. "No, I don't. You're afraid this Perry might escape and come after me again, aren't you?"

"Yeah," he admitted softly. "I'm afraid." Then he moved closer and took her by the shoulders. "I just don't understand Blevins's reasoning on this. He ordered me to release you and tell you that it's safe to go about your business. I can't lie about that. You are *not* safe, Mary."

She watched him closely as she questioned, "Did you tell him about the dolls?"

"He doesn't know you heard the tape, or that you know we suspect you. I mentioned I'd asked you if Antonio gave you anything that night. I told him you said it was two dolls, but I don't even think he heard me," Ford admitted. "He kept insisting I turn you loose and let you make the contact."

Mary scoffed. "Well, I'd be stupid to do that now, if I did have the diamonds. Which I don't."

Ford paced, grinding one fist into the opposite palm, as though it helped him to think. "We caught the perp who shot the owner of the gems. An undercover agent took his place and passed them on to Antonio so that we could follow through and catch the couriers. Antonio didn't leave after he took possession of them from our agent. We have that on tape. He closed shop and had no customers that night or the next day."

Then he turned and shook one long finger in her direction. "No one but you and his killer came there that evening, and you say you don't have the gems. And Perry didn't have time to search for them before the police arrived."

"So?"

Ford regarded her with one brow raised. "So, they must either be inside your dolls or in that shop somewhere."

"Didn't your people search the place?" Mary asked, finding it hard to believe such an oversight. Wasn't a murder scene always inspected for clues?

"Two of our guys did," Ford answered, "but maybe not as thoroughly as they should have. We were convinced you had the gems."

"'They?'" Mary scoffed. "Didn't you search? You're an agent, too! Just where were *you* when all this was going on?"

His lips tightened in a wry smile. "Following you, of course. We were so sure you had possession after hearing that conversation. I was supposed to detail your every move the minute you left the interrogation room. I did, too."

"How commendable of you," she remarked acidly.

He ignored that. "For what it's worth, your story does make sense. To me, anyway."

"So what do we do?" she asked, willing now to help in any way she could. It seemed he might be sincere, after all, about giving her the benefit of the doubt.

"I guess our best bet is to hang loose here and hope they're located. Then you'll be in the clear. At any rate, you can't go on your merry way until Perry's behind bars. He can't know for sure that you didn't see his face when he shot Antonio."

"Cheery thought," she said in a shaky voice.

"Look, Perry's slippery as mercury. He's already been picked up a couple of times in other cities and released. Even if they do haul him in, they don't have enough to hold him without a positive ID from you. He located where you teach. He'll know where you live."

She held up her hand. "You're right, I know. But he won't find me unless I go home. Suppose you take me to my fiancé's apartment. I'll be as safe there as here."

Much safer, she thought, since Ford Devereaux stirred up feelings she didn't welcome at all. Every time he touched her, she tingled. Every time he smiled, her knees went weak, even when she was angry with him. It was probably just adrenaline or some such nonsense, but she could certainly do without it.

She watched his troubled gaze rest on her left hand and then return to her face. "Shoot, I forgot about that. You're engaged." He looked disappointed and frustrated. For some reason, that gave Mary a jolt of pleasure.

"Yes," she said, rotating the two-karat solitaire around and around on her finger. "For six months."

"Six whole months? What's wrong with him?"

She ducked her head to avoid his probing glare. "He's still working on his degree."

"A college kid," he said, scoffing. "Damn, you would pick a kid."

"Jim is not a *kid,* he's twenty-nine! He's an assistant professor working on his doctorate in theology."

"Oh, great! You picked a preacher?" He laughed and slapped his forehead with the heel of one hand.

"No, he plans to teach. And don't you make fun of him!"

"Tell me, Mary, what's the Bible-schooler gonna do for you when he answers his door and Perry shoves a nine-millimeter up his nose, huh? Pray?"

"That won't happen! If I go to stay with Jim, that man won't find me."

"I hope you're right," he said, shaking his head. "Tell me, if you're so crazy about this fiancé of yours, why do you still live alone?"

"That's none of your business!" she declared, pushing herself up from the sofa. "But it would hardly be proper to live together, considering his chosen profession, now would it? Besides, Jim needs the solitude to work on his thesis. I stay where I stay because I choose to, and I do *not* choose to stay here with you! Your supervisor told you to allow me to go, so let me go!"

"What about other family? Could you live with them for a while?" he suggested.

"No, that's not an option." She stuck out her hand. "You'll have to give me money for a taxi since my purse is still at the school."

"I'm not giving you squat!" he declared. "We'll just go and see about this Jim guy and what kind of protection he can provide you. I'm not letting you out of my sight until I know you're safe. You got that?"

She turned away from him and threw up her arms in disgust. "Let's just get out of here!"

"Oh, all right. Come on." He scooped up his jacket and the keys from the bar and headed for the door. "But just for the record, I don't like this, Mary. I don't like it at all."

Other than providing Jim's address, she had nothing more to say to Ford during their ride. She noticed how he watched the mirrors and took numerous unnecessary detours across town. Not once did he increase his speed or show any sign of concern that anyone followed. Mary finally relaxed.

When they arrived at Welton Towers, Jim Whalen's high-rise apartment building, Ford parked in the underground lot. He got out and went around to open her door and then escorted her to the elevators.

"You definitely are not coming up with me, Ford," she said firmly.

"Think the boy wonder will go berserk with jealousy? Maybe break a commandment or something?" he asked dryly. "Sorry, but I gotta meet this guy."

"No, you do not have to meet him! It's just not necessary and I don't feel like explaining you to him the moment we get up there. If you insist, Ford, I will complain to your superior. You have no right to do this."

"Suppose he's not home?" Ford argued.

"He's here. You parked right next to his car."

"Then I'll just go up with you and make sure."

Mary rolled her eyes and pushed against his chest to keep him out of the elevator. He pushed right back and entered to stand beside her, arms folded, calm as you please.

She glared up at him.

He shrugged. "Okay, I promise I'll wait down the hall. The second his door opens, I'll leave. He won't even see me. Fair enough? I just don't want you stranded here in case he's gone out somewhere with a friend or something."

Mary nodded once. "All right, that sounds reasonable. Just don't let him see you. I'll explain it all to him myself, once I'm inside."

He grabbed her right hand and slipped a card into it. "My cell-phone number. Call me if you need me. I won't be far away."

"Right," she said, almost spitting the word.

His face softened and he took her other hand, as well. "I mean it, Mary. Promise." He refused to release his hold on her until she responded.

"All right!" she said, exasperated.

Before she knew what was happening, he leaned down and planted a firm kiss on her forehead. "You stay out of trouble, hear?"

The elevator doors parted and she rushed out, unwilling to look back at him.

She knew Jim worked at the college until four in the afternoon, then came directly home and rarely went anywhere in the evenings. His car was in the garage. He must be here.

What would he make of all this, or should she even tell him at all? Yes, she supposed she had no choice. He would need to be prepared in the event there was trouble. Could he handle it if anything happened?

Mary couldn't help but contrast Jim's polite, cautious nature with that of the man she had just left holding the elevator door. There was certainly nothing polite or cautious about Ford Devereaux.

That devil-may-care charm of his probably attracted women in droves. She smiled wryly at her own reaction to it. Give her a safe, tame theology professor any day of the week. She'd had enough excitement today to last her a lifetime.

It reminded her of the time she'd taken that Zugspitze slope on one ski. Not a planned thing, and certainly not an experience she would care to repeat.

Mary rang the buzzer at Jim's door and waited. The chain inside rattled, so she turned, nodded and waved Ford on his way.

What would Jim think of her showing up here unannounced?

Then the door opened and Mary guessed immediately what his reaction was going to be.

A curvaceous and partially dressed blonde filled the gap

between the edge of the door and its frame. *Diana Seacomb, Jim's adviser's wife.* Though Mary had never met the woman formally, she immediately recognized her.

"Take your time, Jimmy, hon, I've got it!" the woman sang out as she thrust a twenty under Mary's nose.

Mary snatched the bill and pocketed it. "Thank you."

"Hey, where is the—you're not the pizza person!" Mrs. Seacomb declared, frowning.

"Obviously not."

"Well? Who *are* you?" the woman asked impatiently, one long red nail tapping against the edge of the door.

"The fiancée," Mary said in a carefully controlled voice.

Mrs. Seacomb's eyes widened as she stepped back. "Jim?" she whined loudly.

Mary wanted nothing more than to break something and run out of the building screaming with outrage. But practically, she knew she had no way to go anywhere else.

With no purse, no credit cards, and only Mrs. Seacomb's pizza money, she felt pretty well stuck. At least until the confrontation.

Automatically, she glanced back toward the elevators. As good as his word, Ford was gone. Thank God. She couldn't bear for him to witness this farce. She should never have come here. Never.

Mary watched with dedicated interest as Jim Whalen, the former soul of propriety, exited the bedroom, his lower half wrapped in a towel. She reveled in the profound shock on his face when he looked up, his left hand arrested in the motion of smoothing back his damp hair.

"Well, Reverend Whalen," she said in her coldest tone, "I seem to have caught you at an inopportune time."

"What— What the—"

"Hell am I doing here?" she finished for him. "You owe me a fifty from last week." Which he had borrowed to pay for the dinner he'd invited her to.

Now that she thought about that, she recalled the countless times he had conveniently forgotten his wallet. Jerk. Freeloader. Bastard.

"If you haven't got fifty, then just give me whatever you have," she ordered. "Now!"

"You—you've come here for—for *money?*" he stuttered.

His eyes darted around the room as if somebody might appear to drag him out of his nightmare.

"Just find your damned wallet, 'Jimmy, hon,' before I go totally ballistic."

He started to say something else, but Mary slowly shook her head in warning. The man never had been very quick on the uptake, but he did realize there was no reason for this present situation except the obvious.

Mary hoped he would opt for action over explanation in his attempt to get rid of her. He did.

It only took him a couple of tense moments to disappear into the bedroom and return. He was wearing a pair of wrinkled corduroy slacks and holding another twenty.

"I'll call you tomorrow, Mary," he said in a pained whisper as he offered her the crumpled bill. "We should talk. I'm so *sorry.*"

"No argument there. You're as sorry as they come. I need change, too. Quarters," she said with a lift of her chin, daring him to question her need for them or what more she intended to demand.

He slid a shaky hand into his pocket and hurriedly fished out three coins. When she took them from him, she saw the frightened plea in his eyes. If word of his little assignation with the professor's wife—obviously not a one-shot deal—ever made it back to the husband, Jim's future at Vanderbilt Divinity School was dead in the water. She only wished she could stand to stick around to watch that corpse float.

Mary smiled the most evil smile she could dredge up and hoped he worried himself into permanent impotency.

She turned to leave, and at the last moment, said over

her shoulder, "I would hurry on that thesis and scare up a résumé if I were you. News like this tends to travel rather rapidly."

His groan as he closed the door satisfied her immensely.

Mary met a pimply faced boy in a striped shirt, carrying a large, flat box just as she reached the end of the hall. "Don't expect a tip," she advised him bitterly. "I think they just lost their appetites."

When he started to brush past her, she stopped him. "Wait a minute. That is for Whalen, isn't it?"

He nodded. With a tug, she drew off the engagement ring Jim had given her. "Open the box," she ordered.

"Ma'am, I can't do that! Unless this is your order."

"Open the damned box!" she demanded through gritted teeth.

He gingerly lifted the lid, his eyes wide as he watched her. Mary plopped the ring on top of the pizza and watched it embrace a mushroom. "I hope he chokes on it!" she declared. "Tell him I said so."

She couldn't even remember taking the elevator. All of a sudden, Mary found herself several streets away from the high-rise and leaning against a phone booth.

For a moment, while still disoriented, she considered calling Ford Devereaux. He couldn't have gone far, and she had his cell-phone number.

Then she straightened her shoulders and shook herself into full awareness. No, she couldn't do that. What would she say—"Come and get me, I just discovered my fiancé's been devoutly screwing somebody else"? Not hardly.

She refused to cry. James Whalen would not make her crazy just because he had decided a little sex was in order. Men required it; that was a fact of life. And she certainly had not done a thing in that department to prevent his embarking on an affair.

But with his mentor's wife? Jim must be stark raving crazy to risk such a thing. She hoped they got caught. It was small of her. Mean, really. Strong as the urge was, she

vowed to herself she wouldn't call the professor and tell
him. But oh, how she hoped somebody would. Jim ought
to suffer for this, big time.

If she really wished that on Jim, could she really have
loved him? He'd never encouraged her to sleep with him,
even though she had told him she wasn't totally inexperi-
enced. He had quietly forgiven her that one mistake when
she had confessed it. Big of him, wasn't it? The sancti-
monious jerk.

Now she knew all that drivel about respecting her had
been just that. Drivel. But why hadn't he just broken their
engagement if he had discovered he didn't want her or love
her?

Well, of course he didn't love her. Anybody with half a
brain could see now what her attraction had been. Money.
He'd insisted on their attendance at various charity balls
and auctions, and getting them involved in the society Mary
had formerly ignored. He'd known she would inherit
Gran's house as well as everything her father owned, since
she was an only child. His interest had to be the money.
And ambition, of course. She wished, now, that she had
told the snob up front what the real situation was, but he
had never asked.

Or maybe he had simply used her for cover. She just
might have been a perfect front for an ongoing affair with
the professor's wife.

Whatever they were, Jim's reasons didn't matter at this
point. Nothing he could ever say would put things back the
way they were. Not that she wanted them put back.

She brushed her face with one hand and found her cheeks
wet with tears. Even so, they seemed generated more by
humiliation and chagrin over misplaced trust than by grief
at losing Jim. She admitted that feeling stupid and naive
was infinitely better than being heartbroken over the whole
thing.

So much for Jim and his greedy intentions. Mary realized
she had more pressing matters to worry about right now.

Like what to do next with only forty dollars and seventy-five cents and no place to hide.

She pounded the glass wall of the phone booth once, hard enough to bruise the side of her fist, and then pushed inside to call a taxi. Surely by the time it arrived, she would have thought of someplace to go.

The banks were closed now, and even if they were not, she had no identification. No ATM card, either. The pre-school was locked at this hour, so she couldn't get her purse until tomorrow.

The money from Jim wouldn't take her very far. Her father would wire her more if she could guess where he was and called him, but she would still need ID to collect it.

It seemed she had two choices. She could phone Ford Devereaux for help, or she had to risk going home.

No contest. She could not imagine having to explain to Ford why she couldn't stay with her fiancé after all. Besides, no one had followed them here. Even if that man had escaped capture and knew where she lived, Mary knew she could sneak inside and out again, undetected.

It wouldn't take long to pack a suitcase and get her extra credit cards and passport. She could be out of state before midnight, and out of the country by morning. Much as she hated the thought of running and appearing guilty, Mary knew she had little choice.

Not only might this Perry guy be coming after her, the FBI would surely be hot on her trail. They would definitely not give up on getting those diamonds. Her flight would probably put her on their Most Wanted List.

Ford might understand why she left once he got over his anger, but his superiors would not.

She'd have to disappear until they recovered the diamonds and she made certain the man who'd tried to kill her was safely locked away—if those things ever took place.

She would call in a few weeks and, if necessary, come

back and testify about all that had happened. It would be
her duty to do that. Until then, she planned to get as far
from Nashville as she possibly could. Tibet sounded nice.

When the taxi arrived, she climbed inside and gave an
address for the street that backed her house. She ignored
the little prickling on the back of her neck.

It wasn't paranoia, she knew that much. Not when everyone *was* truly out to get her.

Chapter 4

Ford still had a job to do, whether he liked it or not. He returned to the parking garage and moved the van to a spot where he could see the street out front. If Mary or her boyfriend decided to go anywhere tonight, they'd have to come down here to get Whalen's car. Anyone intending to go in would have to park in the garage or across the street, which he could clearly see.

He reclined the seat a little and got comfortable while he thought about everything that had gone on today. The most puzzling of all were his orders. "Turn her loose, tell her she's safe, and watch her like a hawk," Blevins had said.

The file on Perry indicated that he was a pro. He went after the big boys—politicians surrounded by an army of security. Difficult hits. True, this theft ring the task force was after included some international dealing, but their hiring Perry to take out an antiques dealer and a schoolteacher seemed weird. Maybe Perry was moonlighting, keeping in practice between political jobs, or just racking up kills for the hell of it. Who knew? But even Blevins couldn't brush off the fact that Perry was after Mary.

Something smelled strange about this whole deal, Ford thought. Blevins seemed convinced that Mary had the diamonds. But a dead suspect—which is what she would be if Perry got to her—couldn't pass them along to anybody. Blevins should have reasoned that if anything happened to Mary, they might never find the gems or the person who was supposed to smuggle them to Amsterdam. If she died, the investigation would end right there.

While Ford had been the one to discover the tie-in between the three jewel thefts, Blevins had been assigned to run the show here in Nashville as agent in charge. The man knew his gemstones, and the Bureau had used his expertise on numerous jewel-theft cases before.

Duvek, the regional director, had kept Ford on this one, as well. Like the victim, Antonio, Ford's mother ran a local antiques shop here in town. Ford knew the business fairly well since he had worked with his mother during his high-school and college years. Also, Nashville had been his home until he'd joined the army, and he knew the city.

These diamonds were to take the route of the other stolen lots. Then the agents would pick up everybody who had a hand in their disposition and have the proof to make the charges stick.

Blevins had really dropped the ball on this play, however. It had been on his watch that somebody—probably Perry—had killed Antonio. He might know all about jewels, but Blevins seemed to be inept as hell about conducting an investigation.

Ford supposed that was why skirting a few rules seemed excusable. Making quick decisions on his own had been a matter of life and death before he joined the Bureau. And now he felt responsible for Mary's life.

He might have overplayed his hand in letting her hear his tape, but he had felt certain she would cooperate after the scare she'd had today. He couldn't very well admit to

Blevins that he had let her listen to the taped conversation without confessing he had made a copy for himself.

Why did he have this gut feeling she was telling the truth about not having the jewels? If she'd lied, she sure had quick reflexes. That story about the dolls had spilled out way too fast to be made up. He had listened to that tape repeatedly while he'd been on surveillance. It was certainly possible Antonio had given her dolls instead of diamonds.

But he still couldn't figure why Damien Perry was involved in this. That first murder during the theft in Virginia seemed to have been inadvertent, and definitely wasn't Perry's doing. The owner surprised the thief rifling his safe and got a bullet for his trouble. Had Antonio's death been planned?

He and the killer had argued a little first, but only a few words had been decipherable, whispered as they were. Why had they whispered? Had they known the place was bugged? Blevins was working on beefing up the sound on that. Hopefully, he was better at that than surveillance.

Ford stretched his legs, trying to get comfortable without letting the van's seat back any farther. He needed to be ready to roll if anything happened. He almost hoped something would. Maybe a lovers' spat, a real row that would have Mary dialing his number, demanding his help. He refused to think about what she could be doing upstairs right now with Whalen.

He'd keep watch, of course. That was his assignment. But he felt as though he ought to do more, to stay closer than he was now, in spite of what Blevins had just ordered.

Hell, she probably thought that her fiancé would be able to provide all the protection she needed. What kind of guy was he, anyway? Would he believe God would provide all the protection Mary needed? Ford winced at that and shifted uncomfortably. If he could show the man pictures of a few of the innocent victims in their files, he might be more inclined to offer the Big Guy a little help down here.

Ford knew he couldn't leave things the way they were.

He had to impress on the man how important it was to keep Mary secluded. She would never be safe until Perry was out of the picture one way or another.

He climbed out of the van and strode back to the elevator. She wouldn't appreciate this after he'd said he wouldn't show his face, but Ford knew he had to make certain this Jim knew how critical it was to keep Mary out of sight.

For such exclusive apartments, they weren't very soundproof. He heard the shouting long before he reached the door. A loud crash from inside sent him running. He tried the knob, found it locked and began pounding. "FBI! Open up!"

Sudden quiet greeted his announcement and only a few seconds later, the door opened. The man who opened it stood there hyperventilating. He looked scared. "Wh-what do you want?"

Ford hadn't thought Mary would have picked a loser in the looks department, given how pretty she was, but this was ridiculous. This guy was movie-star handsome. He was a tall, wiry sort, barefoot and wearing only a pair of unsnapped corduroy pants. Ford wanted to break his caps—teeth and knees.

"If Mary's hurt, you are dead meat."

"Mary?" the man asked, glancing over his shoulder. "She isn't here."

"The devil she's not!" Ford growled and pushed his way inside past lover boy. "She came in here not half an hour ago and I just heard her yell!"

He scanned the room and stopped at the sofa where a petite blonde sat hunched over, wringing her hands. Not Mary. Relief took his breath away. Then sudden dread made him suck it back in. If she wasn't here, then where the hell was she?

Ford swiveled around and backed the guy against the doorjamb with an arm against his throat. "Where is she, Whalen? Where did she go?"

He gasped for breath and Ford let off a little. Very little. "She—she came here, but then she left. I don't know where she went. What do you want with her?"

Ford looked again at the sexy little blonde. It wasn't really that hard to imagine what had taken place here. Mary had caught preacher boy with his britches down. Was the man a total idiot? How could any guy in his right mind prefer that little piece of fluff over there to Mary Shaw?

He released the man before he gave in to the urge to pound him into the carpet. "If anything's happened to her, you son of a bitch, you'd better find a real good place to hide."

Ford hurried downstairs to find her. She would surely need him now, because she couldn't possibly be thinking straight. Either she'd be too angry to remember she was in danger, or crying too hard to see where she was going.

He didn't mind her needing him in this way, he told himself as he began searching in earnest. Defending Mary was his job. Ford took that to mean defense against any and every thing that threatened her. This didn't feel as impersonal as a business-as-usual assignment, however. Not when he thought of what that bastard, Whalen, had done to her. Probably wrecked Mary emotionally.

Lord, that had to be a shock—to find the guy she loved making it with somebody else. Sweet little Mary, who really worked hard at being courageous when it went against her nature to be that way. He admired that in her.

An hour later, he knew he wasn't going to find her. He had searched everywhere—both stairwells, the basement, the roof, even the alleys nearby—fully expecting to find her curled up in a corner somewhere, licking her wounds. Mary had no money and no transportation. Where could she have gone?

Ford went back to the van. She might have set out walking, but where? Not his place. Too far away and, besides that, Mary wouldn't want to face him and admit this. Would she go home? Surely she wouldn't risk that. But in her state of mind, she might have discounted the danger. Hell, maybe she just wouldn't care.

He had to check it out.

The silent beeper he wore on his wrist vibrated. Ford reached into his pocket for his cell phone and punched Blevins's number. "Devereaux here."

"What's the deal?" Blevins asked. "Is she still with you?"

"Nope," Ford admitted. "I took her to the boyfriend's place and she left there on foot. Might be headed back to her house. I'm on my way there now. Did you get Perry?"

"Not yet," Blevins said, hesitating a beat. "Maybe you'd better find her and stick a little closer to her for a while."

"Now why didn't I think of that?" Ford said dryly.

The phone went dead.

He drove along the route he figured Mary might have taken, searching both sides of the street, praying for a glimpse of her. It took him a while to reach her house, which appeared totally dark. No sign of Mary. Nothing. She had vanished.

The stone fence in back of the house loomed high, too high to scale without a ladder. She had waited for a long time, concealed behind a high ligustrum hedge, until she felt certain no one had followed her from the street where she had exited the cab.

Mary eyed the huge trash can sitting in the alley beside her back gate. If she climbed up on it, she might be able to get a leg over the wall. And then she just might break that leg or both of them when she dropped to the ground on the other side.

With a sigh, she quietly rolled the big rubber container to a likely spot. It wasn't as though she had much choice here, she reminded herself. Maybe the thick grass would break her fall.

Once she stood on top of the thing, she realized it wasn't

as high as all that. Only when she straddled the wall and looked down did she hesitate again. "No point dreading it," she mumbled to herself and jumped. For a moment, she lay there trying to reclaim her breath. Except for the promise of a bruise on one hip, nothing seemed damaged.

She located the fake stone containing her extra key just to the left of the flower bed. Her stealthy entrance through the mudroom would have done a cat burglar proud, she thought with a grin. She could just imagine the encouraging smile Ford Devereaux would have given her if he had been here.

All of her important papers were in the desk drawer in the study, so that was her first stop.

Her heart thudded frantically when she noticed that her desk pad and several items on the surface had been disturbed. The drawer was unlocked. Someone had searched the place. She looked around carefully, shivering at the thought of a stranger pawing through her things. The streetlight shone through the window, illuminating the room enough that she could see there was no mess.

Whoever did it had been fairly neat, so it probably wasn't an ordinary robber. Mary supposed the police or the FBI had been here after she had left for school that morning. Looking for those dratted diamonds, no doubt. She rolled her eyes in disgust.

Her extra credit cards and passport were still inside the small manila envelope right on top. Mary took the whole packet and stuck it in her pants pocket.

Then she felt her way up the stairs and along the darkness of the hall toward her bedroom. The light coming through the windows would be enough to pack by. She couldn't wait to leave. The thought of someone ransacking her personal belongings made her furious. At least she had the satisfaction of knowing they couldn't have found what they were looking for.

She entered her room and gasped. Even the near darkness could not hide the damage done to her collection of dolls.

"Oh, no," she moaned to herself, stricken. A few lay on the floor, decapitated, others sprawled about on the bed and dresser, gutted or broken. Out of the two dozen, Mary couldn't see one that remained whole. For a long moment, she mourned her childhood babies and the recent little friends she had bought because they appealed to her.

Mary soon realized that the condition of her toys should be the least of her worries now. Whoever had done this might come back. Or they might still be here.

Her skin prickled when she reached for the closet door. The shock scenes from every horror movie she had ever watched ran through her mind. With a determined jerk, she threw open the door and jumped back. Nothing flew out at her. Nobody lunged with a knife or chain saw. She let her breath out in a rush.

Mary entered between the rows of hanging clothes and felt around, quickly selecting what she thought she might need for the next few days. With several pairs of slacks, and a couple of shirts and sweaters over one arm, she returned to the bed and deposited them there. She scooped up the dismembered dolls and laid them on a pillow, out of her way.

When she turned to go back to her closet for her carry-on bag, a huge silhouette loomed between her and the window. She ran. It tackled her before she made it to the door.

Breathless and scared out of her mind, she fought for all she was worth, going for the eyes or where she thought the eyes might be. Strong hands pinned her wrists to the floor.

"Mary, it's me!"

Ford. She went limp beneath him, struggling to swallow the heart lodged in her throat.

"Are you crazy coming back here?" he asked in a fierce growl.

"Wh-what are you doing here?"

"Looking for you. I checked the alley and found your step stool by the fence. Oh, and I talked to the saintly fiancé right after you left. Real slick, that guy." Ford's voice held such blatant disgust, Mary knew he had figured out exactly what had happened.

"So you met Jim," she whispered.

He moved off her, sitting up and massaging her wrists where he had gripped them. "Oh yeah. I ripped his pretty face off and sold the bimbo to the nearest whorehouse. That okay with you?"

"Fine with me," she said, smiling in spite of herself. "Just keep what you got for her. It can't be much."

"Two bits and I feel overpaid."

Mary laughed, amazed that she could find any humor at all in the situation. Ford could be a tonic at times. She went to the closet and dragged out her smallest suitcase, a carry-on with a shoulder strap.

"We really need to get out of here," he said seriously.

"I know. Just let me pack these things."

"What's this?" he asked, picking up the headless body of the smallest Effanbee from her pillow.

Mary sniffed, determined not to cry. How silly, with her life in danger, to cry over a doll. "That one was Ruthie, my favorite. My first."

Ford lifted another, leaning toward the window so that he could see them better. "Damn. I'm sorry, Mary," he said, replacing the small figures on the pillow as though they were real babies.

"Don't worry about it."

"Where are you going? I'll drive you," Ford offered.

She couldn't very well tell him she planned to skip not only town, but the entire country. He would definitely think she was guilty then. He would stop her, too.

"Thanks," she said. "I've got my credit cards. Just take me to a motel."

He made a wordless sound that definitely didn't indicate agreement. Mary figured he would fight her on this idea, but she would hold firm. His boss had told him to let her go, and he would have to do that.

He might as well drive her since he'd follow anyway.

She knew that. She also knew how to evade him once he thought he had her settled for the night.

Mary looked around the room one last time. Ford's fellow agents had done this. He had told them about the dolls Antonio had given her and they had come here tonight, searching for the damned diamonds. Her fury outstripped her fear, now that she realized.

She could take care of herself from here on out. Perry couldn't know where she was at the moment and she would be perfectly safe once she got a flight out of here.

While she folded her clothes into the carry-on, Ford wandered around the room, picking up things and examining them in the semidarkness.

"Your people have already done that," she informed him. "They searched the study and this room, for certain. I assume they went through the others, as well." Mary zipped the case and hefted the strap over her shoulder. "Thankfully, they were neat about it," she said, pausing. "Except for my dolls."

The faint light through the window illuminated his frown, but he didn't reply. After giving the room another careful once-over, he reached for her bag. "Let's go."

He pulled her across the hall to the bedroom at the front of the house. Separating the blinds ever so slightly, he peeked out. "There's a car down there that doesn't belong. Come on."

"Perry?" she asked, almost too breathless to speak.

"Safe bet," he said evenly.

"Could it be FBI?"

"Not hardly. I'm the one who's supposed to be watching you, remember?"

They quickly made it downstairs and out the way Mary had entered. When they reached the stone wall, he hefted her bag and pitched it over, then lifted her high enough to climb up. She watched in amazement as he backed away and executed a sort of bouncing leap, landing neatly on top of the wall, straddling it.

"Gymnastics?" she asked, amazed at his agility.

He laughed softly. "Got too big and tall for it at fifteen, but it still comes in handy sometimes. Impressed?"

"Show-off," she groaned. "I hope you have a good dismount." She peered below at the paved alleyway.

He dropped immediately, landing as if on springs, and reached up for her. "Just fall. I'll catch you."

She threw her leg over and fell. The moment her feet touched the ground, he grabbed her bag and propelled her toward the end of the alley at a ground-eating run.

In moments they were headed north, back toward the city, out of the exclusive Brentwood district. Mary finally caught her breath. Her eagerness to part company with him and go it alone had died a swift death once he'd discovered that car in front of her house. "Where to now?"

"We'll pull in here for a few minutes and see if he's tailing us." Ford wheeled into a small shopping center and parked between two other large vehicles. He kept an eye on the four-lane access road while he punched in a number on his cellular phone.

"Devereaux here, about nine twenty-five. Ms. Shaw's with me. We left our perp parked in front of her house, but he may be moving now. Check you later." He thumbed another button and pushed the antenna down against his thigh.

"Your supervisor?" Mary guessed.

"Yeah."

The phone chirped and he answered. "What?" His brows drew together as he listened for several seconds. "Parked on 31 South right now, north of Brentwood.... No, not to my place, but I'll come up with something. A motel, maybe... Yeah, all *right!*"

He broke the connection again and tossed the phone on the dash. "Blevins says I'm supposed to stash you somewhere tonight and call back to let him know you're okay. I guess we'd better go and find us a foxhole."

"My grandmother's house is near Franklin. We could go

there,'' she suggested. Maybe, in familiar surroundings, she wouldn't feel so inclined to cling to him like a terrified cat.

''I go there sometimes when I want to get away from things. This surely qualifies as one of those times.''

''Why the hell didn't you say so earlier? I could have taken you there instead of—''

''Don't start in on me! You didn't actually give me any choice about the matter when we went to your place, did you? And I thought going to Jim's would be preferable to being alone out in the country! Everybody's allowed one mistake. That was mine, all right?''

He shot her a look that said he understood. ''Okay. Sure you're okay with it now? To go there, I mean? With me,'' he clarified.

''I guess so,'' she responded without much enthusiasm as she watched him reach for the phone and punch Redial.

''We're headed for Franklin,'' he snapped into the phone. ''Call you later.''

Mary raised a brow. ''That had to be the shortest conversation in history. He must really love your attitude.''

''Hates my guts,'' Ford admitted cheerfully as the phone chirped insistently. He ignored it and it finally stopped. ''That makes him crazy.''

''Isn't that risky?'' she asked, grinning simply because he was.

He nodded as he drove, still watching the road behind them. ''Yeah, well, some days unemployment sounds pretty good.''

''I'm not crazy about him, either, since he's the one who ordered my house searched. He should have asked, and done it while I was there. It was a waste of his time, at any rate. I don't even have any rhinestones, much less diamonds. I prefer pearls.''

Ford glanced again into the rearview mirror, then back at the highway, frowning in concentration, terrifying her with that look of worry he wore.

''I just wish this were over,'' she said, half to herself.

Mary pinched the bridge of her nose in a fruitless attempt to quell the burgeoning ache behind her eyes.

"Hey, you okay?" He spared her a quick glance.

Well, if she didn't count the headache, a possible hip fracture from her jump off the wall and the hysteria she had battled since early afternoon, she probably was.

"I'm fine," she said with a firmness she didn't feel. "Just fine."

"You are one tough cookie, you know that? Went over that wall like a soldier, and all by yourself the first time. Now, that took guts, hon." He reached over and squeezed her knee, his thumb making little circles that sent shocks right up her leg. "You'll survive all this. Trust me."

"Don't call me *hon!*" Mary ordered, batting his hand off her leg, not daring to respond to the praise. Or his touch. Her awareness of him as a man irritated her, and he was only making things worse by being nice. She wasn't tough at all. She had guts, all right. They were all tied up in knots that would do a sailor proud. Trust him? What else could she do, since he held her life in his hands?

Her trust must go deeper than she thought. She had just suggested going to a secluded house in the country with him for God only knew how long. A truly dumb move on her part, when they could have stayed at an out-of-the-way motel in separate rooms. Maybe safety hadn't been the only thing on her mind.

Despite her bruises, aches, fears and anger, Mary could not remember ever feeling as turned-on as she did now, with the two of them strapped into bucket seats, sailing down a deserted highway, watching for a murderer in the rearview mirror.

Unreal as that seemed, her wanting him made a weird sort of sense. Ford wanted her. His eyes said it. All those little touches said it. If she gave him a chance, he would follow through. The way Jim never had. Jim's rejection of her was behind these feelings for Ford, Mary knew.

Identifying the reason behind her misplaced desire made

no difference whatsoever in her state of arousal. But any civilized woman would see it for the anomaly it was and fight it, she told herself. She would concentrate on the other, more imminent danger—the threat of death. That ought to cool her off in a hurry.

Ford seemed to think she was capable of dealing with all this, and she meant to live up to his belief for as long as she could manage. It was that or fall to pieces like an upended puzzle.

"Hang on to what you've got, kid," he growled, and abruptly gunned the van into high gear. "We've got company."

She heard a loud clunk and it sounded as if the muffler suddenly quit working altogether. With her luck, the insides of the van would fall out on the ground. She could just imagine coasting to a smoking stop and then getting shot.

Mary bit her lips together to keep from screaming. That wouldn't help a damned thing. And Ford would think her a wuss. Instead she said, "Lean forward so I can get the gun."

He laughed and leaned. "Atta girl."

"*Girl?* You are the most politically *incorrect* man I've ever met!" she shouted over the roar of the engine. "But if you fix it so that I don't have to shoot this thing, I'll forgive you!"

"No promises!" he said. "But I'll do what I can."

Mary clutched the weapon with both hands as they tore down the curving road, the van's speedometer locked on the right margin. Thank God there was no other traffic right now. In the right-hand mirror, she could see the lights of the car behind them.

Ford sailed across the intersecting Highway 431, barely missing the rear end of a large truck. Mary squeezed her eyes shut on a short, wordless prayer, certain that one of the idiots on this road would kill her.

Then, out of the darkness on her right, blue-light salvation roared into action. A state trooper. "Ford, look!"

"God bless you, Smokey!" Ford shouted at the top of his lungs.

He slowed, laughing, when the car following them caught up and sped around them, racing on toward Franklin. "Choose your target, man," he said at the pursuing trooper. "I don't even care which one of us you stop!"

As it happened, Ford was his choice—probably due to the loud muffler and the fact that Ford had been out front in the chase. He braked and finally rolled to a stop on the grassy embankment.

"He'll have called this in," Ford explained. "Hopefully, they'll catch our pal on down the road."

He brushed a hand over Mary's arm and took the gun, replacing it in the well beside the emergency brake. "Better not let Smokey see you with that." Then he drew a folded map from the side pocket of the door and laid it over the pistol.

Ford rolled down the driver's window as the trooper approached with a flashlight, his other hand on his weapon. He looked awfully young, she thought.

"Step out of the car, sir. Ma'am? You stay right where you are and keep your hands where I can see them."

As Ford got out, Mary thought of the gun they had just concealed, and how these lawmen risked their lives every time they stopped a car and approached it this way.

"Let me see your license, sir. You want to tell me why you were flying?" the trooper asked politely.

"The other bird was after us. I'd appreciate it if you could— Uh-oh!" Ford pointed up ahead. "Here he comes. He may be armed, kid! Take cover! Get down, Mary!" he shouted at her.

She glanced up and saw the lights barreling toward them. The trooper had dropped to firing stance, sheltered behind the open door of the van.

Mary cursed him for it. Ford must be standing out there in the open with no place left to hide.

Chapter 5

Mary quickly grabbed the hidden pistol, opened the passenger door and slid out to crouch on the grassy bank, hoping to see Ford come around the back of the van. Where was he?

Deafening bursts of gunfire riddled the vehicle, shattering glass, thunking into metal. Mary pushed away from the van and rolled down the shallow embankment through foothigh weeds, choking on silent shrieks and pure fright. When she came to rest against a wire fence, she lay flat on her stomach and buried her head in her arms, shaking.

"Good instincts," said a voice just behind her. "Quick, he might be back!" Before she could react, Ford dragged her upright and flung her bodily over the fence and into a thicket. Briars scratched her arms and face as she struggled to make her way deeper into the trees.

Suddenly she found herself surrounded by his arms, huddled into a crevice formed by several large boulders.

Almost immediately they heard a car peel away. A siren

blared. For a brief time, faint blue flashes penetrated the trees and illuminated the top of their stone cocoon.

Mary swallowed hard and buried her face in the crook of one elbow. The heavy pistol clunked against her head. She had forgotten she held it. As tightly as she gripped it, she might have shot them both. She hurriedly groped for Ford's hand, found it and placed the gun in his palm.

He smoothed her hair once and she felt his lips against her crown. "Wait here," he instructed.

"No!" she pleaded, grabbing his arm. "Don't leave!"

He patted her shoulder and untangled himself. "I'll be right back." With that, he disappeared.

Shortly, Mary heard an engine cough to life, briefly emitting the rumble of a faulty muffler. Then it fell silent. That had to be Ford trying the van.

At least there were no more shots. Long moments passed with nothing but crickets to break the silence. Temporarily removed from the worst danger, Mary tried not to think of snakes, spiders and other large crawly things that might be anticipating the taste of her exposed ankles and hands.

"You tired of this place yet?" he asked softly.

"Ford!" she groaned, uncurling to leap at the sound of his voice. She threw her arms around his neck and squeezed. "They're gone?"

"Yeah, the kid took off after him. We need to get out of here, though. During that little delay in pursuit, I expect he called for backup and gave them our location. Let's go find your grandma's house."

They made it through the small town of Franklin without incident. Mary pointed out the first road leading them to Fernshaw Farm. After two more turns, traveling on a narrow two-laner without any traffic, she indicated he should go left. A few minutes later, they reached the entrance to the property.

Mary hopped out when he stopped, unlatched the gates, waited for him to drive through, and closed them again.

Well, here they were, for good or ill, she thought with a fatalistic sigh.

"You'd better park around back," she said as she climbed into the van.

"Holy cow!" Ford breathed out the words, staring owlishly at the house in the glow of the headlights. "*This* is where your grandma lived?"

"Where I grew up," she admitted. "Well, some of the time. I don't have my key, so I'm afraid we'll have to break in. But that's okay. It's mine now."

"Yours," he said with a click of his tongue. "Figures."

He threw the van into gear and rolled slowly up the long, curving drive. "Your other house looked pricey enough, but this is a freakin' mansion. And to think, I'd about decided you were just a regular person."

"What do you mean by that remark? I *am* a regular person!" Mary snapped.

"Yeah, right. In jet-set circles, maybe," he said, laughing at her furious glare.

"But not in yours," she retorted, annoyed by his assumption.

"Honey, my social circle's so small, it barely qualifies as a dot."

She smirked and rolled her eyes. "And includes only you, I'll bet. I wonder why that is. Could it be your way with an insult?"

"Wouldn't be a bit surprised," he answered with a grin and a wink. "Why don't we go on up to the big house, Miss Gotrocks? Maybe you can teach me some manners."

"I doubt that's possible!" she declared, crossing her arms over her chest.

"But you'll *try,* anyway," he said with a low chuckle. "Civilizing the uncouth rabble, and all that."

"Why, Agent Devereaux, I do believe you are a snob."

"Nope," he said with a sigh. "Just a realist."

Ford drove past the huge white mansion with its six majestic columns. He noticed, even in the dark, that the shrubbery adjacent to the paved driveway probably cost more than he'd agreed to pay for the new condo.

In the course of his work, Ford occasionally visited some very expensive homes. He had searched more than a few, plundered through them from the bottoms of toy boxes to the backs of underwear drawers. But unlike the plush palaces of the nouveau riche he had investigated, this particular house indicated old money.

"Lawsy, Miss Scarlett," he muttered, unaware that he'd spoken aloud until Mary laughed at him.

"It's a little ostentatious, I admit," she said, her gaze locked on the old home place illuminated by the headlights.

"Right out of *Gone With the Wind*," he agreed.

He followed the curve of the driveway around to the back of the mansion.

"Just park there behind the carriage house," Mary instructed, and pointed to a structure that stood perpendicular to the main house. He pulled close to the back of the smaller building.

Quickly, he replaced the pistol in his belt and the cell phone in his jacket pocket. Then he got out and went around to open Mary's door, not really surprised that she waited for the gesture, though most women didn't these days.

From the first, Mary had struck him as an old-fashioned girl, one accustomed since birth to having doors opened for her. Like Nan. But was she really like his ex-wife? Was he being unjust to lump Mary in the same category with her?

The inborn haughtiness seemed to be missing in Mary, but then Nan had been sweet, too, at first. She'd tried sugar to start with, then tearful pleas, then whines and demands. All women weren't like Nan, Ford knew.

It didn't matter all that much what Mary Shaw turned out to be like, anyway, he told himself. Why should he care? He wouldn't have to deal with her for long.

Mary had handled herself pretty well up till now, but

Ford still figured she would probably fold up like a fan
once she had time to stop and think about everything she'd
been through today. Some were like that. Delayed reaction.

He would have to offer a little sympathy when it happened. Standard procedure for him. But he would keep a
comfortable emotional distance, no matter how appealing
she was. It didn't help that she seemed attracted to him,
too, even though he knew why. She had to depend on him
to stay alive. That provided another excellent reason to
keep her at arm's length.

For his own sake as well as Mary's, he needed to ignore,
if he couldn't extinguish, whatever seemed to be drawing
them to each other. Self-preservation had ranked high on
his list of priorities since his divorce.

Mary led him to the back entrance of the house through
a little flower garden. The first frost hadn't yet arrived to
strip it of blooms. The heavy scent of roses reminded him
of his mother's perfume, the kind she always bought on
special at Wal-Mart. He chuckled to himself. Yeah, he had
so much in common with Mary Shaw, it was downright
laughable. Not that he was *trying* to find anything in common with her.

"Here," she said as she stooped and lifted one of the
good-size rocks that bordered the flower beds. "Break a
window."

"Surely you've got an alarm," he said, hefting the stone
in his palm.

"A three-minute delay. I know the code. Go ahead."

Ford wished he had his pick tools, but he didn't. He
shrugged and tapped the glass pane in the back door that
was closest to the knob, and had them inside in less than
half a minute. "Terrific security," he commented. "A burglar's wet dream."

Mary ignored his crudity. She opened a small cabinet
beside the door and punched in the numbers. "We don't
get much traffic out here, so security's not a problem.
Haven't had a break-in since 1865. You recall that unpleas-

antness?'' He could hear the smile in her voice. ''Mr. Knoblett checks on the place every other day to make certain everything's all right.''

''Who's he?''

''He runs the little store we passed about five miles down the road. His wife was Grandmother's housekeeper. They're family friends.''

Ford's reply went right out of his mind when she flipped on the lights. ''Good God, it's a restaurant!'' The kitchen contained enough space and appliances to accommodate an army of cooks and at least eight diners at the trestle table near an enormous bay window. And there would be a formal dining room, too, Ford was sure. ''How big did you say your family was?''

''We used to entertain a lot.'' Mary went to the refrigerator and retrieved two bottles of Perrier. She handed him one. ''Sorry, water's all we have to drink.''

''Ah, just simple folk, huh.'' He opened it and sipped. People actually paid good money for this stuff in bars. Wasn't bad, he admitted. Wasn't good, either. It was just water.

''The place isn't very well stocked,'' she explained. ''I've been trying to make up my mind to sell, but I haven't cleared anything out yet. There are some canned goods, I think, and a few things left in the freezer from before— before Gran died.''

''That's okay. We'll make do,'' he assured her, not encouraging the grief that flashed in her eyes. He didn't want to get tangled up in her life or her mourning for the woman who raised her. All he had to do was protect Mary, just as he would anybody else he was responsible for on a case. Stick to the job, he told himself firmly.

While she rummaged around in the walk-in pantry, Ford ran a hand over the smooth gray marble counter, shaking his head in wonder. He couldn't imagine why she would even consider getting rid of a house like this. Did she have something even grander in mind? Her place in Nashville seemed downright modest by this standard, though even that exceeded by far any place Ford had ever lived in.

Don't even think about stepping out of your league here, boy. He dismissed any lingering notions of pursuit. It wasn't that he thought Mary was too good for him just because she was rich. Ford simply knew firsthand the problems involved in trying to blend two such disparate lifestyles. Even a casual relationship wouldn't work for long.

He forced his mind back to business. "We'd better kill these lights, just in case. Nobody followed us, but there's no use advertising our presence."

"Come with me," she said. Clutching several cans and an opener in one arm, she led the way, pausing only to open a drawer and fish out a couple of spoons and forks.

The flip of a switch as they left the kitchen threw them into total darkness. He felt her grasp his hand as she spoke. "We'll stay in the den. It's an interior room and the lights won't show."

He was deprived of his sight, but the scents of lemon wax, expensive leather and potpourri invaded his nostrils. The place even smelled rich.

He felt her draw him through a doorway and heard the solid click as it closed behind him. No glaring overhead lights for this room, he saw, as she flipped a switch. Four antique lamps, each different, each perfectly chosen for its location, shed comfortable warmth evenly around the paneled walls and over the thick Persian carpet—an inviting page out of *Country Estates*.

"Hungry?" she asked brightly. "I'm starved." Not waiting for an answer, Mary whisked around the side of one of the huge leather sofas and plunked all the cans down on a low, round coffee table of inlaid wood. "Do the honors, will you?" she asked, handing him the can opener. "I'll be back in a minute."

Ford did as he was told. Absently, he glanced down at the can he had just opened. Asparagus? It must be a joke. Poor Mary sure wouldn't find the way to a man's heart with this. Not that she'd ever be looking to find her way to his, of course. Did rich guys like this stuff?

He grimaced and picked up another, expecting artichoke hearts or something. It was good old-fashioned spaghetti and meatballs. Ah, now she was talking. And canned peaches, just like Mom used to make.

Leave it to a nursery-school teacher to put together a balanced meal, he thought with a short laugh. She'd probably bring out the crayons next to keep him occupied. Another playtime activity that would suit him better popped into his mind. Ms. Shaw would probably give him a time-out just for thinking about it.

Ford didn't want to think about it, but he couldn't seem to get that kiss out of his mind, no matter how hard he tried. He reminded himself of Nan and all that had gone wrong because he had wrapped his life around her. But that memory of kissing Mary continued to hang in there, bothering him.

In spite of everything, Ford wanted to do it again, and do it right this time. Maybe ego figured into it. Maybe he just wanted to make sure Mary knew he could kiss with the best of them when he wasn't in a hurry. He had to laugh about that.

His physical attraction to her was a joke on himself. Even if Mary were interested, he couldn't afford to be. No woman had stirred him up this way in years, but he knew it was just because she was forbidden fruit. She intrigued him. That was all.

"Um," she said as she reentered the room. "That spaghetti is calling my name. You want to—ah—wash your hands? The bathroom's that way," she said, pointing behind her.

Later, they ate in relative silence, sitting opposite each other on the matching sofas, passing the cans back and forth since she hadn't brought any plates. It seemed an oddly intimate thing to do, he thought, as their fingers brushed.

"I didn't think. I could have warmed this in the microwave,'' she said belatedly, plopping her fork in an empty can.

"We didn't need it heated." That was for *damned* sure. She raised the temperature of everything in the room by a good twenty degrees as it was. He added, "I like it cold."

When they had finished, Mary asked, "So, what do we do now?"

Ford fished around in his pocket for his cell phone. "Call in. Gotta follow procedure." He flipped it open and punched in the number, his gaze unwavering on hers, his words rapid. "Devereaux here. We had a shooter on the road, probably Perry. He's got a Smokey on his tail. Check and see if he got him. Catch you later."

He disconnected and returned Mary's grin when they heard the urgent trill that followed. A flick of the On/Off button silenced it.

"You're going to get yourself fired with little tricks like that," she warned with a chuckle.

"Then you can hire me. Need a chauffeur? Gardener? Gigolo?"

What a laugh she had—low and sensuous, as stimulating as a touch in the right place. And his right place responded, damn it all. Nothing would equal crossing the eight feet of space that lay between them and giving way to that response. Not an option, unfortunately.

"If you ever need a reference as a bodyguard, I'll write you one that glows," she offered.

"Thanks. I'll keep it in mind." He leaned back against the soft, chocolate-colored leather and felt it squish comfortably. The determination to keep his distance grew fainter by the second. "We should get some sleep, I guess. You must be tired."

"I am," she admitted.

She looked it, he thought, as he watched her gather the fringed afghan from the corner of her sofa and knead the velvet cushion next to her. Her long, dark lashes drooped with exhaustion. The circles beneath her eyes looked like bruises, and her movements were slow, as though her muscles protested her efforts.

Without further ado, Mary lay down, knees tucked nearly to her chest, pulled up her cover, and sighed. She blinked up at him and smiled. "Good night, Ford."

The urge to go to her, to brush a kiss across her lips, to tuck that long strand of silky hair behind her ear so that it wouldn't drape across her cheek, almost undid him. He fought it—a fight as difficult as any physical confrontation he'd ever experienced. He'd had some doozies, too.

"Good night, Mary," he said softly.

He watched and waited until her breathing evened out in sleep before he got up and turned off the lights, then tried to rest.

One by one, he began ordering his muscles to relax, an old technique he had used time and again when coming down from an adrenaline high. The problem was, there was enough danger on that other sofa to keep his blood rushing indefinitely.

Ford could understand why he wanted to kiss her again. But his powerful fascination for this woman baffled him. It could very easily jerk him right past his decided line of demarcation. He prided himself on his iron will, but it seemed that had gotten a little rusted out somewhere along the way—enough so that it felt as if it might crumble any minute. Strong as the attraction was, he just couldn't figure it out.

Mary was a beauty, that was for sure. And she moved like a dancer, slender and as graceful as a ballerina. Yeah, but he hated ballet, Ford reminded himself. That, and opera. *And* the theater. All things she probably loved. He was strictly a two-step, bluegrass, video-and-popcorn good ol' boy. They were total opposites, and she was off-limits in just about every way he could list. What was he doing even thinking about this, anyway?

All he needed to do was keep Mary alive and kicking until Blevins and the guys rounded up Perry and found those damned stones. Then he could say goodbye, send her a dozen roses just for the hell of it, and get on with his next case.

He drifted off, imagining Mary opening a box of long-stemmed American Beauties, smiling down at the roses, trailing one finger over the petals. Just the way he wished she would trail it over his—

Ford woke with a start when he heard the door click shut. Silently, he drew his Glock from under the sofa pillow where he'd placed it, rolled to the floor and crept to the other sofa.

Mary was gone. He decided she must have left by the door to the hall, the way they had come in, and he quietly followed.

Just outside the kitchen, he heard her moving around in the dark. Her breathing sounded as though she might have come down with a cold. A small red light blinked on and seconds later, he heard the gurgle of the coffeemaker interspersed with her sniffles.

Ford remained still against the doorframe while his eyes adjusted to the weak moonlight. It defined the huge bay window with its comfortable padded nook made for lounging and enjoying the view. Eventually the faint glow outlined the furniture in the eating area.

He strained to see Mary, who remained a motionless shadow against the counter beside the slowly dripping coffeemaker. Her breathing sounded unsteady, still giving way to those frequent sniffles. Was she crying?

A compulsion to go to her and put his arms around her surged through him again like electric current. He grasped the molding on the doorway to ground himself.

She might not appreciate his sympathy. Hadn't she sneaked out and come in here so he wouldn't hear her? Or maybe she would appreciate it too much. Either way, he really didn't need to get involved with this woman on any personal level. Protesting too much, he thought. Not a good sign.

He heard a long sigh, so forlorn it wrecked his sanity. Before he knew what he was doing, he had crossed the kitchen. She gasped in surprise when he first touched her, then grabbed fistfuls of his shirt and began to cry in earnest. Oh, Lord, here it came. He had expected this.

Ford said nothing. He lifted her and went to sit on the deep-cushioned seat built in the alcove formed by the bow window.

Mary didn't weep gently, he noticed. Instead of soft sobs and pretty moans, she sounded furious. He remembered his sister Molly crying like this when Spike Macer had thrown her brand-new book bag in a ditch full of water. The next year when Molly had grown bigger than Spike, she had nailed the bully. Punched him right out without any warning at all. It was a pity that Mary was as big as she was ever going to get.

While she cried, he gazed out at the panoramic view of the foothills, black silhouettes against the moonlit sky.

Stars twinkled, but none of them were the shooting kind. Ford wished anyway. He wished Mary happy and free of danger. He wished he'd never met Nan, who had made him so cynical. He just wished things were different. And that he and Mary were not.

She felt warm against him, her arms more relaxed now and circling his waist. Her bottom snuggled against his lap. Comfortably for her, it seemed. Definitely not so for him.

No point in asking her what the matter was. *Everything* was the matter. This one day had upended her life. Her privileged, perfect, well-ordered, carefree life. She had suffered his abduction and accusations, her fiancé's betrayal, and had nearly gotten shot. And all through it, she had kept her cool.

The whole mess was sinking in now. This was perfectly normal. Hell, he'd felt like crying himself at times when things finally wound down.

Only things hadn't exactly wound down yet, he thought

wryly. Who knew what tomorrow might bring? That, in itself, was reason enough for her to cry.

Ford threaded one hand through her silky hair, smoothing the tousled strands, caressing her head, sliding his fingers down to knead the slenderness of her neck, the delicious curve of her back.

The scent of her teased him, an exotic blend of perfume and Mary herself, so elusive it always drew him closer, craving more of it, driving him crazy.

His other hand, which rested on her thigh, just above her knee, seemed to take on a life of its own, smoothing upward toward her hip, exploring the curves through the supple fabric of her loosely fitted slacks. With determination, he forced his hand back to its original position, but not hurriedly enough to miss the replay of sensation beneath his fingers.

Mary shifted and he could feel her breath against his neck. Then her lips. Full-blown desire shot through him, a rush of hot liquid in his veins. His body pulsed with it, even as his brain fought to remain calm and unaffected.

She can't realize what she's doing here, he told himself sternly. *Don't take advantage.*

He tried to set her away from him, but either she clung too tightly, or caution deserted him. He had no time to decide which as Mary pressed even closer, moving suggestively against him. Her small, firm breasts rubbed enticingly against his chest.

"Please," she whispered, raising her mouth within reach. Ford covered it with his own, tasting more fully all that he remembered from that first brief kiss at the school. God, how he had wanted to do that, all day long. He delved deeper.

"We can't," he gasped when they broke apart for breath.

"We can," she argued, taking charge of the next kiss herself. Ford surrendered without any fight at all. What could it hurt, just another kiss? She needed kissing. Hell, *he* needed kissing. Badly.

He felt Mary shift her body, making him loosen his hold on her as she straddled his lap. Her arms slid around his neck and she kissed him again, almost desperately this time, her small tongue exploring the recesses of his mouth, inviting him back into hers.

Ford drew away—a belated attempt to gain some control. "Mary, we'd better think about where this is going—"

"Here," she whispered, roughly dragging one of his hands between them and placing it on her breast.

In spite of his good intentions, his fingers closed around her and squeezed. *Heaven.*

She raised herself a little, and somewhere in the back of his brain, Ford thought she had come to her senses. Then he realized she had only done so to bring them more fully in contact. The heat of her banished whatever reservations he might have had left.

He enfolded her as tightly as he could without breaking any bones and groaned as she moved against him, rhythmically riding the waves of pure pleasure.

Mary released his neck and rapidly drew her sweater over her head, returning her mouth to his with hardly a pause. With one hand, she unsnapped her bra and shrugged out of it. Her urgency fed his own, and his already proved ravenous.

This was all wrong. He had to douse this fire between them before things went too far. Hell, they had already gone too far, but he had to salvage what he could. She would hate him for this in the morning. He would hate himself.

"Mary," he whispered against her ear, "we have to stop now."

"No," she argued, breathless, branding the word against his lips as she found them. Her fingers worked the buttons of his shirt, baring his chest nearly as fast as she'd bared her own.

Words flashed through his mind. Welcome words. *When a woman says no, she means no.* Thank God.

Chapter 6

Ford's breath came so fast he couldn't speak. The feel of her bare softness against him undid him completely. He couldn't deny Mary any more than he could himself.

She pushed him back against the wide floral cushion and trailed hot, openmouthed kisses from his neck down to his belly. Her lips were hot, driving him mad, while her hands worked at his belt buckle. Then he felt the zipper slide down, the release of pressure a relief and also a stimulant to his overwhelming arousal.

She rose to her knees beside him, a goddess bathed in the blue-gray light of a waning moon, silvery hair catching what light there was. "Beautiful," Ford whispered.

Mary turned from him for a second and sat down, her hip brushing his. As he smoothed one hand over her back, he heard the swish of fabric as she removed the rest of her clothes.

Then she twisted around and lay fully on top of him, her entire length melding with his as though they were one body. "Please!" she whispered into his mouth.

Ford lifted her into position, thrust into her immediately and devoured her cry of pleasure.

It had to be a dream, he thought briefly as he grasped her hips and held them. Nothing real had ever been this good, this perfect. If he could freeze one moment in time, real or not, it would be this one. His mind recorded it, indelibly, even as he began to move.

She met his every thrust—offering, giving, demanding, taking—until suddenly her body contracted around him, pulsed and shuddered so violently, he thought he might lose his mind. He held back until she peaked and he felt his own rush threaten. At the critical instant, with the last, small vestige of reason he possessed, Ford quickly withdrew and spent himself outside her body.

Long moments, filled with gasps and building regret, followed as they lay still. He could not make himself release her. His arms felt boneless, but his muscles seemed locked in place.

Finally she broke his hold on her and moved away to one side. Wordlessly, she gathered up her clothes, stood and backed away from the window seat where he lay unmoving, watching.

"Mary?"

"Shh," she whispered. "Don't say anything."

On soundless feet, she left him there, lying in the moonlight, wondering what the devil he was supposed to do now.

Following her back into that den with those big, wide sofas sure wasn't an option. He'd compound his error to hell and gone, no doubt about it.

But he knew she'd had what she needed and was ready to distance herself. Unhappy as that made him, it was the smartest move for both of them, so he let it stand.

Never in his life had he fooled around with a subject on a case. Breaking the rules of the job didn't bother him nearly as much as breaking one of his own. He needed a clear head, and this kind of distraction could get somebody killed.

He also had a sneaking feeling that what he and Mary had just done could never be classified as "fooling around." That implied short-term fun and games. This was short-term, all right—not destined to last any longer than this one occasion—but the experience went so far beyond fun and games, it scared the ever-living hell out of him.

No, it couldn't happen again, he wouldn't let it. First thing tomorrow, he would make that very clear.

Exhausted and moving like molasses, Ford finally got up. He discovered a small bathroom just off the kitchen and reluctantly showered away Mary's perfume and the scent of their lovemaking. No sense driving himself any crazier than he already was, he reasoned.

He dressed, poured himself a cup of the coffee Mary had abandoned, and dragged out one of the Windsor chairs that flanked the table. The sun would be up in about two hours.

As much as the events of it troubled him, Ford hated to let go of the night.

Mary dreaded facing Ford. What had she been thinking, flinging herself at an FBI agent, especially one she barely knew? She hadn't been thinking at all. That was the problem.

What in the world could she say to him that would explain her bizarre behavior last night? She shuddered at what he must be thinking of her. Probably not much worse than she was thinking of herself.

She hugged the sofa pillow between her chest and updrawn knees, wishing she could just curl into a ball and die.

How could she go into that kitchen and face him? He might be sitting there wearing a devilish smirk, expecting more of last night's activities. Or he could be lying nude, right where she had left him, God forbid.

That particular image of him seemed permanently embedded in her brain. Would she ever be able to forget it? Not likely.

She knew why she'd done it, of course. Jim's affair. His not wanting her. Well, at least Ford had wanted her. Or maybe he'd just pitied her. "Oh, God!" she moaned, looking up toward the ceiling. "Please don't let him do that! I'd rather he thought me a nympho or something!"

No, she didn't want him to think that. What she really wanted was for Ford to acquire a sudden, permanent case of selective amnesia. She'd like to have one, too.

Okay, she had gone off the deep end last night, but possibly only to her way of thinking. Was she a prude? Maybe it wasn't all that unusual, after all. People had sex all the time, didn't they? Not sex equal to that, of course. If they did, nobody would ever get to work in the mornings, Mary thought with a protracted sigh.

The pillow went sailing as Mary uncurled herself. "I might as well get this over with," she mumbled to herself. "Damn."

She would just march in there, make a pot of coffee and act as though nothing out of the ordinary had happened. Diving into shark-infested waters would be preferable, and she'd done just enough of that to know how unpleasant it was. Not that she had much choice in that activity or this one. Better to jump right in and have done with it.

Her dad had always promised her that the dread was the worst part. Mary hoped that applied here, but the problem was, Dad had been dead wrong on more than one occasion.

Ford looked up as she entered. He sat at the table, one of her grandmother's mugs in front of him. "Coffee's ready," he announced, his face as expressionless as a newscaster reporting on the stock market.

"Good," she replied succinctly, heading for the pot.

"Mary—"

"Don't talk about it." She kept her back to him, hoping he wouldn't notice her shaking hands as she poured. "You want another cup?"

His chair scraped back against the tiles. "What I want is to get something straight here."

"Everything's straight!" she said hurriedly. "I'm sorry. I went a little crazy, okay? No harm done. Please, just forget it."

His large hands cupped her shoulders from behind—his body was so close—and she could feel the heat building. "You weren't crazy, Mary. It was all the tension yesterday. And the shooting. God knows you had enough going on around you to—"

"Leave it alone!" she demanded, trying to shrug out of his grasp. "Can't you see I'm embarrassed?" She covered her face with one hand and shook her head. "To have done what I did. And with you, of all people. I'm mortified."

He released her and backed off. "'Mortified?' I see. Well, okay." He sounded insulted. Gravely so.

Mary turned around then, nearly reaching for him before she thought better of it. "Oh, I—I didn't mean that the way it sounded."

"No?" he asked, wearing a defensive look. "Well, this is a first for me. I don't believe I've ever mortified anybody before."

She bit her lips together and felt tears forming. "I'm sorry."

He exhaled a curse and stuffed his hands in his back pockets as he turned away from her. "No, *I'm* the one who's sorry. That was uncalled for. We'll forget it, like you said. Never happened, okay?"

"All right," she whispered, clasping her hands together to keep them still. And off him. "Thank you, Ford."

"Hey, no problem," he replied with blatantly fake cheerfulness. She darted a look at him and noticed he was fiddling with something on the kitchen island, his movements abrupt, maybe a little angry. His words sounded that way, too. "You want to scout out the food? I'll get the can opener." In three strides, he left the room as if he couldn't wait to get away from her.

Who could blame him? Mary felt terrible. Not only had she used Ford in the worst way, now she had hurt his feelings. Her ill-chosen words haunted her the whole time she plundered the pantry for something to feed him.

But she *was* mortified, no denying that. Not because she had made love to Ford in particular, but because she had thrown herself at a virtual stranger. And loved every mind-reeling second of it. That was the truly bad part. Deep down, even with all the resulting self-reproach and embarrassment, she couldn't make herself wish it had never happened.

"What you got there?" he asked, making her jump. "Tell me it's not more asparagus!"

She glanced down at the can she was holding. *Pearl onions.* Her arms curled inward, clutching the can to her chest as she peered up at him and then hastily looked down to avoid his eyes. "Ford, it's just that I don't know you. That's what makes it so—not bad, exactly, but—awkward. But in spite of everything, last night was—it was wonderful. I want you to know that."

He expelled a harsh breath. "Look, Mary, you just said—"

"We'd forget it, I know. We will, but I just wanted to tell you so you'd know."

He brushed one long finger down the curve of her cheek and tipped up her chin. Then he took the can of onions from her hands and replaced it on the shelf. "I thought so, too," he said, his eyes searching hers.

The moment ended as suddenly as if someone had slammed a door between them. He severed the connection by looking past her at the rows of cans. "How about finding us some fruit or something, unless you meant to make martinis for breakfast?"

Ford's willingness to dismiss what had happened between them alleviated some of her chagrin, but it also pricked her pride a little. He could forget it just like that? No problem, he'd said. But in the back of her mind, Mary knew Ford had been affected by what had happened between them.

She also knew that it could all too easily happen again if they were not careful. It would simplify matters if they could blame the tension, adrenaline, and being thrown together as they were. But that had only heightened the already monumental physical magnetism between them. If they had met anywhere else, under normal circumstances, the attraction would have been there. Avoidance would have been easier in that case. Now, unfortunately, it was next to impossible.

Obviously, neither of them wanted a relationship with the other. Ford was the antithesis of what she wanted in a man. And she knew instinctively that he felt the same way about her. They would need to be very careful until they could go their separate ways.

When she realized she had unconsciously selected a tin of smoked oysters, Mary quickly shoved them to the very back of the shelf and out of sight. Oysters, he didn't need.

Ford hurried back into the kitchen. If he hadn't, he would have kissed her. Next thing they knew, they'd be repeating last night, right there against the canned goods.

Why couldn't he forget it the way she'd told him to? He shook his head, but it wouldn't clear the way he wanted it to. All he could see in his mind was Mary in the moonlight, her eyes closed, her lips parted, that glorious body tensing with passion.

Even if it had been a mistake, Ford knew he would always measure any future encounters with other women against what had happened last night. Never in his life had he wanted anyone the way he had wanted Mary; the way he *still* wanted Mary.

The anger he felt over that surprised him. Why had she done this to him, made him feel this way? He might never enjoy sex again with anyone else and she'd made it pretty clear that she was no longer interested. Mary had ruined him for other women; it was that simple.

* * *

They ate canned pears and corned beef as they watched the news on the small kitchen television. At least it filled the ponderous silence. Ford felt rumpled, exhausted, and in no mood for conversation.

"How about a nickel tour?" she asked, a little too brightly, after she had cleared away their dishes. "I could show you around the place so you could check out the security."

"It's nonexistent," he grumbled. "I've determined that already."

Ford knew she was offering this to try to alleviate some of the tension between them. He ought to cooperate and get his ill humor under control. There really wasn't anything else to do other than explore the house. Nothing sane, anyway.

"I've already checked the perimeter," he assured her, "but I guess it wouldn't hurt to look around inside."

Mary pretended excitement as she led him down the hallway past the door to the den. The fact that she was trying so hard to establish a different kind of connection between them dissolved most of his resentment. Mary hadn't set out to undermine his future love life. And not only had he let it happen, he'd participated—an understatement to end them all, he thought with a grunt of wry humor.

"The house was built in 1848," she informed him, sounding just like one of those guides out at Andrew Jackson's Hermitage. "Though Union soldiers did set fire to it, we are fortunate that they didn't stay to make certain it burned. This is the foyer."

"And what a foyer it is," Ford said as he cocked one brow and looked around. Light spilled in through the clerestory window over the double front doors, highlighting the intricate pattern of the inlaid oak floors, the richly carved molding around the ceiling, and gleaming antique furniture that looked original to the house.

He touched one of the small chairs flanking a marble-topped hall table. "Late Georgian?"

"Very good!" she said, smiling up at him.

"Mom sells antiques," he explained. "Used to drag me around to all the auctions to lift and tote. You pick up stuff, literally and figuratively."

"Ah," she replied, pleased. "An appreciative audience."

"You've done this before, haven't you? Shown the house, I mean."

"Yes. Gran and I used to conduct tours for architectural and design students and a few historical groups." She proceeded toward a door that led into the dining room.

Ford took it all in—the brocade wallpaper, the matching drapes, the ornate silver service on a highly polished buffet. There were sixteen chairs set against the walls and two more bracketing an impossibly long table in the center of the room.

"Barbie's convertible zoomed really well on that, but it did leave tracks," she confided, trailing a finger along the edge.

He tried to imagine that. It wasn't hard to see her as an impish little sprite testing her limits. "That was allowed?"

"No," she said with a wry chuckle. "But at the time, I liked living on the edge."

Ford wondered if she still liked it. She would say not, of course, but he couldn't be too sure after last night. Somehow she'd made it past that and all the preceding events of a nerve-racking day without becoming the basket case he'd expected.

The crying didn't count. That was just her safety valve. Much as Ford hated to admit it, he suspected their lovemaking had served as a confidence boost and maybe provided a little revenge on her ex-fiancé. If nothing else recommended it, at least Mary seemed okay now. Seeing her at the moment, no one would ever guess all she had been through yesterday and might face in the coming days.

He listened while she continued around the room, chattering about this and that, introducing objects more as dear old friends than proud possessions. To Mary, these were more than just expensive things to show off.

Her attitude made him more comfortable with it all, and Ford supposed that must have been her intention. He liked her for that. This girl had so much class it humbled him.

She pointed out a huge dent in the cherry breakfront. ''Rode my tricycle into that and got the spanking of my life!'' she declared, shaking her head and laughing at the memory. ''Even so, Gran never repaired it. She said it gave the piece character!''

Ford laughed with her. ''I rode mine off the end of the back porch. Chipped my front teeth.''

''Oh no!'' she cried, leaning forward to peer at his mouth. ''Thank goodness it was your baby teeth!''

''Yeah…'' Ford's smile died. Her sweet scent enveloped him. Her hand on his arm shot a current of need through him that threatened his good sense.

His swift intake of breath must have warned her, because she deserted him immediately, turning toward the floor-to-ceiling windows of the dining room. ''Here! I wanted you to see these. They could be a problem. The levers are so old. What do you think?'' She rattled one up and down as if desperate to get out.

Ford approached her from behind, determined not to touch her, but to set her at ease. ''I think we could hide in this house till the cows come home. He would need a map to find us even if he did manage to get inside.''

''If he does, there's the wine cellar,'' she said, quickly skirting him and heading directly for the door. ''Come see! We could retreat there if he breaks in. It locks!''

''Take it easy!'' he said, following her. ''You're safe, Mary. No way could he know where we are.''

But Ford knew that might not be true for long. What if Perry decided to check the county records and found out she owned this property? Since it was Saturday and the records office would be closed, they had two more days and nights—unless Blevins could block the information.

Then they could stay here where Mary felt at home, until the task team caught Perry and found the diamonds.

"I need to call in," he said, heading back toward the kitchen where he'd left his jacket with the phone inside it.

"You can call from here," she said, pointing to the phone, a Victorian replica.

Ford declined. "I'll use my cellular."

"Is that safe? Even *I* know people can monitor those using scanners," she said, using her schoolteacher tone. "What if—"

"Mine is encrypted. Safer than your land line," he replied, nodding at the fancy phone. He left her there in the hallway and went back to the kitchen to make his call.

"Where the hell are you now?" Blevins demanded.

"Near Franklin," Ford said. "Did the patrolman catch Perry?"

"No, but we'll get him. Look, Devereaux, I need your location."

"I told you," Ford said, and then started to relate the details of the shooting incident.

Blevins interrupted him immediately. "Damn it, *exactly* where are you?"

Ford decided not to tell him. He was fed up with Blevins's overbearing attitude, and furious about how he'd destroyed Mary's doll collection. There was no doubt Blevins had done it or had it done, since nobody else knew Antonio had given her two dolls that night.

The fool had alienated every Tennessee Bureau of Investigation agent and local cop he'd met since arriving in Nashville. The only men who would have anything to do with him were his junior agents, who had no choice. Blevins could go hang.

"Moving around," Ford hedged. "I'll call you when we get settled." Tomorrow night, he would call, and not a minute before. And then he and Mary would leave immediately after. The fewer people who knew where she was, the better.

"Have you found the diamonds yet?" Ford asked.

"No, have you?"

"She doesn't have them," Ford said.

"You heard the tape. He gave them to her."

"I told you he gave her dolls, which she stuck in her purse, by the way. You had no call to—"

"Don't worry about it," Blevins said. "Your job is to stay with the woman. Find an out-of-the-way place to hole up and then call me back immediately. That's an order."

Ford hung up without acknowledging.

"Don't worry about it?" It seemed a little out of character for Blevins to be more concerned about Mary's safety now than finding the diamonds. And he didn't seem all that gung-ho on catching Perry, either.

Blevins had botched everything right from the first, and Ford couldn't see matters improving. Squabbling over who got the job of heading the task force wouldn't have done Ford's new career any good, however. He had several years less time in the Bureau. Also, Blevins *was* supposed to be the gem expert, as well as the computer wizard who coordinated with headquarters and the teams on the other robberies.

The TBI and Nashville's finest had all but thrown up their hands and quit since Blevins had ordered them to bug off several times too many. The two members, other than Ford, on Blevins's team were fresh out of training at Quantico, green as gourds. No help there.

After discovering the common thread among the widespread thefts himself, Ford felt responsible for winding up the investigation with some satisfaction. He had a feeling that his fumbling leader was only getting in the way of that.

Team sports had never been Ford's thing, anyway. He'd been pretty much on his own when he was military. They gave him an assignment and turned him loose with it. Sharing all the info on this case with three other people didn't come naturally, and he was tired of working that way.

He just wondered how in the world he could find the diamonds, get Perry out of action, and keep Mary safe all at the same time. It would take some juggling, that was for sure.

Chapter 7

"I phoned Mr. Knoblett," Mary said as she came in. "He's bringing some groceries."

"You did *what?*" Ford shouted.

She sighed and rolled her eyes. "We needed some things we don't have here, all right?"

"No, it's *not* all right!" Ford argued. Even without sex, the woman was going to drive him nuts. "How am I supposed to hide you if you tell everybody and his brother where we are?"

"I only told Mr. Knoblett! I impressed on him that no one else is to find out I'm here. He's just a nice old man who runs a store, for goodness' sake, not some...some *criminal!*"

"Is he coming out right away?" Ford demanded, wondering if he should take the man into custody when he arrived, to make certain he didn't spread the word.

Mary seemed to relax a little now that he'd lowered his voice. "Soon as he gets the things together. Less than an hour, I'd guess. It's so early, he hadn't even opened the store yet.''

Ford forced himself to calm down.

Thirty minutes later, they saw a gray pickup truck creep up the long drive and disappear around the side of the house. Mr. Knoblett knocked at the back door off the kitchen.

He wore faded overalls, a checkered shirt with sleeves rolled up to the elbows, and weathered brogans. Ford thought him somewhere in the neighborhood of sixty, maybe sixty-five, with a thin, wiry body, a head of stiff white hair and a farmer's tan. Age hadn't been kind to the man, but he didn't seem to mind.

"Mary, Mary, quite contrary!" the fellow said with a lopsided grin that exposed a gold tooth. "We've missed you, girl!"

"Hi there, Mr. Knob! How's Miss Thelma?"

He stepped inside and nodded a curious greeting to Ford as he answered, "Thelma's doing good. She come over with me Wednesday and give the place a quick goin'-over. Got rid of the dust and then packed up some of Miz Lisbeth's clothes for you."

A flicker of grief darkened Mary's eyes as she thanked the man.

Knoblett acknowledged the thanks, but didn't mention her grandmother again. Instead, he shoved the box of groceries toward Ford. "Well, here's your stuff. Didn't have no fancy water so I brung juice. That do?"

"That's just fine," Mary said.

Ford accepted the heavy cardboard box full of items and went to set it on the kitchen counter.

"Mr. Knoblett, I'd like you to meet Ford Devereaux. He's with the FBI."

Ford shot her an incredulous look. *Tell him the whole story, why don't you?* Before he could finish shaking the dry, gnarled hand of their visitor, she was well into doing just that.

"Lordy, you two got yourselves in a mess, didn't you?" Knoblett said when she paused for breath. "You ort to be all right if nobody don't know you're here. I'll call you if I see any traffic head up this way."

"We'd certainly appreciate that, Mr. Knob," she said. "Would you put the groceries on my account? I left my purse at the school."

He nodded at her and narrowed his eyes at Ford. "You married, son?"

"Uh, no, I'm not," Ford answered uncomfortably.

"Well, you behave yourself, then," Knoblett warned. "Always felt like Mary was partly mine and Thelma's. Don't want to have to come after you with no shotgun!" He spoiled the warning with a hoarse laugh and a wink. "She's a beauty, though, ain't she, boy?"

Ford couldn't keep his face straight. "Yes, sir, Mr. Knoblett. She surely is that."

Mary blushed bright red.

"I'll see y'all," Knoblett said as he ambled back toward the open door. "Holler if you need anything else."

They stood, silently watching through the panes on the door as he climbed back into his truck and backed away with a final wave.

"Well!" Mary said with a clap of her hands. "I'll bet you money Knobby put some candy bars in that box, and I'm starving for chocolate. He knows I love it."

She left him standing there, wondering if he'd made a mistake letting the man leave. But something had convinced Ford that it would be safe to trust the old guy with their secrets. Mary's "Mr. Knob" had seen a lot more of life than tending a roadside grocery in rural Tennessee.

Despite that country-boy uniform he looked so comfortable in, the wise old eyes and the *Semper Fi* tattoo on his wrinkled brown forearm attested to that.

Knoblett admitted a proprietary interest in Mary, too. That meant he wanted her protected. Ford found that reassuring. He feared that the old couple down the road might be the closest thing to family she had to rely on.

Her grandmother was dead and Mary didn't even know where her father was. Ford suspected that even if she did it wouldn't matter. They obviously weren't all that close. Ford really hated to think that no one would be looking after Mary when all this was over.

There was no way he could do it, even if he did feel himself leaning in that direction.

He wished like hell he'd kept more to himself on this case and not gotten so involved with her. She had wormed her way right under his guard in less than twenty-four hours. So much for his self-discipline. Something about that deceptive fragility of hers had driven him toward her with the speed of a runaway train.

He had given up his first career to try to meet Nan's needs and demands. And here he was again, trying to make everything right for a woman. Ford leaned against the kitchen wall and crossed his arms over his chest, his mind in turmoil.

Mary hadn't asked for any of this, he reflected, determined to be fair. She had been busy teaching, minding her own business, when he had barreled into her life trying to save it.

How could he even think about blaming her for anything that had happened since then? Mary didn't expect him to offer her a lifelong commitment of protection or anything else. Especially the "anything else." She would probably laugh her pretty head off at the very idea.

She was not his type and he was definitely not hers. They had absolutely nothing in common. Except the greatest sex he had ever experienced in his entire thirty-two years.

And he was supposed to forget about that? Right.

The day wore on as Ford created opportunities to put a little distance between Mary and himself. He had spent most of the afternoon outside, but now it was time to go back in. It would be dark soon. The muffler on the van worked now, though the fix he'd applied was temporary. Molly would have a fit when she saw all the bullet holes, but he couldn't do much about those.

He noted the patch where he had broken the window on the kitchen door, and shook his head at the woeful lack of security. A child could break into this place, he thought. He'd done it with a rock. All anyone would have to do was cut the power and the alarm would be useless.

Ford regretted having to take Mary somewhere else, but he decided he had little choice. One more day shouldn't hurt, though. That might give her time to get herself together. This current mood of hers was about as forced as a smile on death row. The edginess of it seemed almost tangible.

Last night's sex was to blame for some of that unease. Ford felt like kicking himself, especially when he admitted he might do it again if she gave the slightest indication she wanted to. He was trying to prevent the opportunity.

Mary needed his reassurance and protection. Maybe she had thought, subconsciously, that she had to ensure that somehow. If he took advantage of that, then he was the worst kind of jerk.

He knew she was upstairs. The water had been running when he'd walked along the hall up there earlier. A picture of Mary, wet and naked, suddenly flashed through his mind. "Whoa," he cautioned himself aloud. "Get a grip before you go ape."

No way would he go looking for her. He'd just go back to the study and watch a little television. That one room was the only place he felt comfortable. He couldn't even go to the kitchen for a snack without that window seat stirring recent memories into a frenzy. The rest of the house made him uneasy, as though he'd wandered into a museum where he wasn't supposed to touch anything. Yeah, the "study"—what his folks called a "den"—that was his best bet.

But what was Mary doing up there after her bath? Was

she crying again or just hiding from him? She might be afraid he would jump her without any warning, expecting her to put out. Couldn't have her thinking that.

His former intentions to leave her alone forgotten, Ford climbed the stairs two at a time.

The bubble bath helped restore Mary's flayed nerves. She had come up to her old room and found it just as she'd left it almost seven months ago, the last time she had visited Gran here.

Hours ago, Ford had gone out to see whether he could repair the van's muffler. Quite clearly he sought distance too. No doubt he hoped, just as she did, that they could make what had flared between them subside and die.

She dressed quickly, determined to ignore the feel of silk next to her body. Despite that, she welcomed the familiarity of the dress and the comforting scent of her grandmother's sachet, which lingered on it. The garment engulfed her and made her feel small again.

Embraced by memories of much happier times, Mary picked up two of the boxes stacked next to her closet door and climbed onto the bed she'd always loved. She gently removed the contents of one box and felt surrounded, protected, and held dear.

Then she heard Ford coming up the stairs. She started to put the doll away, but decided against it.

''In here!'' she called out.

A moment later, he appeared in the doorway. He looked pointedly at the Madame Alexander she held in one arm. One eyebrow went up and he pursed his lips as if to keep from smiling.

She held out her treasure. ''Snow White,'' she said. With one hand, she smoothed down the jet-black hair that shone just as brightly as it must have when her mother had opened the box on that long-ago Christmas.

Ford nodded as he walked over to the tester bed and sat down beside her on the floral comforter. He reached over and moved one of the doll's arms up and down. "So you haven't lost them all, after all."

"These are the most special," she explained, indicating the stack of boxes she had retrieved from the closet. "My mother's."

He smiled softly, his eyes still on the doll. "You make a pretty picture," he said, "with that outfit on, sitting here in the middle of the bed. Like a little girl playing dress-up."

Mary shifted uncomfortably when he made her aware of what she must look like. She had appropriated one of Gran's dresses after her shower since her travel bag was still down in the study. She resented his making fun of her, telling her she looked juvenile. Goodness knows, she felt more grown-up right now than was good for her with Ford around.

"'A little girl'? Well, I certainly hope you don't entertain any fantasies in *that* direction!" she said with a toss of her head.

Ford laughed and tapped her nose with his finger. "Not on your life! I just meant that you look cute." He lifted the unopened box lid and looked inside. "Now who is this little friend?"

"Parian," she said. "Very old. Pretty, isn't she?"

"Beautiful," he commented, looking directly at her.

Mary knew she had to change the subject, bring up something that would turn his thoughts well away from where she could see them heading. "Ford, what are we going to do? We can't just sit here in Gran's house waiting for that man. What if your people can't catch him? What if they never find those diamonds? Much as I love this place, you know we can't stay here indefinitely even if it is safe. Both of us have lives we need to resume."

He leaned back, bracing himself on his elbows, his waist brushing against her knee. "Yeah, I've been thinking the same thing. We sure can't count on Blevins to make it happen."

"Your supervisor?" she guessed.

"Team leader," he clarified, turning to regard her with a very serious expression. "Mary, I'm going to spell it out because your life's the one at stake here. I figure this is a need-to-know situation if there ever was one."

"Tell me," she urged, leaning forward. "What can I do to help?"

He smiled then, a wonderfully sad smile that made her heart leap. "If we don't get off the bed this minute, these dollies of yours are going to see that you're not a child anymore."

Mary froze for a moment, tempted, then scrambled off the bed in haste, shoved the Snow White back into her tissue bed, and headed for the door. She heard Ford laugh ruefully, but didn't dare turn around until she got down stairs away from the beds.

He followed her into the study where she had taken ref uge, holding a sofa pillow in her lap and trying to catch her breath.

"Close call," he commented with raised brows. He stood with his hands in his back pockets, the second sofa between them. "Sorry."

"That's all right," she said, feeling the heat rise from her neck to her face. She decided a further explanation might help. "Ford, the thing that worries me most is that I really don't know you very well. And what I do know— Well, you don't want us to get involved any more than I do." She risked a glance up. "Do you?"

"No," he stated truthfully. Mary knew he meant it. She was dying to know why. He rounded the sofa opposite her and sat down, crossed his arms over his chest and rested one ankle on his knee. "It could be dangerous, Mary. I'm supposed to be looking after you, keeping you safe. We can't let ourselves start something here, or I might forget that. Forgetting it, even for a minute, could make the difference between saving your life and not. Do you under tand? It has nothing to do with how I feel about you personally, or rather what I'm trying not to feel.''

Mary nodded with enthusiasm. "Right! Absolutely ight.''

He shrugged. The foot crossed over his knee waggled up and down, betraying his lack of calm. "Might as well admit t's there, though. I don't think it's going away by itself.''

She ducked her head and squeezed her eyes shut. How ould they be having this conversation? "I've never done anything like last night. I can't imagine what I was thinking.''

"You weren't thinking, and neither was I, but it's done. Okay, here's the deal,'' he said, uncrossing his arms and eaning toward her as though preparing to negotiate. 'Whenever one of us feels—you know—attracted or whatever, we say so. With a warning, we can back off quick. Remind each other what a bad idea it is. Okay?''

"Fine,'' she muttered, her voice catching in her throat. 'I can do that.'' Unless they both got caught up in that overpowering feeling at the same time. Then what?

When Mary finally dared to look at him, Ford seemed infinitely proud of himself and his grand solution. She had o fight back the urge to do something to shake his confidence, to make him run for cover. A childish thought, since he had her best interests in mind here, but he affected her hat way with this smugness of his. Maybe because he reated the whole issue like just another bothersome problem to solve with tactics—well-practiced tactics. He'd probably been fending off women when they got too serious for the better part of his adult life.

"Now back to business,'' he said, relaxing, stretching his arms out across the back of the sofa. "I honestly don't believe our situation will alter for the better unless we make t happen.''

"What do you mean?''

"Until Perry is out of commission and the stones turn

up, we're stuck with each other. Worst case, Perry will find us first.''

''Best case?'' she asked.

Ford snorted. ''Perry drops dead of heart failure and Blevins trips over the gems accidentally?''

''Neither a likely occurrence,'' she said, stating the obvious. ''So what can we do?''

''Only two options. Hole up and play it safe, or get out of here and take care of business.''

Mary considered. Staying here, secluded with Ford, might appear to be the safer course, but she doubted it. Every moment they spent waiting around increased the chances of Perry finding them. The other, though less lethal, danger of this forced togetherness with Ford, could prove almost as disastrous. ''I vote we do it,'' she said, smacking her palm against one knee. ''Let's find those diamonds!''

Ford rewarded her with the huge grin that always did funny things to her insides. ''I just might have misjudged you, Mary Shaw! Now go get out of that damsel-in-distress outfit and find something suitable for breaking and entering.''

Mary brushed her hands over the floral silk clinging to her legs and sighed regretfully. ''Black's not my color, but I'll see what I can find.''

''Emma Peel, look out!'' Ford exclaimed when Mary reappeared dressed in black stretch pants and a long-sleeved pullover. She had braided her hair and tucked it up beneath a dark blue beret. When she cocked her brow and slapped a pair of dark gloves across her palm, he laughed.

''Overdone?'' she asked, her voice as sultry as ever, but laced with uncertainty.

''Perfect, just perfect,'' he answered, shaking his head ruefully. ''You just surprised me, that's all. I didn't expect you to go all out this way.''

''Well, I'm trying to look the part anyway. I'm not sure

how effective I'll be at this. Are we going to break into the shop?''

Ford sobered. ''The school first, I think, so we can get those dolls. If the diamonds aren't in them, then we'll hit the shop.''

She started for the door, her stride resolute, but he stopped her. ''Wait a minute. We need to get everything straight before we go. I need to ask you some more questions.''

Mary rolled her eyes, looking for all the world like one of the jaded chicks in a James Bond movie. ''Okay, shoot.''

''Why did you really go to Antonio's that night?'' he asked, indicating that she should take a seat since this might take a while.

She curled up on the sofa like a lazy cat. Ford beat back the heat with an effort, forcing his mind to focus on her answer and not those legs.

''Antonio called. He said he had to see me, that it was important.'' She tried to contain a shudder, but Ford noticed.

''Why didn't you go out through the street entrance when you heard someone break in?''

''No time, I guess.'' She shrugged. ''Antonio had all these locks on the front door. If they were all engaged, as they must have been, it would have taken a while to unlock them. He sent me to the back office while he went for the pistol he always kept near the register. I think he thought—''

''That he could handle whoever it was,'' Ford finished, pacing back and forth at the side of the sofa where she sat. He paused for a minute to think, then asked, ''I know you said you didn't overhear what they said, but did you get the idea that Antonio knew the man?''

She considered that and a little light seemed to dawn in her eyes as she looked at him. ''He must have! He didn't shoot. I was so busy trying to muffle any sounds from the phone while I dialed the police that I didn't pay any attention at all to their initial meeting. When I got around to listening, they were speaking in whispers." Her brows furrowed. "Why would Antonio do that? Shouldn't he have been shouting, if not shooting?"

"An interesting observation," Ford admitted. "Did you tell the police about Antonio going for his gun?"

"Yes," she said. "I think so. I was so flustered at the time, I don't recall exactly what they asked. It wasn't much, considering all that had happened."

"The lights were on in the shop?" Ford asked.

"Only one, near the back, that Antonio always left on at night." She closed her eyes, leaning her head back, as though trying to remember the details. "I parked in the alley like he told me to do, knocked on the back door, and he let me in. He didn't fasten the dead bolt after me, just closed the door."

Ford kept his voice low so that he wouldn't break her concentration. "The killer came in that way?"

"Yes, he must have bumped against something in the kitchen."

"The kitchen? I didn't see a kitchen."

"Oh, it's not now. The shop originally was a restaurant. Antonio uses—used the room to store items that needed restoring before he put them out in the shop for sale."

Ford nodded, compiling his mental notes. "And he gave you those dolls as soon as you got there. Did you get the idea that he had something else important to discuss with you?"

She pursed her lips and raised her head, thinking back. "Yes, I do. He had given me dolls before, as I said. If it were just that, he probably would have said so on the phone when he called. He did the other time, and he didn't seem so urgent about it then."

She looked troubled as she met Ford's eyes. "But what? What could have made him call me to meet him after closing? I had already begun to get ready for bed. I told him I didn't want to come out that late, but he insisted."

"You could have refused," Ford said, experiencing an unwarranted stab of anger that she would go to so much trouble for the old guy.

She smiled sadly. "I hated to. Antonio was always so kind to me."

"Kind enough to leave you everything he owned. That's pretty kind, all right," Ford muttered.

"What!" she gasped, sitting upright, one arm braced against the back of the sofa. "What are you saying?"

Ford knew nobody could fake the kind of shock visible on her face. "His will. We got a court order to see who would benefit most from Antonio's death. He left you everything."

"Oh, God!" Mary covered her face with her hands. "Oh, I had no idea!"

"Well," Ford said, disturbed by her reaction, "you would have found out soon enough. Maybe he had a premonition that something would happen to him. Maybe that's what he wanted to tell you."

"Now we'll never know," Mary whispered. "Poor Antonio."

Ford grunted. "Yeah, poor in luck. Dollarwise, too. But the inventory in the shop's another story. He knew his business, from what I could see. Very little junk there."

She nodded, crossing her arms over her chest. "He had excellent taste."

"In friends, too," Ford said, forcing a smile he didn't feel. "Exactly what was he to you, Mary?"

Her eyes widened as she realized what he was asking. "You think—? No, Ford. We weren't lovers, not ever! He thought of me sort of like a daughter. He even introduced me to Jim at a charity auction we attended almost a year ago. Antonio approved. He wanted me to be happy."

But she didn't really believe that, Ford could tell. She wanted to, but she knew better. Though she might not acknowledge it if she didn't return the feeling, a savvy woman like Mary would have recognized the man's hidden motives.

Ford remained silent, a slightly amused and knowing gaze trained on her, using one of the techniques he'd been taught to intimidate a subject during interrogation. And that was exactly what this was, he realized. He was treating Mary just as he would if she'd been hauled in for questioning. The need to put her at ease, tell her to forget it, nagged at him. He ignored it.

She reacted as any suspect would, going on the defensive. "He always treated me with the utmost respect, Ford! Antonio was almost old enough to be my father!"

Ford shrugged, still pinning her with his eyes. Jealousy surged through him like a dark tide, drowning his scruples.

For some reason, he needed to make certain Mary hadn't loved Antonio back. If she could love one man while engaged to another, then she must be as faithless as Nan had been. He could never trust a woman like that.

That thought proved an instant revelation to Ford. He'd always thought he blamed Nan's unreasonable demands and instability for their breakup. He had capitulated to her every wish, probably to make up for the fact that he didn't really love her as much as he ought to.

If Nan had sensed that, no wonder she had left him. Ford suddenly realized that Nan's unfaithfulness had affected him so much that he'd pushed it to the back of his mind and displaced it with other, less painful excuses for their divorce.

He had substituted other reasons for his cynicism and mistrust because if he admitted the real cause for her leaving him, he would have to accept the greater part of the blame for it. But now he was projecting whatever sins he attributed to Nan onto Mary, and that was wrong.

If his mind was this screwed up, he surely didn't need to start up another relationship. He would be wise to back off, and to warn Mary to do so, too.

She had flounced off the sofa, and was now pacing, her back turned to him.

Maybe because he was angry with himself, Ford persisted even while he knew he would regret it. "He must have loved you to leave you everything he owned. Along with the rest of it, those dolls are yours now, free and clear. And they could be full of very valuable diamonds, a wealth Antonio meant for you to have."

"Yes," she said, turning to meet his glare head-on, surprising him with her agreement. "You're probably right. Let's go straight to Cartland's and get those dolls."

Chapter 8

Mary crouched on the floorboard of the van, which Ford had parked behind a Dumpster a block away from his condo. She hardly had time to curse him at any length for leaving her when she heard him return. He tossed a gym bag onto the seat behind her.

"Got it!" he said as he drove out of the dark parking lot that surrounded a less-than-desirable apartment complex.

"I still don't see why you had to risk coming here," she muttered.

He hummed, looking both ways at an intersection. "For some clothes. And my tools. With picks I won't have to break any windows," he explained. "Don't want anyone to know we've been there. We'll just get in, grab your purse and get out as fast as we can. We need to make a run by the museum first, though."

"The museum? Where we hid?" She curled into herself, staring out the window, still expecting bullets to fly any minute. "That's crazy, Ford."

"I've got to pick up my Jeep," he said, ignoring her protests. "If it hasn't already been towed."

Luckily, it sat right where they'd left it and the streets looked clear. Ford drove by twice before he finally parked.

"Can you drive a stick shift?" he asked, jingling the two sets of keys in one hand.

Mary nodded, and he handed her one ring. "Good, you follow me in the Jeep. Keep close. If we get company, I'll draw him away. You take this," he advised as he placed his cellular phone in her hand, "and find a place to hide. Then hit Redial on this and tell Blevins where you are."

Mary clutched the keys so hard they bit into her palm. "Where are we going?"

"Molly's house." He seemed to realize how unnecessary she thought this additional venture was and added, "She'll want her van back and we might need my four-wheel drive."

Mary couldn't imagine why, but she had to trust that he knew best. She held off arguing about it, hopped out and got into the Jeep. A few minutes later, they were back on the freeway.

The subdivision where Molly lived caused Mary a few pangs of longing. Here was exactly what she had always dreamed of in a home, she thought as she drove down the streets lined with half-grown trees, past houses surrounded by flower beds. Normalcy. She imagined Molly's home would be comfortable, filled with laughter and love, and as friendly as the woman herself had seemed.

Ford pulled into the driveway of the light-colored two-story house with dark shutters and a small portico on the front. Mary pulled in behind him and waited, watching as he got out and went around back.

No interior lights came on, but it was after one o'clock in the morning. Normal people would be sound asleep at this hour.

When he returned, Mary got out to let Ford in the driver's seat, then climbed in on the passenger side. "Did you wake them?'' she asked as he pulled back out onto the street.

"No, no point in that," he replied with a grimace. "Molly can kill me later. She's not going to be too happy with all those holes in her pride and joy. Insurance ought to cover fixing it, but guess who gets to foot her deductible. Got a hard heart, that girl."

"I'll pay for it!" Mary rushed to offer. She had no inkling what an FBI agent made in the way of salary, and had never asked what Molly's husband did for a living, but she felt responsible for the damage to the van. "If it hadn't been for me, this would never have happened."

He shot her a look. His eyes narrowed and his mouth kicked up on one side. Snide. This man could do snideness like no one else. "And have you do without lunches? No way."

"Peanut butter is cheap," she countered.

Ford laughed out loud and pounded the steering wheel with the heel of his hand. "You just slay me, Mary Shaw. You really do."

She dearly wished she could smack him. He was treating her like a rich bitch again, when he had no more idea of her financial situation than she did of his. "I'll pay! And that's the end of it!"

"Okay," he said with one last chuckle. "I'll let you."

They rode in silence until they reached the community where Mary taught. It looked so alien at night, she thought. Very few rooms were illuminated in the homes they passed, but outdoor security lights glared over the manicured yards.

"Are you sure nobody will be watching for us?" she asked, scanning the driveways for cars. Few remained outside the garages, and none looked like the one that had followed them.

"No reason for them to keep up a surveillance here. Nobody would dream of your coming back to the school until all this is over." He hesitated, then added, "One way or another."

She was wringing her hands she noticed, and promptly separated them, deliberately relaxing her fingers.

"You don't have to come in if you'd rather wait for me."

"Again? I don't think so!" Mary huffed, recalling how terrified she had been when he'd left her alone behind that Dumpster.

"It'll be okay," Ford promised. "Only the two of us know that you left your bag at the school, so Perry has no reason to think we'd come here. Neither does Blevins."

He turned onto the street where Cartland's Preschool was located. Instead of stopping, he drove right by it at normal speed, taking in the surrounding area. "See? No one watching and no lights on, which means there's probably nobody inside."

"Inside? It's two o'clock in the morning. Why would you think anyone might be there?"

"Janitors usually work at night. Painters, sometimes exterminators and plumbers," he explained. "We'll park a few blocks away and come back on foot."

He left the Jeep in a small treed park where nearby residents did their morning jogs and mothers strolled with their children in the afternoons. Silently, they crossed the street and threaded between the widely spaced houses, keeping near the hedges and trees until they reached the school.

"I wish I had my key," Mary whispered while they hugged the shadows beside the front entrance.

"Now you're sure there's no alarm?" he asked. When she nodded, he opened the miniature tool kit he'd retrieved from his condo and had the door open in less than two minutes.

He carefully closed the self-locking door, led the way to her classroom and ushered her inside. The spotlights from the back of the closest house shone through the windows, reducing the room by night to stark gray and black.

Mary hesitated for a moment, glancing down at the big pillow she had been sitting on when Ford had first barreled into her life. The memory of that kiss tingled on her lips. It had been urgent, consuming, and more than a little scary, just like their every action these past two days. And like tonight's escapade.

She shook off the feeling and went straight for the cubbyholes bearing boldly printed names that stood out, even in the near darkness.

Since it was the weekend, most were empty. She noted little Libby's forgotten bunny in one, and Sarah's wadded, fuzzy security blanket in another. Mary didn't envy Sarah's parents their weekend without "banky," she thought with a frown.

Her own roomy tote bag nearly filled the open compartment bearing her name. Catching it by the wide strap, she pulled it free. Through the leather she could feel the sharp edges of the two foot-long boxes that held the nine-inch dolls.

"Looks like a weekender instead of a handbag," Ford commented.

"Because I bring show-and-tell surprises for the kids every day," she whispered as she hooked the strap over her head and settled the bag comfortably against her side. "All set! Let's go," she said, patting the purse.

Ford clutched her elbow and pulled her toward the door. "Come on, we'd better get out of here."

They quickly left the way they had come. A patchy fog had drifted in, granting them more cover than they'd had on the way in. As a result, Ford took a more direct route to the park.

Only moments later, Ford pulled out of the park slowly, so their exit wouldn't draw attention. Soon they reached the on-ramp to 440 South and were absorbed into the late-night traffic. Mary watched him forcibly relax, flexing his fingers on the steering wheel, shifting his chin to unclench his jaw.

Then for miles, he kept his eyes on the highway except for frequent glances in the rearview mirror.

Mary hoped this would be her last excursion into the world of breaking and entering. She sighed, leaned back against the headrest and closed her eyes.

"If you're bored, I'll take you home," Ford said with a chuckle.

Mary laughed, too, and some of her tension dissipated. "Give me a break. I'm not used to this. Please tell me our crime wave's over for tonight."

"Yeah, I think we've had enough excitement."

With a last look behind them, Ford took the next exit and pulled up beside an all-night Texaco station. They sat there for a while with the engine idling, watching the off-ramp until Ford decided they hadn't been followed.

Though he had assured her repeatedly that neither Perry nor Agent Blevins would expect them to turn up at the preschool, Mary knew Ford was exercising every caution in the event that he was wrong.

"Looks like a successful heist!" he declared finally and pulled around to one of the pumps. "Come on," he said as he opened his door. "You can hit the ladies' room while I gas up the Jeep and get us some coffee."

Mary wondered how he knew she needed to go. Was he that attuned to her? Nonsense, she thought, laughing to herself. It was only that they had been busy for several hours now, and had downed numerous cups of coffee in preparation for their little adventure. He'd be feeling the results of that, as well. She shrugged her purse strap higher on her shoulder and followed him into the station.

Once she had taken care of business, Mary washed her hands and looked in the mirror over the sink. Her face was as pale as a death mask, surrounded by several dark strands that had escaped her beret. She unzipped her bag to find her hairbrush.

The doll boxes rested on top of everything else. Open. And empty. "Ford!" she cried, rushing out of the rest room and through the aisles of toiletries and snacks. "Ford! They're gone!"

He turned from the counter, warning her to silence with a look. The clerk glanced back and forth between them, curious.

Mary shrugged. "Can't find my glasses," she explained. "Maybe I left them in the car."

"You'd better go see if they're there," Ford said. He handed her one of the capped plastic cups, plunked down a twenty and a five, and calmly awaited change.

Mary rushed out and climbed into the Jeep. She set the coffee in the cup holder and began emptying the contents of her bag onto her lap, though she knew the dolls were not in it.

Ford got in, slammed his door and settled back to watch her. "Any theories?" he asked, peeling the lid off his cup.

Mary slumped back in her seat and closed her eyes. "Somebody obviously figured out the dolls were there. Nothing else is missing." She roused herself and began replacing the items she had scattered in the futile search.

He reached over and took one of the boxes, examining it.

"They were left open," she told him. "Whoever took the dolls must have been in a hurry."

"Not one of the teachers, then," he said thoughtfully.

"No, of course it wasn't!" Mary said, aghast. "I don't work with thieves!"

One of his dark brows shot up. Mary realized his thought before he voiced it. "Don't you?"

"Don't be an idiot!" she said defensively, crossing her arms over the purse.

"Maybe I have been already," he said, sipping the hot coffee and staring out into the night. After a moment, he recapped his cup, set it in the holder and reached for the ignition key. "Guess we'd better go and get some sleep."

The silent ride back to her grandmother's house worked on Mary's already frazzled nerves. What could she say to convince him that she had nothing to do with the dolls' disappearance?

"We'll talk about it tomorrow," he said when they ar-rived. Then he sent her into the study where she spent a restless few hours alone.

Mary finally gave up trying to sleep. She showered and dressed in comfortable navy slacks and a pullover. Since she had her purse now, she applied a little makeup. It was the closest thing to armor she had, and she needed to pre-pare for the battle that was about to ensue. The only weapon she could wield against Ford's suspicion was the truth. Somehow, she didn't believe it would prove ade-quate.

Ford leaned his forehead against his palms and ran his fingers through his hair. No matter how he figured it, she looked guilty as hell. No one knew she had left those dolls at the school but Mary and himself. Except the person she must have phoned after they got here.

She had called Knoblett yesterday without his knowing what she was up to, and could just as easily have called the courier she was supposed to meet with the diamonds. Whoever took them had to have broken in exactly as he had done, gotten what he was after and split. It couldn't have been a regular break-in because nothing else had been disturbed.

"He might have realized I didn't have time to get my purse," Mary said. "If Perry thought I had the diamonds, where else would he think they'd be but in my handbag? Or it could have been Blevins, for that matter! He might have figured it out."

"Into mind reading, are you?" Ford asked, glaring at her. She had no right to look that great with only three hours' sleep. He felt like hell and looked it, he was sure.

Mary sighed and slid into the chair to his right. "I can't imagine what else you'd be thinking about," she replied wearily.

"Try what we're going to do next," he said wryly. "Even if you're telling the truth and are right about Perry, he's still going to want you dead. You saw him kill Antonio.''

"*Heard* him do it," she corrected, stealing a sip from his cup of coffee.

"Yeah, but he doesn't know that. I gotta tell you, Mary, a hit man wouldn't waste time doodling around in your cubby for loot. He'd think it was beneath him. Somebody else is involved here. I can't play this little game right if I don't have all the cards. Who'd you phone to pick up those dolls?''

"Nobody!" she assured him, reaching for the long roll of cookies he had opened earlier and taking several. She nibbled thoughtfully. "Who says a killer can't also dabble in other things?''

Ford watched her, looking for signs of guilt. He saw none, but that didn't absolve her. He was hardly objective when it came to Mary Shaw.

She nodded twice, slowly. "I think I've got it figured out. Try this. Perry found out about Antonio's part in the theft ring. Maybe he approached him about sharing the diamonds instead of passing them on as Antonio had done in the past.''

"Not possible," Ford argued. "Somebody might have done that, but I'll bet you money it wasn't Damien Perry. If what we have on him is any indication, wealth means nothing. He probably lives in a little monk cell somewhere fondling his high-powered scope between jobs. With men like him, it's the kill they enjoy.''

Ford could see her picturing the monster he'd just described. Her wide eyes and tremors affected him so much, he felt obliged to change the subject. Scaring women made him sick.

"Want to guess why your buddy put them in those dolls?''

Mary got up and poured him another cup of coffee, since she had drunk half of his already, and fixed one for herself.

"We don't know that he did put them inside," she said,

glancing at him over her shoulder. "If he did, then maybe that's the way he shipped the others. Antonio deals with shops in other countries all the time, seeking or supplying specific requests by customers. There might not be another courier at all. Had you thought of that? He could have intended to mail the dolls to wherever they go. Amsterdam, you said?"

"Diamond city," Ford explained. "Lots of expert cutters there who can alter the gems so that they're no longer recognizable when they hit the market." He paused. "And no, I don't buy his trusting the postal service with gems worth millions. Would you?"

"Good point. He didn't with other expensive items."

Ford went on instant alert. "Who did he hire?"

"Didn't," she explained. "He hand-carried or the buyers sent someone to get them."

She rejoined him at the table, leaning closer as though they were telling secrets. "If the diamonds *were* in the dolls, and if Antonio gave them to me, it's because he knew I would keep them safe for him until he told me what he meant to do with them."

"What did he do with the others you took care of?" Ford asked.

"He gave them to me for a charity auction benefiting cancer research. For the children, he said. They brought a magnificent sum."

"No sparklers in those, I'll bet," Ford muttered.

He couldn't restrain a smile. Mary was talking her way right past his mistrust again. The girl was good. She might still be guilty as hell, but she was definitely good. "Okay, I'll rent that for a minute. Tell me how you think Perry figures into it."

Her brow furrowed while she worked it out. When she answered, she paused between sentences as though testing them for plausibility. "Someone else must be involved. Antonio refused to give up the gems to whoever that is. He wasn't the type to renege on a deal, you know. So, this person who had approached him failed to get his cooperation. Then they probably hired Perry to kill him and steal the diamonds. I prevented Perry's searching either Antonio or the shop when I called the police. The sirens alerted him and he ran.''

"So why would he or the man who hired him go looking for the dolls Antonio gave you?"

She bit her lips together, searching for an answer. There wasn't one. Wide-eyed and appealing, Mary placed her hand on his arm, squeezing it. "Please, believe me, Ford. I had nothing to do with any of this."

God help him, he wanted to believe her. He wanted that so badly it hurt. Probably because he wanted *her*. But he had a job to do that involved more than keeping her safe.

"Innocent until proved guilty" might prevail once suspects got into a court of law. But until then, when officers or agents were in the process of eliminating possibilities, that rule was reversed.

Mary did not have the diamonds at the moment, he knew that much for certain. If she knew who did, she wasn't going to tell him. Ford couldn't see spending however long they had left together locked in a debate over her guilt or innocence. She would certainly be a lot more cooperative if she thought he believed her completely.

"Okay, Mary, your theory makes sense," he said. "At least we gave it a shot, huh?" Forcing a grin, he punched her gently on the shoulder. "By the way, you did fine tonight."

Mary shuddered in response and hugged herself, triggering anew Ford's urgent desire to protect her from anything that might threaten her. That included doll manglers, murderers, and even the justice system he'd sworn an oath to uphold.

Could he disregard the law for her? Bending rules was one thing; aiding and abetting, quite another. Could he justify not telling Blevins everything that had happened when he knew it would solidly implicate Mary, right up to those lovely eyebrows? He had only a few hours left to decide.

"Well," Mary said, closing up the roll of cookies and reaching for both cups, "what are the plans for today?"

Getting to know you better, Ford decided. Somehow, he had to come to a decision he could live with. Either he would keep Mary hidden and throw all his energy into proving her innocence, or turn her over to Blevins and do what he could to get her a reduced sentence.

He knew he was playing judge and jury here, and without any objectivity at all. Maybe if he ignored the beauty that all but struck him dumb, and pushed aside the memories of fantastic sex with her on the window seat, he could discover the real Mary Shaw.

Would he find a little rich girl, battling the boredom of the straight and narrow by indulging in grand larceny? Or, as he hoped, would she turn out to be exactly what she appeared to be and what he devoutly hoped she was?

Ford clicked his tongue against the roof of his mouth, shook his head sharply, and puffed out a breath of resignation. He didn't think he had ever wished the role of victim on anyone before, but he did it now. He prayed Mary was a victim of circumstance, caught up in all this by chance.

"Got any games?" he asked, deliberately forcing his mind from the games he'd love to play with her. "You know, cards, board games? Something to pass the time?"

"Of course!" She brightened like a kid on the way to recess.

She found several upstairs and brought them down to the study. They settled on the floor on opposite sides of the coffee table. He rejected an unrecognizable game with a French title, another in English that he'd never played, and settled on an old standard, guaranteed to kill a few hours.

After a couple of rounds of Monopoly—which he had always hated—Ford established the fact that Mary cheated shamelessly. But she did so poorly, and fairly openly. And crowed with delight when she won.

It proved nothing, Ford told himself. Everybody did it. He'd done it himself once after Molly had creamed him for the third time in a row. Thinking about his sister brought family to mind. Maybe if he learned more about Mary's, it would give him a clue what she was really like.

"Enough of that. How about pictures?" he asked, dumping the play money back into the Monopoly box without separating it. "Got any photo albums?"

This time, she didn't appear all that enthusiastic. "Why?"

"Just curious. Want to see what you looked like without your front teeth, whether you had freckles on that classic nose when you were nine."

Mary smiled and rolled her eyes, causing his breath to catch and his chest to tighten. Among other things. "You would leave me no pride," she complained.

"None at all," he agreed, laughing. "C'mon, be a sport."

"You asked for it," she said, rising and striding languidly to the bookshelves near the corner of the room.

Ford watched, enjoying the way she moved. Like a runway model, only not so theatrically. Her hips thrust forward just the least bit, giving her walk a grace and balance most women didn't possess. That wonderful posture of hers made her seem taller than she was, too. And elegant. Probably learned all that in charm school with a stack of books on her head, he thought.

She brought back a thick leather-bound album with her name engraved on the front. Mary Vanessa Ellington-Shaw. At his questioning look, she wrinkled her nose and explained, "Mother felt compelled to hyphenate, but she got over it."

Together they turned through the pages and reviewed her infancy and early childhood. The only thing Ford learned was that Mary had always been beautiful. For her, there had existed no awkward and ungainly phase like what his sister and her pals had suffered. But then, the photos stopped at age twelve.

Ford took the album from her and went to return it. Another rested next to the vacant spot and he pulled it from the shelf. "Now!" he insisted, shaking his finger at her cry of protest. "Now we get at the truth, right? I'll bet your first boyfriend's in this one, and he looks like Eddie Munster."

"No, he's not in there," she said, her reply subdued. "Would you excuse me?"

"What's wrong, hon?" he asked as he laid the album down on the table and sat beside her. Without thinking, he took her hands in his and leaned forward, his face only a few inches from hers.

She pulled away and stood, one hand massaging her forehead. "If you don't mind, I'd like to take a nap. We didn't get much sleep last night, and suddenly I feel sort of wrung out."

"Sure," Ford said, thinking guiltily about how he had disconnected the phone lines in anticipation of something like this. "Go ahead. Why don't you go upstairs where you can sleep in a real bed for a change. It's okay during the day when I'm keeping watch."

"Thanks," she mumbled and left the room. Her walk to the door looked more as if she were making a trip to the gallows. But still, in all, Mary had taken things in stride when it counted. Anybody would be a little bummed out after last night's escapades.

Ford left the album on the coffee table, sat cross-legged on the floor, leaned back against one of the sofas and opened the second book.

Five minutes later, he slapped it shut, then immediately opened it again, unable to resist seeing the rest.

"Baby Rambo," he mumbled, and added an expletive for good measure. He looked up as if his wondering gaze

could reach through the ceiling and into her upstairs bedroom.

How in hell could he equate these pictures with the
woman he had thought Mary was? Smuggling diamonds
would seem like kid stuff compared to what someone had
caught her doing on film.

Chapter 9

Mary awoke cold, thirsty, and in the dark. Just in time, she remembered not to switch on the lamp beside her bed. Only in the study did Ford allow that. Why hadn't he wakened her earlier, she wondered?

She stumbled into the bathroom, splashed water on her face and ran a comb through her hair, even though she couldn't see what she was doing. Then she felt her way back through her bedroom and headed downstairs. She shivered, as much a result of nerves as the sudden drop in temperature.

Hopefully, her decision to come upstairs had distracted Ford from looking at the album. That had been her intention, anyway. Snatching it out of his hands would have made him even more curious and determined to see it.

Gran ought to have gotten rid of it years ago. Mary understood why she hadn't. Her father would want the pictures since they were the last ones taken of her mother.

The questions Ford would ask and the memories those

pictures would summon, were not what Mary needed to face right now with all the other things going on.

The moment she entered the study, she knew her tactic to divert Ford's interest had failed. His expression made her feel defensive. "Will you stop looking at me as though I'd grown two heads?"

He cut that piercing gaze of his toward the coffee table bearing several sandwiches and two bottles of cranberry juice. "Sit down and eat first."

Mary laughed bitterly. "First? Before the inquisition?" But she sat and ate anyway, needing fuel, and needing to postpone the inevitable. She knew he'd require an explanation, but couldn't imagine what would have made him angry when he saw the pictures. He looked ready to chew nails.

To his credit, Ford did wait until she had finished before he began.

"Why the act, Mary? Simple schoolteacher who swoons over a preacher. Demure little rich girl who never gets her hands dirty. Scared of guns. That was a lion you shot, for Chrissake! A lion!"

He picked up the album and slammed it on the table between them. "Explain it to me! Tell me that's your evil twin or something!"

"It's my evil twin," she said, deliberately stretching her arms out across the back of the sofa as though she hadn't a care in the world. She drummed her fingers on the leather, looking at him from beneath lowered lids, challenging him to get even angrier than he was—so angry that he would walk out on her.

She thought for a moment he might just up and leave, but he sucked in a deep breath and glared at her. When he did speak, his calm voice belied the fact that he looked ready to explode.

"When was this?" He turned a couple of pages. One long, tanned finger stabbed at a picture of her at fourteen, holding her father's bolt-action Webley, her booted foot resting on the carcass of the giant cat he had shot in defense of their native guide.

Mary shrugged. "That was on safari in Kenya. I didn't kill the animal. Dad just thought that would make an interesting picture."

"Right," he bit out, flipping to another page. "And this—this must be trick photography?"

He tipped the book so she could see the photo of her hanging by a rope, feet toed against the vertical rock, fingers clinging in the narrow fissures. Her mother braced below her in the same position, waving up with one hand. Her father had reached the top and aimed straight down to get the photograph, capturing the full depth of the gorge below them. Mary's insides quaked, just looking at it.

She quickly averted her eyes.

Could she ever make him understand? Why should she try? It was none of his business what she'd done, and not her fault that he thought he'd misjudged her.

She sighed. "Well, they certainly weren't going to climb the kiddie face just because *I* was with them!"

A look of confusion almost replaced the one of anger. Quickly he turned through the album, thankfully skipping over the skydiving and shark studies, and looked at the last page. "How old were you in this one?" he demanded, showing her the photograph on the last page, one similar to the other shot, but on a more difficult climb in another location.

"Fifteen," she informed him curtly.

Thank God there were no photos of her last excursion. "Not long after that, I came to live at Gran's." *Ready for a straitjacket,* she didn't add.

"I can't wait to see what you graduated to as an adult, though I'm afraid I already know! That climbing experience must come in pretty handy when you scale tall buildings. I gotta wonder how many of your jobs are on the books unsolved! Ever worked Miami, Palm Beach? We've got a couple hanging there we can't connect yet. I should have guessed when you dressed the part so well last night."

"Don't be an ass, Ford," she snapped. "I couldn't climb to a second-story balcony if my life depended on it. No now."

He smirked. "Yeah, well, you did okay on that fence behind your house, didn't you? You sure didn't need my help when you went over it the first time."

Mary shrugged. She couldn't deny it.

"So where's the next volume?" he asked. "I couldn' find that one."

She looked away. "There is no next. Mother died and Dad sent me home to Gran's."

For a long time, he said nothing. Quietly, he closed the book and laid it aside. "I'm sorry about that. I didn't know What happened?"

Mary pushed up off the sofa and picked up the album. Only when she had carefully replaced it in its niche on the shelf, did she turn and speak to him.

"It was off a relatively easy face in Oregon near a friend's ranch. Just a practice climb. Didn't anchor her be-laying pin well enough and fell a little over a hundred feet. Lived about forty-five minutes." *Forty-three, to be exact. In agony, with no rescue expected and only a teenage bas ket case for comfort.*

Ford looked upset. She felt nauseous herself, just think-ing about it. For years she had tried to forget what had happened and had succeeded for the most part.

"Well, that's that," she said, trying to shake off the im age of her mother's broken body and her own hysteria "So, what you see is what you get now. Supergirl retired."

He watched her as though he thought she might crumble but Mary knew she wouldn't. That had already happened a long time ago.

"If you say so," he said doubtfully. After a long pause he added quietly, "I want you to pack your things, Mary We're leaving in the morning."

She raised one eyebrow in question.

"I'm taking you in," he said, his voice as flat and unemotional as she had ever heard it. "I'll do whatever I can for you, but I need some distance to do that."

Mary nodded. No point in arguing with him. She could see that Ford had made up his mind.

Seeing those photos had given him ideas she hadn't even considered. Explaining about her mother's death was what she had dreaded. His supposition was far worse.

He had obviously decided that if she had gone to such great lengths to deceive everyone about the kind of woman she was, then she must be lying about everything else. What other reason would she have to make herself over into someone she was not? A cover, of course, for her life of crime.

The notion would be downright funny if it were not so plausible to Ford.

He wouldn't believe the mental wreck she was after that last fateful summer with her parents. A summer that had turned an all-or-nothing, cocky, athletic teen into a cringing crybaby who couldn't face anything as risky as a ride on a Ferris wheel. Only Gran had understood. And now there was no one left who would.

Mary went into the bathroom off the study to gather the things she had hand washed yesterday. Her travel bag contained everything else she had brought with her from the house in town.

Returning to the study she stuffed the few items in one of the side pockets and set the bag on the sofa beside her purse. "I'm ready," she said.

"We'll stay the night here," he said. "That will give Blevins time to arrange…accommodations."

Mary wondered whether she would see Ford again after tomorrow morning. Of course she would see him, she thought with a huff of resignation. He'd probably testify against her at her trial.

"Grand theft" and "accessory to murder," he had said.

With the tape of her conversation with Antonio, Ford's certainty that the diamonds were in the dolls, and the empty doll boxes in her purse, they'd probably have enough to get her arraigned.

Why wouldn't Agent Blevins just put her in jail tomorrow and be done with it? Or maybe that was the plan, and Ford didn't want to tell her yet. A dauntless daredevil like herself might try an escape, Mary thought wryly. Well, why not?

Mary contemplated it. She could go to Mr. Knoblett's and get him to give her a ride to the airport before Ford even knew she was gone....

"Don't even think about it," Ford said, a look of grave disappointment darkening his features. "A little free advice, Mary. Don't *ever* play poker."

So much for that. Now she'd erased any chance of convincing him she was innocent. Mary sank onto the sofa and closed her eyes, deliberately relaxing the muscles of her face into a non-expression while she tried to think of an alternative plan.

Ford couldn't believe he had been so gullible. From the moment he had seen Mary sitting on that cushion reading a storybook to the kids, maybe even before that when he first saw her photo in the file, she had skewed his thinking. Helpless, my foot, he thought.

She had altered her appearance and attitude drastically. It didn't take Einstein to figure out why, either.

He decided that physical risks, merely pitting herself against the forces of nature, must have paled for her, so she'd gone for something a lot more daring. Federal offenses, at that; not small stuff like shoplifting. The possible penalties would have to be disastrous to get her interest.

Building her cover must have taken a while. That in itself would have excited her. Ford knew. He had experienced that himself, getting ready for undercover gigs.

He understood the anticipation she would have felt preparing, waiting for the job to begin, the itchy inner need to throw herself into something that could result in either immense satisfaction or total, maybe fatal, failure.

Ford shook his head and puffed out a harsh breath, recalling the rush that excitement provided. Mary was hooked on it, as surely as if it were hard drugs. A danger junkie. It took one to know one.

Ford admitted to himself that he hadn't kicked the craving yet or he certainly wouldn't be where he was, doing what he was doing right now—not as hair-raising as some of his exploits down in South America, but then the job wasn't over yet.

Mary's alterations certainly succeeded. If he hadn't seen her caught in the acts on film, he would never have believed Mary capable of such feats. Just looking at the damned pictures of the things she had done made him cringe.

Though she hadn't looked overtly muscular in those photos taken with her parents, she had given the impression of sturdy youth, fearless and lithe, ready for any challenge. Now here was this willowy, graceful example of feminine vulnerability. Remarkable.

She'd taken him in, all right. He wondered just how long she had worked on this false image. Long enough to get herself in a mess of trouble, that was for sure.

Even now, with all he had just learned about her, Ford knew he would go to just about any length to keep her out of jail, and certainly to keep her alive.

But he couldn't stay here with her and do that. He had to trust the rest of his team to put her somewhere safe so that he could eliminate Perry; so that he could find some way to explain away the evidence against Mary. Right now, it was nothing more than highly circumstantial. Not even that, officially, unless he added his two cents' worth.

They only had the recording of her little talk with Antonio. Ford could add her admission that the man had given her dolls, probably stuffed with the gems. He could tell them about Mary's opportunity to phone an accomplice to pick them up, and then he could produce the empty doll boxes.

If he volunteered this information about her thrill-seeking exploits, they would have a motive in addition to any monetary gain. She hardly needed that last reason to get involved, her attorney could argue. But a lawyer couldn't refute those pictures. She sought danger. Thrived on it.

Was all this a recent lark? Or would he find out that she had helped organize the whole thing, maybe even participated in robberies they hadn't connected to the ring yet?

What he would do about this newest development, Ford couldn't guess, and that scared him. How far would he go to protect Mary? Could he compromise his own integrity to get her out of this?

Yeah, he needed a little space between them to get his head straight. The only way he could get that would be to take her to Blevins and let him hide her.

Before he could change his mind, he picked up the phone and punched in the number.

"Where are you?" Blevins demanded.

"You really gotta chill out before you get an ulcer," Ford said, then held the phone away from his ear and let him rant awhile.

When the invective stopped, Ford resumed. "We're at her grandmother's house near Franklin, but you won't need the address. I'm bringing her to you first thing in the morning."

Blevins argued at that, still demanding their exact location. Ford ignored it.

"Look, boss, this is going nowhere, and security here is the pits. Maybe you can get one of the TBI safe houses and a couple of their guys to baby-sit. Will you free me up for a shot at Perry? He could have those gems."

Ford didn't think so, though there was a remote possibility. *Somebody* had the damned things, but he figured it was the mysterious courier, the one Mary must have phoned to pick them up.

After a long silence, Blevins agreed. "Okay. Keep the woman there tonight while I arrange something. Stay right where you are. And keep that phone turned on. I'll call you as soon as everything's set up."

"Roger," Ford agreed, and cut the connection. Why, he wondered, were the small hairs on the back of his neck standing straight out?

He clicked on the television and settled back to watch. Peter Jennings barely registered and might as well have been relating the news in Swahili. Ford's thoughts remained on Mary and the question of his feelings for her.

Now and then he glanced over at her as she reclined on the opposite sofa. What drew him to her, and sparked this almost-obsessive desire he felt? Lust, yes, but it was something far stronger than that.

That made him mad as hell, as much with himself as with her. He was a veteran when it came to seeing through people, not some kid, green off the farm; but he sure couldn't prove it by his initial assessment of Mary Shaw. She'd really had him going. Even so, he couldn't stand the thought of caging her up with hardened criminals, no matter what she had done.

He had some decisions to make here—big ones that would affect him for the rest of his life. If he protected her completely, he would have to resign. No way could he do this job, knowing he had suppressed evidence. That would be difficult to live with, no matter what he did afterward.

And of course, he would have to take charge of Mary then, a permanent commitment, so that he could make certain she never broke the law again in any way. He'd be responsible.

Ford couldn't believe what he was thinking. Maybe he had skirted a few rules in his time. Okay, a lot of rules. But he'd never seriously considered breaking the law. Laws should apply to everybody, even the woman he…what? Needed to protect? Wanted more than air and food? Loved? Could he bring himself to withhold what he knew about

Mary—information that would strengthen a case against her—when he wasn't even certain why he was doing it?

Programs on the TV screen slid past in slow succession. Even when Mary went into the bathroom and back, and later got up and fiddled around in the desk drawers on the other side of the room, Ford didn't pay much attention. Soul-searching took time, and he wasn't finding what he was looking for.

"Ford?" Mary said, as she came over and sat down on the sofa beside him. "I thought of someone who can corroborate my story."

"And which story is that?" he asked, his mind still focused on his inner turmoil.

"That I'm not some burglar in disguise. And that I would never get involved in anything as perilous as jewel theft, either as a perpetrator or an accomplice," she said. "I sort of lost it after Mother's accident. It ended any desire I ever had for taking risks. Would you call my therapist? She can verify how Mother's death affected me."

Ford shot her a look of disbelief. "You want me to call your shrink? Are you still seeing her?"

"Not officially, but we still talk now and then." She laid her hand on his arm and looked directly into his eyes, searching, almost pleading. "Ford, I'm not what you think. I promise I'm not." With her free hand, she held out a business card. "Call her."

He beat back the urge to grasp at anything that might indicate Mary was telling the truth. More than anything, he wanted proof that she hadn't deliberately deceived him and everyone else.

"Well, I guess it wouldn't hurt to check it out."

He got up then, dislodging her hand. He felt reluctant to touch her or have her touch him, especially when their emotions were so highly charged. The feeling of her cool palm and fingers against his forearm lingered.

"Stay here," he instructed, and left the room. He would reconnect the phones. A three-way conversation with this therapist might not settle matters the way Mary thought—the way he hoped—but it could reveal something one way or another.

If nothing else came of it, maybe having the phones working again, and giving Mary private access to one later, might get him the number of her accomplice—provided she had one.

He realized his mind had already latched on to the hope that she didn't, but he had to know for sure.

Once he had reestablished the phone service from the main connection, Ford brought the portable from the kitchen so that he and Mary could speak to her former doctor concurrently.

After trying the number for the third time and getting no answer, Mary left a message asking her to return the call. Then she sighed deeply and her shoulders slumped with defeat. Her eagerness to call the therapist further encouraged Ford to believe that Mary was telling the truth about how and why she had changed so much.

He felt inclined to try to make her feel better, anyway. "It's only seven-thirty. Maybe the doctor's out of town for the weekend and not home yet," he suggested. "We'll try again later."

"If you talk to her and she backs up what I've said, do you still mean to take me back to town?" Mary asked.

The loud ring and chirp from two phones startled both of them before he could reply.

Mary fumbled for a moment before she answered, "Yes? Hello?" Her eyes widened as she handed the instrument to Ford. "It's Mr. Knoblett. He wants you."

Ford took the call, watching Mary as he listened, hating that her features wore that worried frown. He issued a clipped "Thanks," then hung up.

"Come on! We've got to get out of here."

"What's happened?" she asked, scrambling off the sofa.

"Knoblett was down at his store for something. While he was closing up, he noticed car lights turn, headed this

way. We've got less than five minutes to clear out of here!''
Ford announced, picking up her bag and his own. "Grab
your jacket." He shrugged into his own.

"We could hide! Or you could surprise him, maybe
catch him!" Mary said.

He knew she wished they could end this business right
now and put it behind them. "Not when he's packing that
assault weapon that tore the hell out of Molly's van! Come
on, you're supposed to show me the back way out of here,
through the field and up an old logging trail. You know
where it is?"

"Yes," Mary said as they reached the door and he
started to switch off the lights. "Ford, wait! Your phone!"

He backtracked and found it. Then they dashed through
the darkness of the hallway and the kitchen.

Ford cursed under his breath while his heart pounded.
No chance it could be a neighbor coming this way. Nobody
knew Mary was here but Knoblett. This stretch of road
didn't go past any other houses. It dead-ended here at the
mansion.

Blevins had no reason to send anyone out, even though
he did have the means to discover the exact location if he
wanted to. Perry must have discovered it, as well. Ford was
afraid he knew how. Fury at the betrayal created a bitter
taste in his mouth and made his gut churn with the need to
retaliate. Later.

They rushed out the back door toward the carriage house
and jumped into the Jeep. "That way," Mary said, pointing
as she clicked her seat belt in place.

It was not yet eight o'clock. Dark as pitch with no moon.
And colder. Ford drove, barreling across several acres of
pastureland Mary had leased to the neighbors. She indicated
an almost-invisible break in the tree line. "There. The
trail!"

They wheeled past an ancient oak and on into the
wooded area, thick with mostly evergreens. Low-hanging

limbs whipped the windshield and undergrowth scraped the sides of the Jeep.

"Should we stop and just hide here?" Mary asked, her words coming in huffs. Her teeth clicked as they bounced over holes and fallen limbs.

"Can't. He'll check out the house first. That'll take a while, but he'll find our tracks across the pasture for sure, soon as the sun comes up. Probably before then. We'll have to keep going," Ford said. "Can we get on a secondary road from here?"

"I don't know!" She yelped when they hit a huge hole, and braced her hands against the dash. "I remember two trails leading away from the old logging camp. One goes to a small cabin about eight or ten miles away. Gramps leased it to hunters when he wasn't using it himself. That trail stops there. I don't know where the other one goes. Maybe to another road."

"Anybody else know about the cabin?"

She thought for a minute. "Mr. Knoblett. Maybe Mr. Cranston. He's the only close neighbor. The hunters Gramps rented it to know where it is. I don't think we should risk going there. I mean, the path leads right to it."

"There has to be another way out of these woods," Ford said. "I can't imagine those logging trucks tooling past the big house. We'll try the other road."

Mary's head hurt. Her heart ached, too, when she thought of that criminal who was probably ransacking Gran's house right now. First those agents going through her father's house, and now this guy violating the old family home. Nothing would be untouched when all this was finally over. Least of all, her.

They bumped on at a slower pace. The logging camp proved to be nothing more than a weed-choked clearing with a couple of tumbledown buildings. The place looked so much smaller than it had the few times she had been here with Gramps. Years had passed since then—thirteen or fourteen, at least. The logging had been in operation more recently than that, but not by much, considering the rusted state of the abandoned equipment.

A deep stream cut through the woods, off to the right, she remembered, and followed the trail to the cabin. She had no idea when the hunters had used the old cabin last. No one had contacted her about leasing it this year since Gran had died. Too risky to go there, anyway.

"Turn there!" Mary said, pointing to the other barely discernible path through the tall loblolly pines. Ford plowed right through the brush. If Perry did follow, he would have no trouble deciding which way they had gone.

Twenty minutes later, they emerged onto another road, crudely paved and unlined. Ford let the engine idle as he looked both ways. "Where are we?"

Mary pointed left. "That probably comes out somewhere near the interstate." Ford wheeled right and picked up speed.

"Wait, you're going the wrong way!" Mary said, turning to look behind them. "I'm sure that's east."

"I love a woman with a good sense of direction," he commented with a chuckle. "But your thinking's way too predictable."

"I think this must be one of the roads that crosses at Knoblett's store," she warned him. "We could meet the guy head-on if he didn't chase us through the woods!"

Ford glanced over at her, his smile wide. "Life's just full of little gambles."

Chapter 10

"Fish out the phone," Ford ordered. "Call Knoblett. Ask him if he can get us some supplies for camping. A tent and sleeping bags, if he's got any."

The idea of camping held no appeal, especially with the cold front that had been moving in all day. After several days of unseasonably warm weather, the temperature had dropped to near freezing since early morning, and it felt like snow. But Mary had to trust that Ford knew what he was doing, here. Surely he only meant to have these things for emergency purposes.

What in the world would Mr. Knoblett be doing with camping stuff? she wondered as she got a positive response for the things Ford wanted.

With the line still open, she repeated what Mr. Knoblett said to Ford. "We're to go to his house and take whatever we need. He's going to stay there at the store and see if that car comes back by."

Ford nodded. "Give him the phone number and tell him to buzz us if that happens." He snapped out the number, and added quickly, before she could resume her conversation, "By the way, tell him which way we turned out of the woods and find out where the hell we are in relation to his place."

Mary bit back a smile as she repeated what Ford had said into the phone. A *man*, asking for *directions?* Then the thought occurred to her that he hadn't asked at all. He had made her do it for him. Maybe he was a little closer to normal than she'd figured.

Several side roads later, Mary motioned him into a driveway in front of the Knobletts' small frame house.

They went inside together through the unlocked back door. Later, armed with a meager amount of food, two down sleeping bags and a small dome tent, they returned to the Jeep.

Ford backtracked when they got back on the highway and headed toward the interstate.

He had just passed the narrow trail where they had exited the woods earlier when Mary noticed the Jeep's motor skip several times. Ford let off the accelerator and veered straight down the steep shoulder. They rolled through the trees for several hundred yards and bumped to a stop in a depression where the ground about them was thick with high weeds and littered with deadfall.

"Why did you do this? Don't you know we're miles from the interstate?" Mary asked urgently when he opened his door.

"Jeep's cutting out. We can't risk getting caught out in the open. You remember last time we stopped on the side of the road?"

"Could be the alternator," she muttered.

"Don't tell me—you were a mechanic in another life."

"I know a little about cars!" she declared, insulted by his condescension.

He gave a half laugh. "Can you fix it?"

"No," she admitted. "Can you?"

"No," he replied with a pained sigh.

"I would have thought that you, of all people would—"

"Know all about hot cars and fast women, being the blue-collar bad boy that I was? Hon, I rode a rusty bicycle until I was eighteen. Then Uncle Sam provided transportation. Where he sent me, wheels usually weren't necessary. When they were, I always managed to find some that worked."

"Oh. I just thought, since you fixed the van's muffler—"

"It came loose. I put it back. Looks like we've got a lot to learn about each other. I hope we'll have time to do that."

"But if we leave the Jeep, where will we go?" she asked.

"We'll go back in on foot, to your granddaddy's hunting cabin."

"If we can find it," she muttered. She could hardly recall what it looked like, much less where it was.

"We'll follow the road back in, but not until our boy gets through with it. A motel wouldn't have been safe anyway. I had planned for us to camp in some remote site. Perry might not have the resources to find out if we took a room somewhere, but whoever hired him to find us just might."

"You figured out who that is?" she asked.

"We'll kick that around later. Hold this." He had handed her the flashlight and stacked all their gear out of the way. Now he was busy piling dead branches around and on top of the vehicle as they talked.

"We really shouldn't go to the cabin," she insisted, hardly believing Ford would risk going there after what she had told him about it. Granted, it was a good twelve miles from the main house, but even that was too close. "That's just dumb, Ford."

"Then he won't expect us to do it. Don't worry. He'll follow our trail out of the woods and assume we've gone on."

She could hear the cocky smile in his voice and, as usual,

it made her want to smack him. Instead, she grumbled "Yes, and he'll come back tomorrow, follow our trail into the woods and find us!"

Ford handed her their bags, loaded the camping gear on his back, and motioned her toward the paved two-lane. "Trust me, he won't," Ford assured her. "At least not until I'm good and ready for him to."

Mary kept the beam from the flashlight low and watched him walk backward, combing up the flattened weeds with his fingers, arranging them so that they looked much as they had before the Jeep had flattened them in its wake.

When they had crossed the road, she shone the light back again and saw no evidence of where they had left the highway. He gently took the light from her and switched it off.

Ford seemed to know his business when it came to concealing trails, Mary thought. But she questioned the wisdom of his decision to stay in an area where they had already been discovered once. Unpredictability was one thing; tempting fate was quite another.

His impulse to do just that frightened her more than anything else about him. She had suffered the vagaries of fate once too often. The dichotomy puzzled her. Ford's presence made her feel safer than anyone else's had ever done, and yet she dreaded his every move, fearing it would cause a catastrophe. He always seemed to take the path of most resistance, to do the unexpected. In this instance, she had to trust that he knew the criminal mind better than she.

"It's getting colder," Mary informed him, as though he wouldn't have noticed. She felt an intermittent spitting of ice on her cheeks and hands. "Feels like snow."

"Yeah, we can always hope," Ford said. "But I'm afraid it might be worse."

Mary didn't pursue that. She didn't want him to confirm that it felt more like sleet.

The night offered no light at all, but the worn asphalt was smooth underfoot and kept them from wandering off into the inky wilderness. Ford held her hand and walked with one foot off the pavement. He soon hit a break in the ground cover.

"Here's the logging road," he announced, and guided Mary into the cover of the trees and brush beside the trail. "So far, so good."

She heard him drop the tent and gear onto the ground. Then he took her bag and purse from her and fitted the straps over his shoulder, combining the load with his own canvas tote.

"Stay right here and watch for his lights," he ordered, pointing toward the logging road. "We should have a good half hour or longer at the least. It will take him a while to find the way across the pasture and into the woods. Listen for his motor, too, in case he's driving blind. The minute you see or hear anything, go flat on the ground and don't look at the car directly. Eyes reflect. Got it?"

"Where will you be?" she asked. The fear in her voice sounded real enough. He supposed it was, in spite of her old escapades. After all, she had no weapon at hand, and no daddy around for backup.

"Setting up a temporary camp," he told her. "You'll be okay. I'll just be about a hundred yards away, a little deeper in. We have to know when he's exhausted this possibility. He might turn around and go back to check that other road—the one to the cabin—unless he did that one first."

"This just might work," Mary said, sounding thoughtful.

He heard the grudging admiration in her tone, and had to laugh at himself. After she had all but called him an idiot, it amazed Ford how little it took for her to make amends. And to make his chest swell like he'd won first prize for smarts.

"I'm glad you're so delighted with this plan, seeing as how one of us is going to have to wait here until he shows, and find out which direction he takes. It could take all night if he waits until the sun comes up."

"That one of us would be me," Mary stated with a sigh.

"That would be you," he confirmed, laughing. "At least until I get the tent popped up. If he hasn't gone one way or the other by that time, we'll take turns."

She reached for his arm and squeezed lightly. "I'm not complaining, and you don't have to stand watch. I slept a long time today and I'm wide-awake."

"And you don't want to crawl into that dark tent while I'm out here by the road," he guessed, covering her hand with his.

"That, too," she admitted. "Why are we camping so close to the roads?"

"Once he's investigated these roads through the woods, he won't be back, at least not tonight. He'll be too busy checking the motels along the interstate. If it doesn't snow tonight, we need to stick around until morning and see how well I've concealed the Jeep and our trail," he explained. "Just a precaution."

"Makes sense. Go ahead and do whatever you have to do. I'll be fine here."

Ford didn't doubt it for a minute, since she now knew he'd be close by. She might be willing to hazard everything in some instances, but she didn't like to do so by herself. One little piece to add to the puzzle that was Mary Shaw. He would have the complete picture before he was through with her. If he ever *got* through with her.

Something told him that even after all of this was over and she was safe, he wouldn't be able to leave Mary alone no matter how much he had learned about her, good or bad.

Doggedly, he plowed his way through the underbrush a little farther in than he had told her he would. It was hilly and rough going, and would provide good cover. As soon as he located a suitable area, he began setting up the small brown tent by feel.

He would never have bothered with it if she weren't along, but females hated the thought of bugs and snakes. Ford doubted there would be any out in this weather, but

Mary would worry about it the way all females did—even women with courage to sparc, like Molly and his mom. They'd as soon face a shark as a spider. He felt safe in assuming Mary would, too. He tried to forget the fact that she had already faced the sharks, for real. The little zip-up dome would at least ensure a good night's sleep for her, and she would need it for tomorrow's hike.

The sleeting increased as he worked. Ford hoped it would turn to snow. That would help conceal any of their tracks he had missed covering in the dark. The air felt colder than ever, stiffening his fingers and making him clumsy.

He had toyed with the idea of leaving some signs on purpose and getting this over with. But if he allowed Perry to find their trail, Ford knew he'd have to hide Mary and set up an ambush. The thought of ending the whole thing now tempted him, but Perry's aptitude for sniffing out a trap was an unknown factor.

Perry had him outgunned at the moment, anyway, judging by the way he'd shot up the van. Ford hoped he could even the odds a little and supplement his Glock. He'd seen all kinds of weapons' magazines at Knoblett's house. He planned to call the old guy later and see what could be arranged. A former marine ought to be able to lay his hands on something more sophisticated than that shotgun Ford had seen in the closet. Taking that had been out of the question. You just didn't mess with a man's only weapon unless he offered it.

As he worked, Ford enumerated all the facts he had on Perry and they didn't make a very long list. The Bureau file on him was brand-new. Ford thanked his lucky stars for that. Otherwise, he might not have recognized the man quickly enough to save Mary.

Perry had a distinctive face and build, easy to remember. Too tall, too blond, and too good-looking to blend into any crowd. Like a Hitler Youth's descendant. Though the instant recognition had come in handy, it bothered Ford. Why would a man like that choose the profession of assassin? Was he stupid or just cocky as hell? Ford hoped for both, but knew he couldn't count on either.

Perry's file lacked anything concrete, was just supposition and too many coincidences. He'd always been spotted in the right places at the right times, had iffy connections to suspect groups and individuals. Very little personal info had been included. He had a brief military background— three years as a grunt—no special-forces training or the like.

However, the years after Perry's army stint remained a total blank. The man could have spent a decade in some off-the-wall survivalist camp, for all Ford knew. He hoped to hell not, or they might be serving each other bullets for breakfast. Or a late-night feast.

One thing Ford did know for sure. Perry had qualified as expert with an M-16 in basic. No surprise there. The automatic used to spray them the other night hadn't taken any expertise, of course. But apparently, Perry did right well with something that shot a .308 Winchester. That was what had been used on two politicians he was suspected of dropping with one shot each.

The thought of Mary getting caught up in another shoot-out chilled Ford's blood. That was one reason he'd elected to stay here on her property, rather than seeking some unknown place in the wilds. Perry would probably find them eventually, wherever they went. At least here, she would have familiar woods to hide in, and stand a chance of running to the neighbors for help, should Ford blow this to hell and gone.

When he did lay the trap, he wanted to be damned certain the man went down as planned. Ford got no charge out of killing, but Perry might not leave him an option. If possible, Ford hoped to take him alive and get the name of the son of a bitch behind all this—a name he suspected might be all too familiar.

No question Perry would come after them, but this way

Ford could control things. Unless he missed his guess, he also knew precisely how to fix the time. He needed a few days to set it up, maximize their chances and prepare Mary for what was going down.

This was Ford's kind of turf, better cover than buildings, streets and alleyways. More familiar to him when engaged in a game like this. If Mary weren't with him, he would actually be looking forward to it. Since she was, an element of dread cooled his anticipation a little. Even so, he could feel the old blood pumping like crazy.

He wondered if she felt jazzed, too. If so, it wasn't exactly a terrific thing for them to have in common. With both of them psyching up for a battle royal, things could get wild. Hell, they already had. He and Mary had that to deal with, as well.

His breath whistled out as he tossed their gear inside the tent and zipped it closed. Mary was waiting out there, keeping an eye out for the man who meant to kill her. And even if she happened to find that a great big thrill, Ford now knew she wouldn't want to experience it all by herself.

Mary lay flat on the ground and squinted her eyes, peeking through her lashes at the car about to exit the old logging road. She watched as it idled for a few moments, then turned left and sped on in the direction of the interstate.

Safe now that the taillights had disappeared around a curve, she pushed herself into a sitting position just as Ford crept up behind her.

"That had to be him," she said.

"You okay?" he asked, running a palm along her sleeve.

"Fine," she replied, her breath rushing out with the word. "You think he'll come back in the morning to track us, don't you?"

Ford put his arm under hers, encouraging her to stand. "If he does, he won't find anything. Not until I want him to. Come on," he said, taking her hand in his and leading her into the woods. "Be careful and don't break any branches or trample anything you can avoid."

"It's dark, Ford! How am I supposed to do that?"

"Just take it easy. Keep your steps light."

"Right. When I can barely feel my feet," she grumbled.

She picked her way through the brushy undergrowth, stepping as gingerly as she could, following his example. Briars snagged at her clothing and scratched her ankles.

Suddenly Ford halted directly in front of her so that she bumped up against his back. The bulge of his pistol slammed into her midriff. He reached behind to steady her. Mary thought he held on just a few seconds too long, but she didn't object. In fact, she automatically clasped one arm around his waist.

"Wait here," he instructed gruffly, pulling away.

The man must have infrared vision, she thought, because she couldn't see a blessed thing. She heard his rustling around and then, thankfully, the unmistakable sound of the tent's zipper.

"Your bed awaits!" he announced. His fingers touched her hip as he searched for her hand and found it.

"I'm afraid I can't sleep after napping half the day," she said, torn between wanting to stay outside near him and needing the haven the small tent offered.

"Well, just climb in there and meditate or whatever," he ordered. "Unless you'd rather sit outside and gather ice."

She felt around for the opening and crawled through it. As much as she hated being alone, she did hope Ford wouldn't decide to follow her inside. Every time he touched her, she came unglued, despite her fear and the danger that threatened them. What would happen if he joined her in such a closed-in space?

Ford remained outside, however, and zipped her in. "Where are you going?" she called out.

"About six feet away," he answered. "If you wake up

and have to go potty, give me some warning so I won't shoot you. I'll have to show you where to go, anyway.''

She could hear the laughter in his voice and cursed under her breath. Ford was enjoying this to the extreme.

"This isn't the first time I've camped, I'll have you know!"

"First time you've camped with me," he replied easily. "This'll be a shade different from your comfy little catered outings with Mommy and Daddy."

Well, he had *that* right, Mary thought as she wriggled out a fairly comfortable spot and rested her head on her travel bag. She would never admit the amenities her former camping trips had afforded, even if Ford had guessed already. If he expected her to rough it, then she would.

Mary really felt that old saw apply—Damned if you do, damned if you don't. If she appeared tough and game for anything, that would verify Ford's belief that she'd lied about her fears and pretended to be different than she was. Didn't he believe that, anyway? If she totally wimped out, he would think it was only an act.

Mary knew she wouldn't do that. She had conquered most of her terrors somewhere along the way. Maybe years ago, once she'd gotten over the worst after her mother's death. No test of that had arisen since then. But the fearlessness her parents had worked to instill in her seemed a thing of the past, and she'd just as soon keep it there.

Once in a great while it flared unexpectedly, causing her to commit rash acts totally at odds with her current character. It certainly had leaped right out with a vengeance when she'd found Jim with the professor's wife. Her boldness later that night had almost gotten her killed, and Ford right along with her.

That proved she was right. Caution made sense. It ought to be a way of life for people like her, without exception. So should prudence. But she had lapsed there, too.

Having sex with Ford, a man she hardly knew, had seemed daring to her at the time. In retrospect, Mary saw that idiocy for what it was. It was not bold at all. Neither was it cautious or prudent. It only qualified as a terrible weakness.

Her life depended on Ford's commitment to protect her. She had craved his closeness and reassurance that he would not leave her alone. Mary had wanted nothing more than to lose herself in Ford that night. Now she was terrified that she'd done exactly that.

The incident only increased the magnetism that had drawn them together right from the beginning. Ford felt it too; she could tell by the way he looked at her, touched her, and teased her. But she now realized how wrong and foolish it had been to give vent to it, whatever her reasons.

Lovemaking should happen only between two people who had at least a strong possibility of building something meaningful together. Ford Devereaux wasn't seeking anything long-term. That was clear. And even if she were seeking that, Mary knew it should never be with the likes of him.

She needed steadiness, stability and safety. Ford was who he was—a man who lived by chance and for the next adventure. It would take an act of God to change him. Just as it had in her case.

But she still wouldn't wimp out, Mary decided firmly. No matter what. For the duration of their time together, she meant to call up every ounce of fortitude within her. And to hell with what he thought about it.

"Mary! Wake up, I'm coming in," Ford warned as he reached for the tent's zipper. He didn't want another tussle like the one she'd put up the last time he'd scared her to death.

He stripped off his ice-encrusted jacket as he crawled in.

"Wh-what is it? What's wrong?" she asked, her voice husky with sleep.

"I'm getting soaked and freezing my ass off out here, that's what's wrong. Move to one side."

Unfortunately, he'd picked the wrong side when he launched himself into the tent. She groaned when he landed on top of her. "Sorry, didn't mean to squash you," he said, taking his time about rolling off. The thought of crawling into that warm, downy cocoon with her and soaking up some heat jump-started his libido.

She'd appreciate that, he thought wryly—him coming on like a polar bear in rut. "Jeez, it's cold out there! Temp's dived a good twenty degrees. Sleet's really coming down now."

He shivered as he dug around for the cell phone and his penlight. When he switched it on, he could make out her worried features.

"Who are you calling this time of night?" she asked, sniffling and running a hand through her tousled hair.

Ford almost turned off the light so he wouldn't have to look at her. Talk about tempted? *Mary, warmth, sex.* In that order. He dragged his hungry gaze back to the buttons on the phone.

"Weather," he said, and then listened for the forecast.

When he heard it, he cursed and stuffed both the phone and the light back into the side pocket of his waterproof bag. "Just frigging dandy!"

"What?" she demanded, wide-awake now and sitting up.

"Ice storm. We've got to pack up and get to the cabin, and we'll have to do it in the dark." He reached out and half encircled her neck with his hand, his caress more apologetic than sensual. "I figure it's around eight miles on foot if we take the crow's route. Can you make it, Mary?"

She sighed. "As long as I don't have to run. I walk about three to five miles several times a week. I can do twice that."

Ford's estimation of her upped several notches. No whiny complaint. No pitiful pleading to uncover the Jeep and find a nice warm motel, which they couldn't do now, even if he thought it safe. She just gave him a matter-of-fact statement of her known capabilities.

Her earlier protests had concerned their safety, not her own comfort. She trusted him to do what he thought best for her. A humbling thought.

He considered whether he might be making a mistake, sticking to his original plan. But the roads would be closing soon if they hadn't already. This whole area would be icicle city by morning.

They both had plastic and ATM cards, but his cash was limited and so was hers. Even if the Jeep held out and got them to a hotel, they would leave a paper trail a kid could follow.

If he only had Perry to contend with, he might have risked it. But if what he suspected was true and Blevins was involved, they would be located in no time. Besides, if the roads were already iced up, they wouldn't get far, anyway. Four-wheel drive would only do so much, even if something else wasn't wrong with the Jeep. The alternator. How the hell had she known that?

This trek to the cabin looked like their only option. It was much closer than going back to her grandmother's house. He dug out the thin poncho that Knoblett had kept packed inside the folded tent, and found the regular flashlight in his bag.

"Put on an extra sweater under your jacket," Ford said. "And extra socks, if you brought them."

She wriggled out of the sleeping bag and followed his orders to the letter and with full attention. Her movements, while a bit jerky and rushed, betrayed very little in the way of fright.

"You're all right, kid," he said.

"Of course I'm all right," she countered, yanking the poncho over her head and settling it around her. "It's only eight miles or so. How hard can it be?" He heard the slight break in her voice, but tactfully ignored it.

"A walk in the park," he assured her.

Two hours later, Ford figured they had come only about three quarters of the distance required to get them to the cabin. Navigating through the trees, and over rocks, and an ice-slick carpet of pine needles had probably added an hour or so to their journey.

In the eerie quiet around them, Mary's breath heaved in and out like a noisy bellows. His own nearly covered the sound.

He stopped for a moment to rest, leaning against a tree. Mary did the same, choosing one close by. The tall pines, most of which had no low branches, afforded them plenty of room to walk between the trees. But sleet and ice had collected on the high tree limbs, weighting them down so they drooped to head level.

Mary's quickly stifled groan knifed through him. He raked her with the flashlight to see how she was holding up. She had pulled the poncho over the top of her hair so that the neck hole framed her face. He had told her to do that so her hair wouldn't get wet and freeze.

The predawn darkness made it impossible to see her face unless he aimed the light directly on it. Which he certainly wouldn't do. Not when mea culpa seemed to have been his mantra for the last few hours. It was his fault they were in this mess, but he couldn't see how they could have done anything else.

"How're you doing, kid?" he asked through numb lips.

"Just fine." She sighed. Her favorite refrain. Ford thought if he heard it one more time he would—

Something cracked. For a split second Ford's mind registered a gunshot. He shoved away from the tree and reached for his weapon.

Then he heard the brush and crackle of a limb falling, striking others on its way down. He swung the flashlight up, then leaped toward Mary with his arms outstretched to push her out of the way. He landed flat on his stomach and felt the hard slap of an ice-laden pine bough pin him to the ground like a giant net.

There was another crack, then more followed in quick succession, until the night exploded with the sounds of a war zone.

"My God, my God!" Mary screamed. "Ford!"

He struggled to move and couldn't. He felt glued to the ground, the frozen weight on top of him enormous. "Don't panic!" he shouted. "Grab a tree and stick to it. Protect your head!"

No use, he thought, feeling his own terror grow. Terror for Mary. She probably couldn't hear him. It sounded as though entire acres of the tall pines were dropping their deadly missiles all over the place. Some of the trees themselves would be snapping in two from the weight of their heavy canopies. There was no safety for her. No place to run.

Suddenly he felt the branches around him move. "Are you hurt much?" Mary demanded, her words cut short by yet another loud snap from above. Ford felt her snaking between the limbs until she finally snuggled next to him.

"I'm fine, just fine," he said, deliberately using her old line. She didn't seem to get the joke. He knew because he could hear her quiet sobs and feel her shaking. "Take it easy. It'll be over soon."

"Wh-what's happening?" she gasped, burrowing under the spiky branches as close to him as she could get. "I've never seen anything like this in my life!"

"Ice storm," Ford said, beginning to feel more discomfort now that the shock was wearing off the body blow he had received. He felt her hand clutching his left arm. "Follow my sleeve and get the flashlight out of my hand."

The cracking began to subside, full seconds passing between echoing snaps and the lumbering crashes as huge limbs struck the ground.

Mary aimed the light straight up. "I think you got the big one. I don't see any others left directly overhead."

Then she began surveying the local damage, skimming him slowly with the beam, sliding her hand between his body and the branches on top of him wherever she could. "Can you move?"

Ford gave it his best shot, rotating his feet and bending his legs as much as the weight on top would allow. "Legs work," he announced.

He twisted his torso a bit and found it still intact. He turned his head to one side and then the other, getting his cheeks jabbed with sharp needles for his efforts. "So far, so good."

Drawing his left arm up beside him from its outstretched position, Ford flexed his gloveless fingers. But his other arm, paralyzed by the cold, wouldn't budge an inch, even when he tugged hard. "Right arm feels pinned down," he said. "Check it out, would you?"

Mary rose to her knees and shone the flashlight over his back and along his right side. Apparently she couldn't see because of the clumps of foliage, so she gingerly worked her way around him.

Ford heard the frozen branches snap off as she moved them for a better look.

And then she shrieked.

Chapter 11

"**J**eez!" Ford shouted. She heard his breath hissing in and out between his teeth. The huge limb pinning him to the ground shifted when he did, jarring Mary back to reality. His voice lowered to an urgent grating. "Knock it off, *please!* Unless my arm's severed. Then you can scream like hell. I'll join you."

"N-no, it's not! Severed, I mean, but—"

"Then for Chrissake, what? I can't feel a damn thing!"

"Blood," she gasped. "There's so much...blood."

She felt herself about to lose it again as she ran the flashlight over the sight, squinting as she looked. "Th-there's a broken branch—sticking through it."

"My arm?" he asked quietly. "Through my arm?"

When she said nothing, he raised his voice. "Mary! Honey, listen to me. It doesn't hurt. I promise you I can't feel it."

His words registered slowly, but Mary focused on them, drawing her breath in and out, compelling herself to stabilize her thoughts.

For a moment there, all the blood had made her see her mother—the crimson flow out of her mouth, on the rocks, smeared on the broken body.

This is Ford. Mary repeated the words over and over in her mind. *Not Mom. Ford won't die. He'll be fine.* "Just fine," she whispered aloud. "Fine."

"Right. I'm gonna be. Okay, hon, now listen to me. Answer me, Mary. Say something."

"Yes," she whispered. "We have to get the tree…off."

He laughed, and she could hear his relief. "Good. You're talking! Now do what I tell you, Mary. Listen up."

She waited, growing calmer. Ford was in no pain. He had said so. Maybe he lied, but she told herself it couldn't be too bad or he would faint or scream the way she had.

"First get these damned needles out of my face, will you?"

Mary frantically snapped off the small frozen branches laden with foliage that surrounded his head, and watched as he turned his face toward her.

"Now shine that light on my arm so I can see the damage. Do it, Mary!"

She did, forcing herself not to look away. A branch about the size of Ford's finger must have cracked on its way down, leaving the sharp edge that had impaled him. It had disappeared into the sleeve of his jacket between his shoulder and his elbow. Blood encircled the branch where it had entered, and pooled beneath his arm.

Ford released a sigh, just short of a groan. "Can't get my jacket off until we get me out from under this mess," he said. "Hurry up, sweetie. I only got so much of the red stuff. Let's get cracking."

Mary jumped up and almost sat down again when her feet slipped on the ice. Quickly, she regained her footing, scanned the main part of the limb and found the broken end. It was twice as thick as her leg. "Cover your face!" she said. "I'm going to drag it off."

"No, wait!" Ford shouted. "Get this thing out of my arm first!"

"Oh!" Mary wondered if her brain had frozen along with every other part of her body. She had to function here, she told herself. *Think!*

First, get Ford's arm unpinned, then pull the limb off his body. She had to do all of that before he bled to death.

She rushed back between the branches and examined the wound more carefully. Nausea threatened, but she pushed it to the back of her mind.

"Lift that limb," Ford told her. "Pick it straight up, the way it went in. Don't—don't break it off in there, huh?"

Mary laid the flashlight down so the beam shone directly on what she was attempting to do. With both hands, she grasped the limb and pulled up. The smaller branch embedded in his arm resisted but then popped free. Without taking time to see the results, she stumbled toward the heaviest end of the broken missile that had fallen on him and began to slide it off.

Portions of his clothing had already frozen to the branches, but with his arm unpinned, he shifted around enough that he was soon free. By the time Mary reached him, he was sitting up, crunching stiffened pine needles beneath him as he tried to shrug out of his jacket.

Ignoring his curses, she knelt beside him and helped him get the garment off. For the first time, Mary noticed the gray dawn sifting through the jagged tops of the trees. The woods around them looked like a winter battlefield. A blanket of ice covered everything and more was falling in the form of mixed snow and sleet. The occasional pop of a limb as it became overloaded rent the stillness, but she figured the worst of it had passed.

"Not too bad, see?" Ford said, but his voice sounded thready to her. "Bleeding's almost stopped."

Mary paid little attention to his words, and focused on his wound. Blood wasn't pulsing out as it would have if an artery had been punctured. There must be black flecks of the pine bark still buried in the wound, but those would have to wait. She prayed they wouldn't cause infection.

The sleet pelted down into Mary's eyes so that she could hardly see, even with the flashlight. She released his arm, handed him the light and began shucking off her poncho and sweater, then her shirt.

"What the devil are you doing?" he demanded. "Are you nuts? You'll freeze!"

With all the efficiency of a stripper on Fast Forward, she unsnapped her bra and pulled it off. "You'd better thank God I didn't wear a lacy underwire today!" she said through chattering teeth. "Hold this on there."

Ford looked up at her, his eyes hot despite the freezing cold. A hint of amusement overshadowed the flash of lust. "Padded cups, Mary? False advertising."

"Just be glad I'm vain!" she declared, shivering back into her other clothes, which were now wet with sleet. Her body continued to shake as she took the bra from him and arranged the thin pads against the punctures. She tied the straps around his biceps to secure the makeshift bandage. "There you go. Now, let's get out of here and find the cabin before hypothermia sets in. I hope you can walk."

"Me, too," he ground out as he struggled to his feet. He stamped them a couple of times. "Good to go. Where's our gear?"

Mary slung all the straps of their bags over her own shoulders and Ford managed the lightweight tent. Together they picked their way around and through the slippery fallen limbs.

If she'd ever been any colder, Mary couldn't recall it. Her hands and feet had no feeling whatsoever.

"Up ahead. There." Ford sounded almost as indifferent as she felt. Her brain must be a Popsicle by now, she thought.

Mary dragged one frozen foot in front of the other until they reached the one-story log house and crawled up the steps on hands and knees. The stone steps were a solid

sheet of ice, but the wooden porch, shielded by the over-
hang, offered enough traction to stand.

"Door's locked," she groaned as she rattled the knob,
her fingers so numbed by the cold she could scarcely grasp
it.

Ford stood and took over. "Move and let me." He
turned the knob all the way to the right and fell against the
solid panel. It flew inward and he landed on the braided
rug with a pained grunt.

"Just as cold in here," Mary said as she stumbled in
beside him and collapsed in a heap.

"Fire," Ford grunted and heaved himself up off the
floor.

Moving slowly, he made it to the stone fireplace and sat
on the hearth. "Drag that black pack over here," he ordered. "Come on, we don't have time for a nap."

Mary did as he asked, then watched as he rummaged
inside the bag. "There's no firewood," she noted, massaging her hands, trying to regain some feeling in them. "What
do we do?"

He nodded toward a chunky wooden stool that sat near
his hip. "We burn that, for starters. With all the limbs lying
around, we won't have to worry about doing much chop-
ping, but they're all iced. When that melts, everything will
be wet. We'll have to bring some wood in to dry out later.
Right now, we've got to get out of these clothes and warm
up. Find me some paper or something to use for kindling."

Mary stirred herself to action, realizing that Ford could
pass out any time from his injury. They would both die
from hypothermia if she continued to sit around doing nothing.

She had not seen the cabin since she had come here once
with Gramps as a child. It looked smaller, but was in better
shape than she remembered. The log structure contained
only two rooms—a combined kitchen and living area, and
a bedroom. If she remembered right, there was a small bathroom set into one corner of the bedroom. The rooms were

small and low-ceilinged, she noted, and should be easy to heat.

There were signs that the cabin had been occupied more recently than she'd thought. Gran must have continued to lease it after Gramps died. Still, it would have been almost a year since anyone had used the place. No one had been here this hunting season, at any rate.

She found a half roll of paper towels in the kitchen, along with a plastic bottle full of fuel for the kerosene lamps. She also dragged one of the four wooden chairs from the eating area over to where Ford sat. "We can burn these, too."

"Whatever it takes," he mumbled, taking the towels and tearing off lengths of them, twisting them into tight coils that he placed under the stool in the fireplace. He added a little of the lamp fuel, fished a disposable cigarette lighter out of the pack and ignited the paper.

Neither spoke as he fed the flame more of the towels and watched it finally engulf the stool. The smell of burning varnish and oak filled the room. Smoke drifted out into the room for a few moments until the updraft began sucking it through the chimney.

"Now we're cooking," he said, turning to her. "Get out of those clothes and put on everything else you've got that's dry. Everything."

He didn't have to tell her twice. In minutes, she had stripped to her skin, not caring whether he saw her or not. If he could maintain any lecherous thoughts under these circumstances, he was a better man than most. The last thing on her mind was staying naked and pursuing any romantic diversions, no matter how diligently her brain had recorded their night together.

Still, as she glanced his way and noted his eyes on her, Mary wondered if sharing their body heat might not be the wise thing to do. A warming fantasy of them cuddling in one of the down-filled sleeping bags raised her temperature a couple of degrees.

Then she remembered his wound. That needed tending

right away, and here she was entertaining thoughts of hot, masculine muscles. She reached into her bag for another of her shirts and didn't stop dressing until there was nothing left there. When she'd finished, she felt like a stuffed sausage. A very cold, stuffed sausage.

"Now you," she said, hurrying to help him off with the jacket. "I hoped it's stopped bleeding," she added, thinking of the bloodstained bra she had tied around his arm. She pulled his shirttail out of his pants and carefully drew it over his head.

"All right, kick off your shoes and stand." She stood as well and, without pausing to think about what she was doing, she unsnapped his jeans and pulled them and his navy briefs down over his hips. He stepped out of the clothes.

"Never dreamed I'd be caught in nothing but a bra," he said, chuckling.

"You're delirious," she replied, wondering if he really could be. No, just making jokes, she decided as she looked up at him and saw his grin.

She dropped her gaze and it caught briefly on that part of him that she had felt in the dark, but never really seen. It lay dormant now, but still looked impressive. Ford was built like a male model, she noted as she took in the rest of him. Not beefed up like a bodybuilder, but strong and solid. So wonderfully male. Heat reached her cheeks and she felt them burn.

"Don't be insulted," he said casually. "I'm excited, but the idea got slightly chilled as it traveled south." He reached down and picked up one of the sleeping bags, loosened the ties that held it rolled, and unzipped the length of it. Mary helped him wrap it around himself with the flannel side next to his body.

"Are you in pain?" she asked, reaching for the bandage she had improvised.

"Not right now. Let's leave it alone until the fire's hot enough to heat some water. Then I'll clean it up."

"I'll do it!" she offered quickly. "I've had courses in first aid. Required for the school," she explained.

He laughed as he snaked his left arm out of his cover, reached for the poker and gently stabbed at the burning stool. "You go ape at the sight of blood, remember?"

"I do not!" she retorted. "It was just that when I saw you lying there, bleeding, it brought back the memory of my mother…when she died and I had no way to save her."

His movements stilled and he swerved to look at her. "You were the only one there when it happened?"

"Yes," she said, avoiding his eyes. "Just me. I'm sorry I sort of fell apart on you. It won't happen again. I wasn't expecting it, that's all."

He reached out and ran his hand over her head. "Hey, it's okay. You were great, hon. You saved my bacon out there this morning. Thanks." His hand captured hers and brought it to his lips. Then he reached for her other hand and squeezed it softly.

Mary felt a smile pull at her lips. "You're welcome."

"Give me your feet," he said abruptly.

"What?"

"Your feet. Those hands are cold, but I think we can rule out frostbite. Let me check your toes."

Mary hesitated for only a moment before she peeled off the dry socks she had donned. He encompassed both her feet in his large hands and began to rub. Tingles that had nothing at all to do with poor circulation ran right up her legs, straight to the core of her. She sighed and closed her eyes, feeling the heat building from the inside out.

He released her feet all too soon. Mary opened her eyes and saw him looking at her with such raw need, she almost fell against him. Catching herself in the act, she quickly turned away and began pulling her socks back on with shaking hands.

That was all she needed—to throw herself at him again. Nothing could go further in proving her guilt in his mind. He would think she was trying to bribe him with sex.

She might have done just that if she thought it would work, but Ford wasn't the type to be swayed in that way. No, he would need proof positive, something irrefutable that declared her innocent, before he would believe it. She must remember that this man thought she was a criminal. He had made up his mind, and nothing she could say or do here would make the slightest bit of difference.

And yet, no matter what he believed her to be, Ford still wanted her. He made no secret of it, either. But it was a situational thing, having to do with availability and his notion of her morals—which couldn't be all that lofty, considering her behavior thus far.

She got up from her seat on the hearth, more eager to put distance between them than she was to enjoy the proximity of the fire. That burned brightly now, throwing inadequate waves of heat only a couple of feet from its source.

The rest of the room had yet to absorb much of it. Mary figured activity would compensate a little, so she began searching for things they would need.

She found a cast-iron pot in the kitchen and dashed out the back door. In moments she had the container filled with broken bits of long icicles that she had gathered from the edge of the low-hanging roof. For good measure, she returned for several plastic bowls that she set on the steps to collect the sleet-and-snow mixture that continued to fall.

Belatedly, she noticed a crinkled tarp bulging from beneath the crawl space under the cabin. She plucked an edge of it away and whooped with delight. Firewood, cut in uniform lengths, lay piled beneath the cabin. *Dry* wood! She pulled out several logs and stacked them on one arm.

Ford met her at the door, gun in hand.

Mary laughed. "Didn't mean to shout. But look what I found!"

An hour later, the main room of the cabin had warmed to a nearly comfortable level, at least near the fireplace. Mary had cleaned Ford's wound as well as she knew how and doused it with the pitiful remainder of a bottle of bourbon she had found in one of the cabinets. He'd turned the air blue when she did that and hadn't subsided much since, still muttering under his breath now and then about her sadistic tendencies.

She had used one of his T-shirts to bandage his arm and helped him dress in the sweats he'd brought in his sports bag.

One of the single-bed mattresses she'd lugged in from the bedroom lay in front of the fireplace. They reclined on it lengthwise, facing each other and absorbing the warmth of the fire.

"Now, if we don't starve to death, we'll be all right," she commented.

Ford lifted the cup of soup Mary had made from the envelopes of dry soup mix he'd appropriated from the Knobletts' kitchen. "Chicken-sleet soup's not so bad."

Mary giggled and sipped her own. "But we can't live on it."

"Nope," he agreed. "I'll scare up something a little more substantial when I get my second wind."

"I wasn't complaining—just wondering how we'd solve the problem. There's no food here except what you brought."

"Soup mix, instant coffee and ramen noodles," he listed.

"Uh-hmm. And the salt."

"Can't have possum stew without that," he said.

Was he serious? Mary knew beggars couldn't be choosers, but she wasn't about to eat an opossum. "I'd sooner eat a house cat," she said, relishing the last mouthful of her soup, wishing it could have lasted for days.

"I'll see what I can do, then."

She glanced at him and saw his expression. He had such an appealing grin. Great teeth. They were strong and white. No caps like Jim. She loved the indentations—almost dimples—that framed his expressive mouth. Just thinking about that mouth seemed too dangerous right now when she felt so languid and relaxed. Remembering what those lips had felt like, what they were capable of…

"Squirrels and rabbits are good," he commented idly, setting his cup on the stones of the hearth.

Mary recovered quickly, shaking off her thoughts of kissing. "I'm sorry to inform you, but I don't eat anything that's cute."

He laughed and lay back so that he was flat on the mattress. "Go to sleep, Mary," he ordered, still shaking with mirth long after she had wriggled out a comfy spot and closed her eyes.

What had she said that was so funny?

The phone's chirp interrupted Ford's X-rated dream. Cursing, he pushed himself to a sitting position. He'd meant to turn the damned thing off. "What?"

"Blevins, here. Where are you?"

"Lost in the wilderness," Ford muttered into the receiver as he yanked the corner of the sleeping bag up to cover his shoulder. The fact that Blevins knew they were no longer at Mary's grandmother's confirmed Ford's suspicion. No proof yet, however, so he played it cool. "Look, we're stranded God knows where, so don't hassle me, all right?"

He made static noises with the back of his tongue and interspersed them with words. "Sorry, almost out of range and I'm losing you. I'll call back." He punched the button, then the off switch and tossed the phone into the open zipper of his sports bag.

Mary watched him, her eyes wide. "Why did you do that?"

"Because he's the son of a bitch who's calling the shots on us. Literally."

She sat up abruptly, pushing her cover down to her waist. "What?"

Ford blew out a breath of frustration. He knew he had to level with her. Guilty or not, her life was at stake here.

"Yeah, think about it. I tell him where we are and, just like clockwork, up pops Perry."

"But why?"

"The diamonds would be my guess. I don't think Blevins was involved in all the heists, but he saw an opportunity here to get his hands on this take without even being suspected. He came in to honcho this investigation late, after I had pointed out the link between the other jobs."

Ford lapsed into thought for a few minutes before continuing. "It's his connection to Perry I don't understand. Why hire a hit man? Hell, Blevins had enough training, he could have taken out Antonio with no problem."

"What about Perry? Do you still think he's the one after us?"

"Definitely at your school. I recognized him the minute I saw him. Blevins could have contacted him easily enough with the information we had on file. Blevins even said he'd hauled him in for questioning once on another case. Never had enough proof to arrest him, and Perry knew that, so he had no reason to hide. Blevins probably hired him to knock off Antonio and grab the gems so they could split 'em."

"But—but Blevins is an agent!"

Ford snorted. "And that's grounds for sainthood? Hey, we can be just as greedy as the next guy. Look at me! I'm ready to chuck a perfectly good government job to join forces with Spider-Woman." He shot her a pointed look. "And don't think I'm hooked because of your sticky-fingered life-style. Diamonds don't mean squat to me."

Mary's mouth dropped open. He just loved that speechless look of hers. Those eyes were so wide he could see the whites all around. The picture of innocence, and maybe she was innocent. He knew better than to bet the ranch on that, but he couldn't resist testing her.

Before she could gather enough spit to speak, he continued. "See, Perry offs Antonio and can't find the diamonds. Then when he discovers you witnessed the shooting, he comes after you. Now Blevins knows you might be able to

ID Perry, which could lead to him. And he figures you've got the goods. So he sanctions the hit on you. They both figure you've told me everything. So now we're a package deal.''

She covered her mouth with one hand and lowered her eyes. Her head shook slowly as though denying what he'd said. When she raised her gaze to him, she looked more frightened than he'd seen her yet. ''Then who can we trust, Ford? Who will save us?''

He could hardly stand for her to look that woebegone. It wasn't as if all hope had died. ''I've got an idea how to get us out of this. My job's probably history anyway, so I guess I don't need to worry about skipping up the chain of command or throwing out wild accusations. I'm going to call the regional director and see if I can convince him.''

''Blevins's boss? What happens if you can't make him listen?''

He met her eyes directly and gave her the bad news. ''Then we play hard to get. Indefinitely.''

No use waffling, Ford thought. Now that he'd laid out his suspicions and plans aloud to Mary, they made perfect sense.

He glanced at his watch. Four o'clock. Since it was Monday, Duvek should still be at his office. Ford reached for the phone again and punched in the number. Might as well find out exactly how they stood.

He worried about how Michael Duvek would take a suggestion that one of the senior agents could be dirty. While it was true that nobody Ford knew of liked Blevins personally, the man had a good rep for his expertise with computers. And no one had ever questioned his abilities or his willingness to jump right in on a case involving gems, either. There could be a reason for that, Ford thought.

A secretary answered on the second ring and passed him through. ''Duvek, here.''

''This is Ford Devereaux over in Nashville. We've got a large problem here, boss. Spare a few minutes?''

"Well, the Boy Wonder," Duvek said with a sigh. "What now? Have you been yanking Blevins's chain again? He was ready for me to pull your badge last time we talked."

"I'm in no position to jerk anybody around right now. But I do have something smelly I'm about to throw at the fan. You're not going to like this."

"Why am I not surprised?" Duvek asked in his upper-class Bostonian accent.

"Just keep an open mind and stay with me, sir. Ms. Shaw's life and mine are on the line here. Someone put out a contract on her and I believe I know who."

"Go ahead," Duvek said seriously.

Ford's eyes locked with Mary's as he related all that had happened. Well, almost all. He didn't give their location. And he certainly didn't include the fact that he had violated rule number one when protecting a witness of the opposite sex. Or a suspect.

Still, when he'd finished, he had a sneaky feeling Duvek had listened between the sentences where that last secret was concerned. His next words confirmed it.

"Devereaux, tell me you haven't crossed the line with this woman," Duvek said in warning.

"Didn't you hear a word I said?" Ford demanded.

"Oh, yes, and I heard how you said them, especially the names. Are you...*involved* with Ms. Shaw? No, don't tell me. I don't want to know about it right now. As for the rest, do nothing for the present. Stay wherever you are. Don't move unless you have good cause."

Ford laughed, more with relief than anything else. "Not much chance of that. I'll call you back day after tomorrow."

Duvek confirmed, stating a time. "I'll get someone on this immediately and see what I can uncover. And Devereaux?"

"Yeah?"

"Keep your head down." He paused for effect. "*Both* of them."

Ford rolled his eyes as he punched off and closed the phone.

"Is he with us?" Mary asked.

"Absolutely. For some reason, I don't think he was too surprised to hear about Blevins. Duvek's a good man, spotless rep as an agent. We can trust him." Ford smiled. "Even if he does talk funny."

"Hmm?" Mary glanced up at him questioningly.

"Can't say his *r*'s. Pure Boston. Sounds like Kennedy. He might be a dyed-in-the-wool Yankee, but he's definitely one of the good ol' boys in my book."

She moved over, either seeking body warmth or reassurance. "This scares me, Ford. What if Perry finds us here?"

"Scares me, too," he admitted, sliding his good arm around her and drawing her close. "But we're safe here. There's no way he can know where we are. Nobody can get to us, anyway, with the roads slick as owl…stuff."

"And when it melts?" she asked in a worried whisper.

He lay back on the mattress and drew her down beside him, carefully wrapping the corner of her sleeping bag close around her neck and resting his hand on top. "We play it as it lays, hon. That's about all we can do. But Perry has no reason to look for us here."

"When do you think that will happen? The melting, I mean?"

"A day or two, a week, who knows? This is a freak storm. I should have paid more attention to the weather forecasts."

"What do we do in the meantime?" she asked, fitting her head into the curve of his neck.

Ford knew she had no intention of setting him on fire the way she was doing. All she wanted was something to cling to in a world gone mad. He certainly understood that.

It was right up there in number-two position on his own list of desires. A little distraction wouldn't hurt.

"We could play Eskimo," he said, dropping a none-too-brotherly kiss on top of her head, and nuzzling her hair. "Want to rub noses?"

Chapter 12

Mary didn't mistake the half-serious tone of Ford's suggestion. She leaned her head back and looked up at him. His thoughts were as clear as if he were speaking them. He wanted her and he knew she wanted him. His hand gripped her waist, long fingers moving in an insistent caress that sent heat surging through her veins.

She slid one palm up his chest, smoothing the thick cotton of his sweatshirt over the muscles of his chest. She explored the bare skin of his neck, feeling his pulse pound furiously beneath her fingertips. His indrawn breath and the flare of his nostrils excited her further.

His mouth descended and she opened hers slightly, anticipating his kiss with a hunger she'd felt with no other man. The power of that hunger frightened her even as she welcomed it.

His salty taste mingled with the sweetness of desire as his tongue invaded. Ford's attempt at gentleness suddenly turned wild. His urgency encompassed her, demanded her participation, evoked all the feelings for him she had tried so hard to deny.

"I need you, Mary," he rasped as his mouth left hers and hungrily tasted her chin, her neck, and the spot beneath her ear that sent tendrils of fire curling through her body.

She drew in a deep breath, hoping to gather some resistance, but it only inundated her brain with a heady mix of pine, bourbon, and Ford's own enticing scent.

Her breasts swelled beneath his impatient hands. She raked her fingers through his hair, urging him to another lengthy, mind-drugging kiss. Craving more.

His phone chirped.

Ford dragged his mouth from hers. "Damn!" He gripped her almost painfully with his good arm and she felt his harsh breath of frustration rush out against her ear.

He released her reluctantly, but held her gaze as he reached for the phone. His eyes told her this was not over. Mary knew that he'd never even entertained the thought of ignoring the call. Their lives could depend on it.

"Yes?" he answered impatiently. Then his eyebrows shot up in surprise.

Mary watched a rueful smile smooth out his frown as he said, "Yeah, she's okay." A small silence ensued as he listened. "Look, buddy, I appreciate the gear and food. We're settled in for the duration. Got plenty of wood, a little grub. Everything's cool.... I might think about it once the ice melts. Any idea when that will be?" He listened for a while, nodding. "Yeah, don't worry. I promise I'll take care of her."

Ford remained silent for another moment. "No, they can't do that. This phone's encrypted. But I am going to stay switched off to save my battery. Don't worry if you can't reach us."

"Mr. Knoblett?" Mary guessed as he closed the phone.

Ford issued a long-suffering sigh and rested his forehead against hers. "The old guy must be psychic. I think that call was as much a warning to keep my hands to myself as it was an offer of help. He guessed where we are. Asked me if I planned to do a little hunting—big game."

Mary drew back so that she could see his face. "You

will, won't you?'' She sensed that Ford didn't intend to run anymore.

''Might have to,'' he admitted.

''You know Perry will come after us, don't you?'' she asked in a hushed voice.

Ford released her hand, turned away from her and stared into the fire. ''Only when I'm ready for him. There's a chance Duvek might find him first, but I'm not counting on that. We've got nothing concrete on Perry but the fact that he followed us the day I picked you up at the school. Hell, we didn't even see him the night of the shooting.''

''It was his car, wasn't it?'' Mary argued. ''The green one?''

''From what I saw, it looked like the same make.'' Ford shook his head as he ran a hand through his hair. ''We have to assume it was. At least we don't have to worry about him until things warm up. Knoblett says the whole county's closed down, and they're enforcing it. No vehicles allowed on the main roads. Nobody's looking for us at the moment.''

''What if Perry has tire chains or something?''

''Wouldn't help on this kind of ice. Even if he miraculously guesses where we are there's no way he could get back to look for us until the roads open. Even then, driving in here would be impossible. He'd have to hike in through the woods like we did.''

Ford's heated gaze reminded Mary that he hadn't forgotten their interlude before the phone call. She also realized he didn't intend to continue it, at least not at the moment. The emptiness inside her ached for him. But she knew the foolishness of pursuing a physical relationship with a man like Ford. It would be short-term, and heartbreaking when it ended.

As though he read her mind, he stated the immediate problem flat out, mincing no words. ''We can't…make love again, Mary. Not until this is over, anyway.''

''Make *love?* It was just sex, Ford. And who asked you!'' she retorted, stung that he had put it so bluntly.

He laughed bitterly as he picked up the poker and stabbed at the fire. "Didn't give you much chance to ask, did I?"

She turned completely around and crossed her arms over her chest, her breath surging in and out rapidly, in both anger and disappointment.

"Mary," he said quietly, "I don't have any protection with me. It's not like I expected anything like this to happen. We could complicate matters big time, you know."

She scrambled up off the mattress, stuck her feet in her shoes, and stalked to the kitchen. There she fumbled with the packets of food, slamming them around on the table's surface and grabbing up the blue packets. "Do you want coffee?" she snapped. "I want coffee."

She turned on the faucet. Nothing happened. She wiggled it furiously. Still nothing. She gave it a final, vicious twist and the thing came off in her hand.

Mary slammed it down with a curse, grabbed the enameled coffeepot from the stovetop and stormed out the back door. She welcomed the bite of frosty air that greeted her heated body and the linings of her throat and lungs. The light snow sprinkled her face, caught in her eyelashes and melted on her lips. Better than a cold shower any day, she thought with increasing fury.

Who did Ford think he was, preaching to her about safe sex, as if she didn't know the chances they had already taken? But in all fairness, she hadn't really given it much thought. She hadn't worried for a moment about anything transmittable. Whatever else Ford was, the man was honorable to the core, and would never have touched a woman if he had anything like that. He surely knew that she hadn't either, since occupations such as hers had such stringent health requirements.

That peril aside, there loomed another she should have considered. He had withdrawn from her to prevent a pregnancy. That age-old method hardly boasted any great success rate. Still, it had been a thoughtful thing to do during a time when any rational thought could hardly have been expected.

Maybe she should be thanking him instead of flouncing off in a huff. But his outspokenness on the whole matter rankled. His explanation should have been tender and sweetened with regret, at the very least. Instead, he'd made it sound as if she were hanging on him, begging for sex, while he—tower of wisdom that he was—resisted for the good of all. *Insensitive dope. Typical man.*

Mary picked her way through the mass of broken pine branches, slipping this way and that, until she reached the small stream she remembered. "A lot of good this did," she muttered, grimacing at the stream covered with ice and littered with pinecones and tree trash.

Ford approached from behind her, slid down the bank and tapped the ice with the ax he carried. He reached out for the coffeepot. Mary thrust it into his hand and watched him dip it beneath the surface. With a wordless but meaningful glare, he handed it back, retraced his steps past her and returned to the cabin.

Only the fact that she knew she would freeze if she didn't, made Mary follow him. All the way, her mind conjured visions of what the next few days held for them. Ford would drive her mad with that nobler-than-thou attitude of his while she practiced avoidance. Not a pleasant prospect for their enforced confinement in such a small place.

But worse problems loomed. Mary was afraid everything would culminate in some kind of confrontation with Perry, leaving one of the men—maybe both, and her, as well— full of bullet holes. The very thought sent shivers of dread racing up and down her spine.

Ford kept out of Mary's way and let her arrange the coffeepot on two logs placed over the red coals she'd raked to one side of the fireplace. For someone who had never had to make do and improvise the way they were doing now, Mary managed very well. He knew he was causing her more grief than the lack of conveniences.

He resisted the urge to take over the task of simulating a campfire and do it more efficiently. She needed the busyness of it to work off her anger. And she was definitely still angry.

He hadn't been exactly what you would call tactful about their not making love again. But, damn it all, she ought to understand. They were stuck out here in the middle of nowhere, isolated, and so hot for each other they could set the cabin on fire. He couldn't afford the distraction. All he needed was to be worrying about whether or not this little piece of togetherness might foster a little complication she wouldn't want.

Not that he would want it, either. An unexpected picture flashed through his mind—one he tried to shove aside. Mary in a rocking chair, her arms curled around a blanketed little bundle. A small mouth nestled against her breast. Her smile... Ford shook his head to clear it of the vision. *Not allowed. No babies, no serious entanglements.*

At the critical moment, he'd done all he could to avoid that. He had wanted nothing more in this world than to hold her in the aftermath, their bodies still joined. But he had forgone that, trying to save her some grief if he could. And how did she thank him?

Maybe it would work out better if she held on to that anger, and he juiced up his own toward her. Not likely they would wind up throwing caution to the winds again if they stayed angry with each other. He couldn't think of any other way to keep his distance when they had to live cooped up in the cabin for a few days.

Once all this was settled and he made certain Mary was safe, he would like to make things right between them. He wished they could start over, date normally and see what developed. But he would probably be heading back to Memphis as soon as this case was resolved, assuming he still had a job. And, unless he implicated her in the thefts by telling all that he knew, Mary would resume her teaching. Maybe find somebody else. That last thought set his teeth to grinding.

Still, he now owned property in Nashville—the new condo he'd bought for his mom. And he would be visiting her and Molly regularly, just as he always had. Maybe…

He lay back on the mattress and folded his uninjured arm beneath his head, watching Mary out of the corner of his eye while she fiddled with the coffeepot. Her slender curves were all but obscured by the layers of clothing she wore. That silky hair looked a tangled mess. Her cheeks and nose were chapped raw from the biting cold. And she was still the most beautiful, the most exciting woman he had ever seen in his life.

The beauty went deep. Soul deep. Ford knew in that instant, with a clarity that left no room for doubt and suspicion, that Mary could never do anything wrong. She was good clear through to her bones. Too good for a man like him.

A powerful craving streaked through him—one that surpassed anything sexual. It shot down his reservations as if they were tin ducks in a carnival game.

He needed her like air. It scared the life out of him, but there it was.

After a supper of artificially flavored ramen noodles and coffee, Mary picked up her sleeping bag and headed for the bedroom without even saying good-night.

"Where do you think you're going?" Ford snapped.

"To bed!" she declared without turning.

Ford leaped up off the mattress and caught her before she reached the door. "You'll freeze your buns off in there." He grabbed her shoulders and pointed her back toward the fireplace. "Sleep there on the mattress. I'll take the bedroom, if you're so afraid I'll jump you in your sleep."

She balked. "I *want* to sleep in there."

Ford ground his teeth. "Do, and I'll haul your butt back in here after you go to sleep!"

"I'll lock the door," she informed him, betraying her real reason for going in there.

"Like that would stop me." He drew in a deep breath, struggling to stay sane in the face of her provocation. "We'll both sleep by the fire, and I don't want to hear another word about it. I promise I won't bother you. Fair enough?" When she lifted her chin and pressed her lips together, he added, "And don't you start anything, either!"

She dropped the sleeping bag and slapped him.

He'd had it coming, but it stung all the same. Mary was a lot stronger than he'd thought. The look of surprise and contrition on her face triggered a spurt of laughter, which he neatly hid by turning away from her and clearing his throat.

"I—I never struck anyone before in my life," she whispered. "It's just that you—you made me so angry." The silence was deafening, and then she said, almost inaudibly, "I apologize."

Ford massaged his jaw and wiggled it back and forth. "Only a couple of teeth loose. Good thing we're not having steak anytime soon."

She rolled her eyes and groaned, swept up her sleeping bag and plunked it down beside the hearth. He fingered the stinging imprint of her hand on his cheek while he watched her bundle up for the night.

As soon as she had settled, Ford zipped into his own bag and nestled close behind her.

"You promised not to touch me!" she cried, jerking upright.

He drew her back down and wrapped his arm around her. "I won't. Not that way. Doing it through two layers of goose down might be safe enough, but somehow it doesn't appeal to me. Now go to sleep before I kiss you."

Ford slept the sleep of the dead and woke feeling foggy and feverish. That was all he needed—to get a blasted infection in the arm. Probably nothing to worry about. A little rise in temp was to be expected with most any wound.

He edged away from Mary to keep from waking her. It

was already midmorning, but she needed the rest. Quietly, he added a couple of logs and stoked the fire.

Ford studied her face, composed in sleep, her long dark lashes like feathery fans, her mouth so vulnerable, so kissable. Ford knew he had to get out of that room before he did something he would regret. Again.

They would need more water. As good an excuse as any, he figured. He pulled on his shoes, annoyed that his movements felt lethargic and clumsy. The arm hurt like hell, worse than that time down in Nicaragua when he'd taken a bullet. With a curse, he snatched up the fire-blackened coffeepot and headed out.

As he bent beside the stream, he thought for a minute he heard the jingle of bells. Right. Santa would be along any minute. He crouched farther down and peeked over the bank. By God, it was Santa, or as close to it as Ford ever hoped to get.

"Mornin', boy," Knoblett called out. He stood about ten yards away. Again, something jingled.

Then Ford saw the dog. Or small pony. The golden retriever gazed up at him, its dark eyes full of friendly curiosity. A bright red leather collar studded with round bells the size of Ping-Pong balls encircled his neck.

Ford cradled the full pot of water in his good arm and strode over to join the old guy. "What the hell—?"

Knoblett chuckled. "I thought you might like a little advance warning we was coming up on ya. Didn't want us to get shot so I let ol' Westy here wear his jingle bells. Thinks he's Rudolph 'round Christmastime."

Ford laughed and shook his head in disbelief. "'Westy'?" He reached out his free hand and let the dog sniff.

"Westmoreland," Knoblett explained. "He just don't never know when to quit. Good ol' soldier."

Ford scratched Westy's chin and watched him yawn, exposing a long pink tongue. "How the hell did you get here? It's got to be four or five miles through the woods from your place."

"More like six. Walked in, just like you did. It's a mess out here, ain't it? Just like this back in eighty-five as I recall."

The thought that Knoblett could make it through made Ford uneasy. If he could do it that easily, so could Perry. Only Perry couldn't possibly know where they were yet, he reminded himself. Not until the ice melted and somebody found the Jeep.

The old man seemed to read his mind. "Don't worry none. The roads are like greased glass. No way anybody's goin' anywheres for a couple of days. Least not in no car. This crap begins to melt off, then you might want to be kinda careful. How're you fixed for defense, son?"

"Got a Glock and two clips. Should be sufficient."

Knoblett snorted. "Maybe. Maybe not. I brought a rifle just in case."

"You planning to hang around, are you?" Ford asked, half hoping he would. Ford didn't feel all that sharp.

"Naw. Thelma might call and think I wuz dead in the bed or somethin'. I could take Mary on back with me, though. They already checked to see if she was there."

"They? Who?" Ford snapped. "When?"

"Young feller called this morning. Asked if I'd seen Mary lately. Said he had a real important message from her daddy."

"And you don't think he was legit?" Ford asked.

"Naw. Evan Shaw don't hardly ever bother to contact her, and if'n he did, I don't think he'd go through somebody with a Nashville number to do it. He'd call me direct."

"You're sure the call came from Nashville?" Ford demanded.

"Got Caller ID. Gotta keep up with the times, y'know."

Ford nodded. "What did you tell him?"

"Told him I ain't seen her in a coon's age, and if she warn't at Evan's house in town, she might've gone to Atlanter to see her cousin."

"She got a cousin there?"

"Not that I know 'bout," Knoblett said, grinning. His gold tooth gleamed.

Ford considered sending Mary back with the man. She would probably be perfectly safe with Knoblett. Then again, she might not. "Sorry," he said. "We can't risk it. Whoever called might not have bought your story."

Knoblett pushed his cap back and scratched his head. Then his sharp gaze met Ford's. "Might not, at that. You're gonna keep her, then."

There was nothing else he could do. "I'll keep her."

Ford needed a contingency plan. "Look, this guy has no idea where we are. The trail in here is totally covered with limbs. He can't know the cabin even exists."

Ford only hesitated for a moment before advising Knoblett of his plan. "Soon as the snow and ice clear up, I'm calling in our exact location, so he'll come for us."

"Settin' him up," Knoblett deduced, and made a little ticking sound with his tongue. "Dangerous."

"When I'm ready for it to go down, I'll send Mary to you through the woods." He noted the direction from which Knoblett had arrived in the clearing. "Due south, right?"

"Yep."

"Your job will be to get her to my boss in Memphis. Drive her there, call the main office and ask for Michael Duvek. He'll find you. Got it?"

"Guess you ought to know if you can handle it or not. You done this kinda thing before, have you?"

"A time or two," Ford replied, scratching the dog's head as he circled around his legs.

"So you know what you're a-doing?"

"I know," he assured the man. "I'll send Mary on and give her plenty of time to get there before I make that call."

Knoblett nodded again and looked down at his dog. "Westy's gonna stay. He can lead our girl back to my place and see she don't get lost. Might be good to have him 'round here, meantime, in case your devil's got more smarts than you think."

"Roger that," Ford replied. "Thank you, sir."

"Nuthin' to it. Left you some stuff over there," he said, pointing to a pack propped against a tree next to his rifle. Again, he pinned Ford with a warning stare. "You mind what you get up to in there. Mary's like one of mine."

"I hear you," Ford replied, looking—he hoped—guiltless. "I'll take good care of her."

They shook hands on it. Ford watched the older man pick his way carefully through the fallen debris that covered the clearing around the cabin and reenter the woods.

Ford wished he could insist on Knoblett's sticking around until just before the showdown. There'd be no problem meeting the attack by Perry on his own, but he could sure use a buffer between Mary and himself in the meantime.

"Look what he brought!" Mary exclaimed as she pulled out several tubes of plastic-encased sausage and a bag of hard rolls. He had also packed a carton of eggs, one of which had broken and leaked all over the stack of chocolate bars and the box of ammo in the bottom. "Cholesterol and bullets," she remarked, laughing.

Ford loved her laugh. Low-pitched and sexy. Everything she did seemed sexy. He wondered where all her anger had gone. It had evaporated like steam when he came back inside with the dog.

She had greeted Westy like an old friend, which Ford supposed he was. After her baby talk and hugs were rewarded by happy whines and tail-wagging from her furry pal, Ford had given her the goody pack from Knoblett.

She had fussed because Ford hadn't wakened her to say hello to the old guy, but then her hunger had kicked in and she'd forgotten to be mad. Right now she was munching a chocolate bar while she made soup with the water he'd brought in. He liked that she didn't hold grudges. And when she pouted, it never lasted long. She packed a mean right, but only used it when all else failed.

The brash self-confidence and daring he required in his

women was missing in Mary. She had courage, but it was the quiet kind. Maybe that was why he goaded her the way he did, just to trigger that little bit of aggressiveness she hid so well.

She was delicate, outrageously feminine, and even cried on occasion. But that didn't seem to matter where his feelings were concerned. He wanted her exactly the way she was.

Her brief spate of adventures had been forced on her by her clueless parents trying to make her into something she was not and never could be. Thank goodness her reaction to her mother's death had put an end to that. Ford felt relieved that she had come home to her grandmother when she had.

Given the type of woman she was, he ought not to like Mary at all, much less feel what he was feeling. Putting a name to that made him uneasy. Couldn't be love or anything like that. They'd only known each other for a few days and under the worst of circumstances. But it certainly affected him the way he thought love might. Maybe it was the fever.

He wiped a palm across his forehead, which now ached like the very devil.

Mary didn't know when she had enjoyed a meal so much. Cooking it in the fireplace must have added flavor. She was licking her fingers free of the sausage grease when she happened to look up.

The expression on Ford's face arrested the motion immediately. His eyes gleamed unnaturally bright, like glittering blue gems. "Don't look at me like that," she warned.

He shrugged slightly and held up his palms. "Sorry." His grin seemed forced. "I think I might be in love."

She snorted. "I think you might be in heat."

"In rut, maybe. In heat's a female thing."

Mary busied herself gathering up the remains of their meal. "Must you be so coarse?" She refused to meet his eyes. "If this is your idea of charming, it's no wonder you're still single!"

"Marry me and I won't be. Single, that is. I'd still be coarse, of course." He laughed. "Just think how rewarding it would be for you, sanding off my rough edges. Missionary work at its finest. That *is* my favorite position, by the way. Missionary."

"You're trying to make me mad, aren't you?" Mary said, secretly amused and a little turned-on by his teasing. "Just in case I was getting any ideas? Don't bother. You're quite safe."

He stretched out by the fire, rubbing his stomach with one hand. She watched that hand, wanting to replace it with her own. With an impatient sigh and a shake of her head, she got up and took the leftover food to the kitchen.

Ford followed. "Mary, do you think we could...well, maybe see each other when we get back to the world?"

The old suspicion reared its ugly head. What did he really want? Was he like so many others who had made a play for her? Was he interested in her or her wealth? Did it really matter, when she didn't intend to enter into anything with him anyway? Yes, it did matter, she decided. It mattered very much. For some obscure reason, she had to know.

Very deliberately, she pushed the food she was rewrapping aside and looked up at him. "Ford, you should know why I was working at the preschool."

"I'll bet you like kids," he said, tracing her cheek with one finger. His gaze felt hot on her face.

She took a deep breath and stepped back. "I do, but there's another reason. There's no money left."

Ford's hand dropped to his side and his brows lowered. The look on his face changed to one so hard she could barely stand to meet his eyes. He said nothing.

"It takes every cent I make to maintain both homes. I need to keep Dad's for him, so that he has a place to come home to. And I can't bear to sell Gran's. There are taxes, upkeep, my living expenses. So you see—"

His dangerously low voice interrupted her. "Money? You think I'm after your freakin' *money?*"

Mary felt lower than low. "I just wanted you to understand. Jim didn't. I never explained it to him."

"Oh, I get your drift, all right," he said, turning away as though he couldn't stand being near her. "Well, never mind, then. What's the point of getting into your pants, if I can't get into your bank account? Rats, and I had it all planned, too. Take her, and then take her for all she's worth!"

"Ford, I know you didn't plan that! I only meant—"

It was too late. He had stormed out of the cabin and left the door standing open. Cold air rushed in but it didn't matter. Her heart already felt flash-frozen by his expression of disgust.

A man like Ford would consider hers the ultimate insult. But she had realized that too late. Her own insecurity, fostered by her former relationships, had prompted her to hurt him.

Maybe it was best that she had. Now he would stop trying to make more of what had happened between them than was warranted. But she ached inside for what might have developed, now that she knew for certain that Ford had never given a thought to her financial assets.

Chapter 13

Ford's blood boiled. The cold didn't begin to faze him, though he could feel his body shivering. At first he directed his fury toward Mary, who dared suggest he was after her money. What had he ever done to her to make her think he was a gold digger?

Sure, he had joked around about the mansion, and made a few comments about her life of leisure. He had done that to remind himself—and her—of their differences, hoping to put a little distance between them, since he felt so drawn to her physically. But then he had made love to her anyway, the minute she had shown any interest.

When he thought of what he'd just said to her, Ford's reason returned. No wonder she had accused him. Taken together, his actions didn't exactly make his intentions seem honorable.

Hell, maybe they hadn't been—not if "honorable" meant considering marriage. Up to this point, he hadn't thought about that. Not consciously, anyway. The words had popped out of his mouth on impulse, surprising him as much as they had her.

He just wanted Mary. He needed her any way he could get her, to have and keep and hold. Well, that sure sounded like a commitment when he put it that way. Maybe he was more honorable than he thought he was.

The shivering increased. He'd forgotten his damned jacket. Ford wrapped his arms around himself, wincing at the fiery stab of pain caused by the sudden movement.

Whalen had used Mary—that was a fact. He wondered how many others had done that in the past. Not that he thought her promiscuous, or even that she granted her trust easily enough for frequent relationships. Still, she must have come across several jerks who had an eye on her bank balance. That could mess up a girl's self-confidence, no matter how beautiful she was.

Had he given her any indication that he was any different? No. All he had done was jump her at the first opportunity, and then told her he thought he loved her. Two days later. And in a joking way. Now he was amazed that she'd spoken to him at all.

Ford leaned against the side of the cabin, trying to decide what in the world he could say to her when he went back in there. Nothing clever came to mind. Mary wouldn't appreciate cleverness anyway. She would expect sincerity. He had always found it damned near impossible to be sincere about really deep feelings. Clowning was easy. Sarcasm, even easier than that.

The time had come to wise up and lay it on the line. If what he felt for Mary wasn't love, it was damned close to it, and need for her figured into it very heavily. Sexual need, yes; but a lot more than that was involved here. How the devil could he say that and not have it sound like a proposition? *Lie down, I think I love you?* Well, that sure as hell wouldn't cut it.

Might as well wing it, he decided. His head hurt too

much to compose any speeches and he needed to get it all said.

Ford pushed away from the cabin. He kicked through the shallow snow and walked up the back steps, dread battling with anticipation. Putting feelings into words definitely was not one of his talents.

"I didn't mean it," he muttered the minute he entered. No preamble. No putting it off.

"Yes, I know," she said, straightening the few items of food on the countertop.

Apparently unsatisfied with the arrangement, she moved things around again. Fiddling. She was fiddling. As wary as he was, probably. That helped.

"Not that I don't think I love you," he tried to explain. God, that sounded lame. "I do think so. *Know* so," he amended, nodding succinctly. "And I don't care what assets you've got or haven't got. It's you I care about. You, as a person. As a woman."

She said nothing, just stuffed her hands in her pockets and went over beside the fire and flopped down. He hated it when she looked so dispirited. He wanted her full of fire, even if it singed him a little.

"Mary, listen—"

She nailed him with a look that silenced him. He could have handled anger. He might have joked his way around disdain. But the hopelessness in her eyes just stopped him cold. She had made up her mind, and not in his favor. "It would never work, Ford. You're not my type and I'm not yours. Just let it go, okay?"

"Pretend nothing ever happened, huh?" He could feel the anger seeping back through the crack in his heart. "Act like we're a couple of strangers stuck out here in the middle of nowhere? The badge and the mark, just waiting it out?"

Her shoulders lifted and sagged in a sigh that looked soul deep. "That's exactly what we *are,* Ford," she said. "And when it's over, you'll go your way and I'll go mine."

"Like hell," he said, his voice rising. "Why don't you

expand on what you just said, that line about my not being your type?''

She looked so sad he wanted to grab her and hold her, then shake her until she came to her senses and stopped looking like that. Her lovely mouth turned down at the corners, her bottom lip just short of trembling. The urge to kiss her nearly overpowered him. Not a wise move right now.

"Ford, the way you live would drive me crazy. *Caution* is a foreign word to you. You never stop to think about consequences. Danger means nothing. Or maybe it means everything. You love it, don't you see? And I hate it. I absolutely *hate* it!"

"Oh, yeah," Ford murmured, staring into the fire, unable to endure the intensity of her gaze. Memories rolled over him, adding to the aches he already felt. "Somebody else said that to me once."

He remembered Nan's words all too well. And how he had argued with her before he'd caved in and given up his army career. If he did the same for Mary, would she leave him anyway, the way Nan had done? He could do without the job and find something else, but he wouldn't. It hadn't worked out the last time he'd made the sacrifice, and it wouldn't work now.

"It just wouldn't work," she said, echoing his thoughts so nearly, he did a double take, which increased the pain in his temples.

"Right," he said, the word like a clean, swift blade, cutting through his hopes. He wouldn't argue this time. A feeling of emptiness engulfed him. He had felt it before, but nowhere near this intensely.

To his surprise, Mary leaned over and placed her hand on his arm. "We can be friends," she offered softly.

Ford laughed—a bitter sound. That was how he felt. Bitter. "Sure we can." He wanted to be gracious about it, but he couldn't. Mary's rejection of him troubled her, he could see that. And he was glad it did. It sure as hell troubled him.

He lay down and stretched out on the mattress, his back to Mary and one hand over his face.

"What else can you expect of me?" she demanded.

"See if you've got any aspirin in that tote sack of yours, will you?" Ford mumbled. "I really feel like hell."

Mary's hand pushed his aside and palmed his jaw, then his brow. "Oh, my God, Ford, you're burning up! Why didn't you tell me you were sick?"

He had thought it must be obvious. He felt as if he were dying right now in more ways than one.

Mary quickly found a tin of aspirin in that storage facility she called a *purse*. "I'm going out to get you some fresh water," she said, pulling on her jacket.

While she was out, he phoned Duvek, who hadn't turned up anything new. Again, he ordered Ford to remain there until he did. As if they had any choice in the matter.

After the call, he switched off the phone and stuck it through a small tear in the corner of the sleeping bag. If he got worse off than he was—which seemed more and more likely with his body cooking from the inside out—he didn't want Mary to be tempted to call in the cavalry. They had to tough it out alone until Duvek got a handle on things.

The rest of the day passed at a crawl. The temperature stayed low and the ice remained. Mary kept the fire blazing, trying to sweat Ford's fever out of him, praying all the while that the firewood would last.

His wound looked seriously infected.

She fed him aspirin and bathed him with cold water when he would allow it. Then he would recover a bit. He managed to drag himself upright several times to visit the bathroom. Mary had struggled with him and argued him down twice when he insisted on going outside to cool off. He ate almost nothing.

He told her that he had phoned Duvek, who had ordered them to stay where they were. She would bet Ford never mentioned his injury. Immediately after he'd called his boss—while she was out getting the water—he must have hidden the phone from her to prevent her calling for help. She couldn't find it anywhere, and he wouldn't respond to her demands for it.

The next day, Ford grew worse, mumbling nonsense and refusing to wake fully when she tried to rouse him.

Frightened that he would die, Mary resorted to what little she had read of folk medicine. She went out and searched for the white willow tree she remembered seeing at the edge of the stream. With Ford's pocketknife, she sliced some of the bark from one of the newer branches.

Mary brewed a pot of willow-bark tea, hoping it might substitute for the aspirin she had used up.

The homemade medicine might or might not prove effective, but she couldn't sit by and do nothing. She nearly had to force him to drink it. Soon after that, he slept again.

He might be a bit cooler than before, she thought, when she checked him an hour later. Or it could be wishful thinking.

In desperation, she hauled Westy outdoors. She pushed and pleaded with the old dog to return to Mr. Knoblett's, hoping he would come to see what was wrong. So much for the Lassie movies. If he'd ever seen the films on television, Westy certainly hadn't paid attention. He merely pawed at her hand, whined and begged her to scratch his ears. Going for help wasn't in his bag of tricks.

She had no earthly idea what to do next. Leaving Ford alone was out of the question. Wandering in the icy woods until she froze to death wouldn't help him, anyway. She wasn't absolutely certain which way to go to find the Knobletts' house, and the road back to Gran's had been completely obscured by the fallen trees and branches. They were stuck here and Ford was dying.

Despite Ford's former assurances to the contrary, Mary

fully expected Perry to show up any moment. She kept Ford's pistol or the rifle within reach at all times. While she hated guns, Mary did know how to shoot. She also decided that she could kill to save Ford and herself, if it became necessary.

She continued forcing sips of the tea down Ford every time he woke, which wasn't often enough.

On the third day after his fever had taken hold, the weather warmed and the ice began to dissipate. Pretty soon, they would no longer be isolated and protected by the weather. The roads would be open.

Ford still felt hot to the touch and slept too much. Maybe if she stopped playing Pollyanna every time he woke up, and assuring him he would be as good as new soon, he would tell her how to find her way out of the woods and bring medical help for him.

She shook him hard, biting back tears of fear and frustration. "Wake up, Ford. Come on! You want to die in this godforsaken place?"

"Where?" he murmured groggily. "Mary?"

She watched as he struggled his way out of the feverish torpor. "Look at me, Ford!" Mary demanded.

"Hey." He breathed the word softly, trying to raise a hand to her face and failing. It dropped lifelessly back to his chest. "You—okay?"

Mary heaved a sigh of relief. For the first time in three days, his eyes looked focused, even if they did appear weak and bloodshot. "I'm fine, but you're *not*. Look, I need to go for help. Your arm's infected. You could— It's serious, Ford. We can't wait on this."

"Water," he growled. "Please."

Mary checked the coffeepot, which she had used to heat the water, and saw that it was nearly empty again, and what was left was hot. She poured it into the cup with more of the bark scrapings. "I'll get some. Back in a minute," she promised.

Thank God, he had come around, she thought as she

worked her way down the slippery bank to refill the container. Maybe after a cold drink, Ford would stay lucid long enough to discuss what they should do next.

Back in the cabin, Ford managed to raise himself to a sitting position. Exhaustion almost claimed him more than once, but he fought it. The determination in Mary's voice had served to shake him out of his fog. He had a muzzy recollection of her doing that several times.

She hadn't been able to conceal the fright in her eyes. Mary thought he was dying. Ford thought she might be right. She was definitely right about one thing—they did have to find some help. He couldn't protect her when he was in this shape. Duvek would come if he knew—

Ford slipped his hand through the slit in the sleeping bag and retrieved his cellular. First thing he needed to do was throw Blevins way off track, maybe give Mary and himself a clear path for at least a day or two. He punched the number, heard Blevins's curt hello, and gave him no chance to say another word.

"Devereaux, here. We're just south of Atlanta, a place called McDonough. Check you later." He disconnected immediately and switched off the phone.

Lethargy overtook him. Ford couldn't remain upright. He sort of melted back into the sleeping bag with the intention of resting for only a minute, just until Mary returned with his water. Next thing he knew, she was shaking him, patting him gently on the face with a cool, wet hand. "Wake up, Ford! Please, don't go out again!"

"Okay," he said, grinding out the word with effort. He pushed the phone toward her. "Call...Duvek. Directions... Helicopter to Knoblett's... He'll find us." Then darkness took him.

Mary stared at the phone as though she'd never seen it before. Where the devil had he hidden the thing? And how was she supposed to call Duvek when she didn't know the number?

After several futile attempts to wake Ford, she gave up. The one bright note in all that had happened was that he felt noticeably cooler. Maybe her homemade concoction was helping a little, but he wasn't out of danger. Far from it.

She started to call Mr. Knoblett, but noticed the battery light blinking. How long did she have? If she switched off the power, would it come back on when she was ready to make the call? No time to doodle around. She would simply call Information, ask for the number of the FBI in Memphis.

Then the word below one of the tiny buttons jumped right out at her. *Redial!* Of course! The call Ford had made to Michael Duvek was the last one made. Relief swept through her as she quickly punched the button and held the phone to her ear.

"C'mon, c'mon, c'mon," she chanted.

"That you, Devereaux?" the gruff voice demanded.

"Oh, thank God! Mr. Duvek?" Mary asked tentatively.

A silence fell. For a moment, Mary feared the phone's battery had died.

"Who is this?" the voice asked.

"Mary Shaw. Mr. Duvek, Ford—Agent Devereaux—has been seriously injured. He's running a high fever and we need for you to send medical help immediately. I'm afraid tetanus or something has set in."

"Just calm down, ma'am. Where are y'all, exactly?" he asked. "Ford wasn't real specific when he called."

"Send a helicopter to Knoblett's store," she instructed, giving him precise directions a child could follow, hurrying in the event the battery died before she could finish.

"So you're at this store now?" he asked.

"No, no! That's just the closest place you can land. We're in the woods about six miles north of there, in my grandfather's hunting cabin. You'll have to come in on foot. Please bring a doctor or medic. I am so worried about him!''

"Of course you are. You relax now, ma'am. Just stay right where you are and we'll come and get you.''

"All right. Thank you, Mr. Duvek. Ford trusts you, you know.''

"Does he, now? Well, that's nice to know. I just wish he'd told me where you were before now.''

"A few minutes ago, he instructed me to call and tell you. Then he passed out again and I can't seem to wake him up. Will you please hurry?''

He chuckled. Mary thought it a strange reaction to her desperation. A sense of unease bore down on her, adding weight to what she already felt.

"You can bet on it,'' he said softly. "I'll be there just as soon as I possibly can.''

Mary pushed the off button and sank back on the edge of the mattress where Ford slept. Thank God. Soon it would be over and Ford would be in a hospital getting antibiotics. And Michael Duvek would find her a safe place to stay, far away from Nashville.

But even visions of a hot shower and a nutritious meal couldn't dispel the niggling fear that something was dreadfully wrong. Something other than Ford's condition.

Should she wake Ford and try to get him into his clothes? He wore nothing except a pair of navy-blue briefs. She hadn't had the strength to keep dressing and undressing him when she'd had to cool his body by bathing him so often.

Maybe he would wake again before Agent Duvek and the medic came. How long did it take to fly from Memphis?

She spent a while trying to calculate that, but finally gave it up. The speed of a helicopter wasn't the only thing she would have to consider. Agent Duvek needed to make arrangements for the rescue, then fly here and land at Mr. Knoblett's. After that, the rescuers would have to make it through the woods. She knew very well how difficult and time-consuming that could be.

Instead of just sitting around, she decided to wake Ford and try to get him to drink more of the willow-bark tea. It certainly hadn't hurt him, even if it hadn't helped much. She poured more hot water over the bark in the cup and covered it to steep.

When Mary raised his head, Ford opened his eyes. "Wh-what is it?" he asked.

"Tea," she replied, and smiled down at him. "I know it's not very good, but I think it helped reduce your fever. How do you feel?"

"Like somebody tied me to a truck bumper and drove forty miles." He managed a swallow and made a face. "Cure-or-kill stuff." His voice sounded gravelly and his breath came in short huffs, but she couldn't tell if his lungs were affected or if it was simply caused by the pain. "Weak," he added. "What day is it?"

"Friday," Mary said, setting the cup aside and urging him to lie back again.

"Duvek!" He felt around for the phone. "I need to call him."

"You did," Mary assured him. "You called on Wednesday, just as you told him you would. And I just talked to him a few minutes ago."

"Thought I dreamed that. I told you to?"

"He's coming. Should be here in a few hours, maybe a little longer. Remember they have to make it overland those six miles or so." Mary patted his good shoulder gently. "Why don't you just rest until they come for us. You seem better."

"Coffee," Ford ordered. "I need to be coherent, and my brain feels like a damn helium balloon."

"No coffee!" She wasn't sure if he should have caffeine.

He didn't waste strength arguing. Instead, he tried to get up, probably intent on fixing it himself.

"All right, then! You win. Lie down and I'll get it." She left him there and went to find the jar of instant brew.

Before she reached the fireplace and the pot of hot water, she heard his steady breathing and knew he slept again.

Men. They could be at death's door—which was exactly where she'd thought he was an hour ago—and the testosterone just kept on pumping like the Energizer bunny. They couldn't admit when they were down, especially not in front of other men.

She looked at him, happy to see that some of his color had returned. His recent exertion probably deserved more credit for that than any real improvement in his condition. Ford remained very ill, and Mary feared he might lose the arm.

"If only you weren't such a wild man," she whispered softly. "I'd really love to keep you."

A smile pulled at her lips as she remembered Ford standing right here in the altogether, wearing nothing but her bra wrapped around his arm. Laughing at himself and at her.

The memory heated her body clear through. Maybe she should have made love with him again. One more time, before they said goodbye. Life certainly would prove dull without him around, she admitted to herself.

Mary felt as though she had lived an entire lifetime since she'd met him. Had it been only a week? A week today, she reflected. Just about this time in the afternoon, he had hauled her right out of her classroom and onto this dangerous roller-coaster ride. Now it was winding down and she would get off, head still spinning, heart thumping ninety miles an hour, an experience to recall and shiver over even after she grew old and gray.

She would never forget the man who had sheltered her, the one who had kept her alive to recall it. And she would also remember how much she had grown to love him in the seven days they'd spent together.

Mary heaved a huge sigh of regret for the farewells as yet unsaid, and curled herself next to him on the mattress. She missed him already.

Chapter 14

Ford knew Mary was gone before he opened his eyes. Westy's snore provided the only sound in the cabin. Mary had gone out without the dog. Little idiot.

No, he wouldn't even think any insults in her direction. That girl—woman, rather—had saved his life.

Even if he hadn't done so by choice, Ford felt guilty that he had left her to fend for herself—and him—for several days now. He cursed the bizarre accident that had landed him here, wrapped in a damned sleeping bag and as weak as a baby.

And there she was, slipping around on the ice outside, doing God knew what. Something that needed doing to keep their bodies and souls together, he'd bet on that.

She was no idiot. Neither was she the dainty little cupcake he'd thought she was at first. Mary had more courage and more initiative than anyone he knew. He doubted even Molly would have been able to cope with all Mary had faced these past few days. Nan would have freaked out from the word go.

He loved Mary. There was just no getting around it. Maybe he would get up the nerve to approach her again about that when all the dust had settled on this case. Until then, he would be her friend, as she wanted him to. He hadn't much choice in the matter the way things stood right now. But later...

He was still weak, but at least he felt a lot better today. Not well, by a long shot, but able to take some of the load off her shoulders.

"Mary!" he called, hoping she had just stepped out for a minute.

His voice came out raspy and weak from disuse. He pushed himself to a sitting position, cleared his throat and shouted, putting more force behind it.

The old body still ached all over, and his arm felt as if someone had run a fiery spike through the muscle there. But his head seemed clear enough. He found he could sit up without getting too dizzy.

Much to his relief, the door opened and Mary rushed in, several pieces of firewood balanced on one arm. Even bundled up as she was, she looked good enough to eat, her nose and cheeks rosy from the cold, and her eyes bright with energy.

"Hi!" she said, smiling with delight. "You look much better today! I really have missed that scowl."

He huffed. "I'd have a spanking to go with it if I could turn you over my knee. What the hell are you doing, running around outside without Westy? What good is a damned guard dog if you leave him snoozing by the fire?"

Her laughter warmed the room as she strode to the fireplace and dumped the wood beside it. "Trust me, he's better at snoozing than guarding." Westy gave a halfhearted bark at the disturbance and then resettled his head on his paws.

"That's the laziest hound I've ever seen," he remarked. "Good-for-nothing rascal. I think Knoblett left him here just so he wouldn't have to feed him."

She patted the old dog's head and scratched under his ears. Westy smiled. "But he's so swcct. Good company, too."

Great lot of help that would be in a scrape, Ford thought, but he didn't bother to argue about it. "It's getting dark," he observed, nodding toward the window.

"And warmer!" she commented, slapping her hands together to clean off the residue of bark. "Above freezing now, for certain. The ice melted today wherever the sun struck it, and the rest should be gone tomorrow. Agent Duvek's people should have been here by now, don't you think?" She glanced worriedly at the door.

Ford remembered then. Mary had called Duvek to come and get them. "What time is it now, and what time did you call?" he asked.

She tossed him his watch. "Nearly five and getting dark. I called around one o'clock."

"They might wait until morning. The woods are treacherous going at night."

"Tell me about it," she said wryly. "Surely they'll come as soon as they can. I emphasized how ill you were to Agent Duvek and he promised he would hurry."

Ford rolled his eyes and blew out a breath between his teeth. "Oh, great. Just the thing I'd want my boss to hear. Put out of commission by a damned tree limb. After this, I'll be lucky if he lets me sit at a desk and answer phones."

With major effort, he pushed himself to his feet. Mary jumped up and quickly covered his shoulders with the abandoned sleeping bag. "You want to catch your death? Where do you think you're going?"

"Bathroom," he said, grinning. "Want to come supervise?"

"Will you be all right?" she asked fretfully, ignoring his joking offer. "I could help you to the door like I did before."

Ford shook his head. "No problem." Mary must be genuinely concerned or she would have thought of some ready comeback. He liked that she worried about him, whether he warranted it or not. He liked it better, however, when she didn't frown that way, when she talked back to him and gave as good as she got.

His bare feet nearly froze to the floor as he trudged through the bedroom. God, how great it would be to have hot water right now. He supposed he should be thankful he didn't have to brave snow and ice in this condition to get to an outhouse.

He entered the tiny closet of a room, not intending to spend any more time in the chilly little place than he had to. The only thing operational was the john. He wished there was a working sink or shower so he could wash. He hated to greet the boss looking like Swamp Thing, even if he did feel like it.

He hurried back to the fire and collapsed on the mattress. Bless her heart, Mary had spread out his things on the hearth. She had found his comb and toothbrush, and had poured steaming water in a shallow dishpan so he could wash. One of his T-shirts lay folded beside it for use as a towel.

She and Westy had gone outside for a walk, he supposed.

In a matter of minutes, Ford had cleaned himself up as best he could. The beard felt scuzzy and looked worse, but he could live with it. Had done that for weeks on end, once upon a time. In spite of everything, he felt better than he had in several days.

Mary returned without the dog. "Westy's exploring," she explained, plopping down beside him so that her hip rested next to his. She bundled the downy sleeping bag around him and tucked it against his neck. At her touch, the old energy level shot up with a vengeance, despite his recent exertion.

Firelight flickered on her face, turning the ivory of her skin to gold. He couldn't take his eyes off her.

"I really thought you might die," she said softly. "And I wasn't sure what I should do."

This closeness of hers definitely wasn't a good idea if she wanted things to stay platonic. He smiled up at her. "If you only knew how I feel right now…"

"Aw, looking for sympathy?" she asked, grinning and shaking her head. "Too late. I've already cured you with my evil willow-bark brew."

"A nasty potion it was, too," he said, making a face. "Gagged on the stuff, but I guess it must have helped. Proud of yourself, are you?"

She raised one eyebrow and pursed her lips, tossing her hair and preening comically. "You see before you a true witch of the woodlands. A healer. A priestess of Mother Earth. Am I handy, or what?"

"Oh, smugness becomes her!" Ford said with a chuckle and a leer. He reached out and drew his fingers along her cheek, twining a loose strand of her hair around one finger, pulling her closer. "You are a little witch, all right. Your spell is working like a charm."

Mary drew away, looking suddenly uncomfortable, and shifted the subject. "Well, I'm glad your boss is bringing medical help. The fever's lessened, but I'll be honest with you—that arm is still a mess."

Her description certainly understated what it felt like, Ford thought. He had shaken the kinks out of the rest of his body once he'd gotten up a while ago, but the arm throbbed like the very devil.

He shifted, trying to get comfortable, covering the resulting stab of pain with an unrelated question. "Did Duvek say anything about Blevins or Perry?"

"No, and I didn't ask. I'm sure he'll fill you in when he gets here."

"Where's the phone? I'll call him now. The office will patch me through to his cellular."

"Can't," Mary said. "Battery's dead."

"Completely?"

"It was blinking red and cutting out when I was speaking to Duvek. Why don't you just wait?"

"Might as well," Ford agreed. He could hardly hold his eyes open anyway, and there was nothing he could do about the situation with Blevins and Perry, whatever it was.

"Go on back to sleep now," Mary suggested, soothing him with her words, crooning just as she would to a baby. "You need your rest."

"You've got the softest voice," he muttered through a lazy smile. "'Song of the South.' What a lullaby." Instead of lulling him into a restful sleep, however, the timbre of her words led him directly into a half-sleep sweetened by memory-enhanced fantasies.

Mary felt a pang of tenderness. She brushed a hand over his cheek, feeling the roughness of several days' growth of beard. She knew she shouldn't touch him when she didn't have to, but she just couldn't help it.

He could be so sweet at times. Most times, really. Underneath all that teasing and blustering, beat the heart of an old-fashioned gentleman. He just couldn't hide it, no matter how hard he tried.

What would he be like under normal conditions, when he wasn't fighting to keep them alive? Would he be a candy-and-roses kind of man? No, not Ford. His gifts would arrive at unexpected times, silly remembrances meant to make her laugh, or sentimental things to make her cry.

Even in circumstances like this, Ford showed a sort of gallantry. He considered her comfort and safety first, naturally, without making a big to-do of it or expecting thanks. And yet, he didn't seem threatened when she asserted herself. He admired her when she did. She could see it in his eyes.

Mary wished she could meet the woman who had taught Ford his manners. She pictured a self-assured Amazon— who wouldn't let much get by her, but had an abundance of love for her rambunctious offspring.

That was probably why Ford had no trouble at all showing affection. He touched, he hugged and praised—gestures that were not always sexual, though he certainly excelled at those when he wanted to. His openness and ready humor drew her to him even more powerfully than did his good looks and sensuality. She would probably love him even if he were ugly.

Love him? Did she really? Or was she merely infatuated with Ford because her life depended on him and his ability to get her through this trying time?

Mary put another log on the fire, then lay down beside him to enjoy his warmth and nearness. This might be the last time they would have together.

He had asked to see her when they returned "to the world," as he called civilization, but Mary knew he didn't really mean it. It was like those people who met in singles bars, had a one-night stand and said, "See you around." She and Ford had come all too close to establishing something deeper than a quick fling, and they both knew it. But once they left here, she doubted she would ever see or hear from him again.

He shifted in his sleep, stretching out his good arm just above her head. Mary snuggled into his embrace, resting her face against his shoulder. The heat of his body seemed more natural now—not dry and dangerous as it had been these past few days.

His arm tightened around her and his hand found her breast. She squeezed her eyes shut and allowed herself to enjoy his touch. The touch became a caress, and she felt his breathing quicken.

He turned his face toward her so that his lips were near her ear. "Love me, Mary," he whispered. "Let me love you."

She raised her mouth to his and kissed him. For several delicious moments, they shared the gentle exploration of tongues and grazing teeth, the fullness of lips against lips. And then he turned into her, trapped her in an undertow of feeling she hadn't been prepared for. Answering need suffused her, stripped away all caution. All reason.

Her eager hands pushed at the puffy fabric that covered him. She pulled up her sweater and pressed herself against his chest.

"Please," he murmured into her mouth, catching her bottom lip lightly between his, moving his hand from her breast. "I want to see you."

Mary drew away and pulled the sweater over her head. She quickly pushed off her pants and underwear, and began tugging his down over his hips and legs. Then she settled back on her heels and drank in the sight of him. *Splendid.*

The bandage on his arm distracted her. "Your arm," she murmured.

"Forget it," he growled. "Come here."

She settled herself against him full length and sighed deeply at the pleasurable sensation of his skin next to hers, with nothing between them except a raging desire as hot as the flames in the fireplace.

With a deft maneuver, Ford rolled their bodies so that she lay on top of him. Before she settled, he grasped her bottom and thrust into her.

Mary cried out, her pleasure so intense, she thought she might come apart. "Oh, Ford," she whispered.

"Yes," he hissed through his teeth, and began moving within her. He squeezed her hip urgently with his hand. Each breath he took grew more ragged and irregular.

She rose above him, bracing herself with her hands on either side of his neck. "Be still," she gasped. "Let me." His fiery gaze locked with hers as she took control and set the pace.

With each lift and downward push of her body, Ford groaned low in his throat. She was so intent on rushing his completion, her own took her by surprise.

The shattering hit her all at once, like a burst of starry fireworks, each prickle of pleasure so intense, she shivered violently.

He plunged upward, into her one last time, and she felt the flood of his release trigger yet another inward shudder that shook her to the core. Her body melted onto his and she lay still, scarcely able to breathe.

A wordless peace descended. Ford's hand trailed languidly from her buttocks, along her back to her neck. His fingers tangled in her hair and rested there possessively. Moments later, his breathing evened out and she knew he slept a sleep of pure fatigue.

She wanted to join him, but knew she had dared too much already. Any moment now, his boss might throw open the door, bringing medics to the rescue, expecting to find Ford half-dead.

Her eyes flew to his face, suddenly wondering if what had just happened had worsened his condition. Guilt gripped her. Oh, God, what if she had added to his injury?

At least he wasn't feeling any pain at the moment, she decided. Even in his sleep, he wore the hint of a smile. His bandage looked undisturbed. She ran a hand over his forehead and down to his neck. Sweat was a good sign, wasn't it?

Quietly, she moved away from him. She found her sweater, retrieved her pants and underwear, and tried to put herself in order for company.

Darkness had fallen completely now. Ford's condition remained uppermost in her mind as she waited for Duvek and the rescue. She shouldn't have made love with Ford. He had so little energy, they should have conserved it. What had she been thinking?

That she wanted him more than her next breath, of course. And that she loved him. The *kind* of love she had for Ford was the question that bothered her. Was it real, lasting? Would it matter if it was? They hardly knew each other—certainly not well enough for the sort of intimacy she had allowed.

Allowed? No, she might as well be honest here. He might have initiated it, but she had encouraged every single thing he had done to her, both times. The decision had been mutual. If she had uttered anything sounding remotely like a protest at any stage of their lovemaking, Ford would have backed off immediately.

Mary considered the fact that Ford hadn't withdrawn from her today, hadn't even tried to do so. Of course, he was not quite himself after the fever, and quite frankly, she'd been too involved to think about it at the time.

A pregnancy wouldn't be the end of the world. She would love to have a child, and Ford's would be doubly precious to her because she loved him. Whether that love proved to be the real thing, or a temporary product of the circumstances, Mary knew she would always have feelings for Ford. Despite her shaky finances and the way single motherhood would change her life, she would manage. And she would be thrilled to have a child—his child—once she got used to the idea.

Her sudden laugh surprised her. Here she was, getting all misty and maternal about a mythical little Devereaux when it was highly improbable that she had conceived. Her subconscious was indulging in wishful thinking, no doubt. Wouldn't a pregnancy force her and Ford into making a permanent attachment? Surely it would. Not marriage—neither of them wanted that—but a shared responsibility. An excuse to keep him in her life and see him regularly.

She did some quick calculations. Well, at any rate, she would have some indication by Monday next week whether the notion was feasible. Not even the catastrophic events of her past had ever altered her body's cycle by so much as a day. There would be plenty of time after that to decide what future course she needed to take, if any. But the wish took hold in her mind, was no longer confined to her subconscious.

Mary poured herself a cup of warm water from the coffeepot. Idly, still lost in worry over Ford and what would happen after their rescue, she mixed instant coffee in the cup and drank it down quickly.

Ford was no longer caught in the clutch of that awful fever. Surely it was a good sign that his body was conquering the infection. He would be fine, she told herself. Ford was entirely too strong and in too good shape to let the injury keep him down for long. A round of antibiotics, a little rest in the hospital, and he would be as good as new.

A smile crept over her when she remembered how he had teased her about her voice. A lullaby, he'd said. A fine one *he* was, to joke about her being so south in the mouth. Not when he had such a wicked Southern drawl...

As suddenly as that, Ford's words about Duvek echoed through her head. *"Sounds like a Kennedy."*

But Duvek *hadn't.* Not when she had talked to him.

"Oh, no!" she wailed aloud, and tore across the room.

"Ford! Ford, wake up!" She shook his legs. She slapped him lightly on his uninjured arm and then his face. "Oh, please wake up!"

He slept on, not even stirring.

"Oh, God, oh, God, what do I do now?" Mary sobbed. She knew for certain she hadn't spoken to Agent Duvek at all. The man who answered had sounded more like Jimmy Carter than a Kennedy.

She replayed the conversation in her head. Why, oh, why hadn't she waited for him to identify himself first? It must have been Blevins. Who else would pretend to be Duvek?

But how could she have gotten Blevins on the phone by punching Redial? Had Ford called him *after* he'd called Duvek? Why would he have done that, and when?

Whatever had happened, Mary feared that either Perry or Blevins might be on their way here, intent on murder, and Duvek would be sitting somewhere in Memphis, totally unaware. There would be no rescue.

And Ford was out like the proverbial light. He would be awake now if she hadn't exhausted him. They would both die right here, and it would be all her fault because she hadn't controlled her damned hormones.

"No, by God, we won't die!" she declared aloud. It

helped to hear her determination voiced. "I'll handle it, don't you worry," she said to the sleeping Ford.

She took his gun from under the edge of his sleeping bag near his head. Then Mary positioned herself behind the door, so that she wouldn't be seen immediately when it opened. Whoever came through that door would get shot, she decided. She wouldn't wait to see who it was. Shoot first, ask questions later. That was what she'd do.

It wouldn't be Duvek arriving, she knew, because he couldn't possibly know where they were. No, like a dummy, she had given excellent directions to the wrong damned man.

Mr. Knoblett would call out first if he happened to come here for some reason. But he would have no cause to come. Not at night, anyway.

So, if anyone opened that door without identifying himself at this hour, he would definitely be up to no good. And he would die.

What if he didn't come in at all? What if he decided to burn them out? She swallowed the lump of terror that nearly choked her. No, not a fire. He would need to make sure he had the right people, wouldn't he? Couldn't leave that to chance. And if he hadn't found them already, he would also want the diamonds he thought she had.

Thanks to her big mouth, Blevins would know Ford was helpless. Maybe he would also believe that she was. That was their only hope.

Perry would probably be the one to come. Blevins would want to keep his own hands clean. Obviously, that was why he had hired Perry in the first place.

The idea of facing down a professional killer, a successful assassin, terrified her.

"I can do this!" she declared aloud, huddling closer to the wall, clutching Ford's Glock with both hands. She slid her finger onto the trigger, feeling the rasp of the cold, scored steel.

She shouldn't have ignored Ford's subtle offer to teach

her about the gun. Did it fire ten rounds? Thirteen? If she just squeezed the trigger hard, would it fire only once or keep firing repeatedly? She pulled the slide back to see if it was loaded. There was a round in the chamber.

Guns frightened her, and she had wanted nothing more to do with them. Her dad had tried to make a marksman of her by taking her to a local shooting range and making her fire his fancy Colt .45 and his .38. A woman ought to know how to handle a weapon, he had said. She hadn't thought so at the time, but now she agreed and wished she'd paid more attention. That had been so long ago.

She could still feel that hated recoil and hear the deafening reports, even muffled as they had been by ear protectors. Mary thanked God that at least those things wouldn't take her by surprise.

"Come through that freaking door and you die," she whispered gruffly, trying to make friends with the hard, lethal instrument in her hands, bolstering her confidence the only way she knew how.

"Okay, sucker, do your worst," she growled, sliding her arms out straight, pointing the pistol. "And eat my lead!"

Within the next half hour, she had used up more four-letter words than an Al Pacino film. Her brain felt tired from thinking up nasty threats. Her arms were weary from holding the heavy weapon. And her stomach contained enough knots to produce a galloping case of nausea. Still she persisted. Couldn't let down her guard. Didn't dare slacken her vigil.

The longer the absolute silence outside the cabin lasted, the more ominous it grew.

Where was Westy? He usually spent less than half an hour out in the cold before he scratched to come back inside. Of course, it wasn't quite so cold out there tonight. Some guard he'd turned out to be.

Mary began to wonder then whether something had happened to the dog. Had someone—namely Perry or Blevins—rendered him useless? Killed him, maybe?

A scraping sound from outside stole her breath. She didn't dare show her face at the window. Slowly she stood, still backed against the logs of the wall.

Wait, she told herself. *Wait and get ready.* A board on the porch creaked slightly. She would never have heard it unless she'd been listening for that sound. Someone was just beyond the door.

"Mary Shaw?" a voice called out. A velvet voice, rich and deep and deadly calm.

Her terrified gaze flew to Ford, who still slept, totally oblivious to the danger that stalked them. *Please, God, don't let him wake up right now.* She looked back at the door.

A moment later, her eyes grew wide and her nerves drew even tighter than before. The doorknob turned—slowly, deliberately, soundlessly.

Show time.

Mary brought the gun up to shoulder level, holding it the way she had, long ago, at the firing range—one hand gripping the weapon, the other supporting it. *Come on. Come on. Come on.* Her mind chanted the words.

The door swung open—freely, as though pushed. Mary glanced at her hands, tightened so on the gun that her fingers looked bloodless. And she remembered the safety was on. *Damn!*

Quickly, holding her breath, she switched it off and regained her stance, legs apart, arms braced outward in front of her.

Westy ambled through the door and made directly for the fireplace. The coals beneath the andirons, a glowing fluorescent-orange heap, and the flames licking at the nearly consumed logs, provided the only light in the room.

Suddenly the man was there, standing in the doorway, lowering his weapon a little and staring across the room at the sleeping Ford.

He took a hesitant step forward, his head turning to examine the far corner of the room—the door to the bedroom.

It was now or never.

Mary swung outward from her position against the wall and fired, squeezing the trigger for all she was worth.

The first shot knocked her off-balance. The next two went wild.

Chapter 15

Shots! Ford's eyes flew open and he gasped as two great paws bounced on his midsection. Westy's continuous barks echoed around the cabin, drowning out everything else. Ford rolled over to grab his Glock. *Gone!*

Mary's keening cries brought him to his knees in an instant. Surely to God he was dreaming. Shadows from the fire danced over the frozen tableau. Nothing in the room moved but Westy, who bounced around the two figures, barking for all he was worth.

For a moment, Ford's mind refused to believe what he saw. Mary stood, arms stiff, holding his weapon aimed at the head of the man on the floor. Perry?

"Hush!" he shouted. The dog ceased his uproar immediately, but Mary continued making that ungodly sound—misery made audible.

Ford dragged himself upright and rushed to her, approaching from the side so she wouldn't shoot him accidentally. He stepped around her and grasped her shoulders from behind. Slowly, he slid his hands down her arms. "Let go, Mary," he said firmly. "Turn the gun loose. I've got it."

Her breath shuddered in. He could feel the vibration against his chest. He liberated the Glock and then released her. She still didn't budge from the spot. Her hands remained outstretched, fingers curled inward now and shaking. "Killed him," she said, the words rushing out in little puffs of air.

He could see the dark puddle of blood between the man's left side and his upthrown arm. Ford moved around Mary, gently shoving her back, farther away from the body.

Then he crouched beside the prone form, pressing his fingers against the carotid artery. Not dead yet or even close. The pulse felt a little erratic, but was strong. Of course, Ford could fix that.

"Devereaux?" the man gasped. "You—you're a hard man to find."

"Got a little more than you bargained for, didn't you, buddy?"

Perry shook and then groaned. "Blevins—he's coming. Came to warn you. Help."

"Yeah, right," Ford said, tearing at the zippered jacket and the shirt beneath to check the damage Mary had wreaked. God, what a woman she was! If he hadn't loved her before—well, he sure had good reason now. Perry could have iced them both without Ford's even knowing it.

"You thought—I was trying to kill you," Perry stated.

"Crossed my mind a couple of times," Ford said wryly.

"I'm with the Bureau," he said, as if that explained everything.

"Oh, *right!* We have a hit squad now?" Ford continued pulling the clothing away from the wound.

"Badge. My hand." Perry ground out the words and then drew his breath in, hissing.

Ford glanced toward Perry's clenched right hand and saw the weapon resting a good two feet away from it. In the left, he held a leather wallet, lying open. The meager light glinted on metal.

"Uh-oh," Ford muttered, picking up the folder. No doubt about what it was. "Jeez, man, what's going on here?"

"Deep cover. Special—"

"Then what the hell are you doing toting ID?" Ford demanded, dropping the credentials and getting back to his original purpose. Now he could see the entry wound in Perry's side just below his ribs. At least he wasn't gut shot, but Mary had done a pretty good job on him, as it was.

"You—wouldn't have believed—me. The file…"

"Yeah, I know all about that. Fake, right?"

"Uh-hmm," Perry moaned. "Had to establish…cover." He clenched his eyes shut. "Will I make it?"

Ford nodded. "Oh yeah, we'll get you patched up. Hang in there, now." He turned then to see how Mary was doing. She had retreated to the mattress and sat with her knees tucked under her chin, her arms encircling her legs.

"It's Perry, Mary. But it looks like he's one of the good ol' boys. Can you give me a hand, here?"

She roused immediately and rushed to his side. Backlit as she was by the fire, he couldn't see her face, but could just imagine those eyes rounded and her pretty lips pressed together the way she did when she tried to keep them from trembling.

"Take it easy, now. You take his feet and I'll get his arms. We're gonna drag him over by the fire where I can see what we're doing. Okay? He'll be okay. We'll fix him up."

She made a murmur of agreement and crouched down to grab Perry's ankles. Her movements were spasmodic, definitely shocky, but she would recover. Perry might not, in spite of what Ford had said.

"Hot water, Mary, and some rags. Shake a leg, hon! I don't have time to baby you now, much as I'd like to."

"*Baby* me?" she demanded, her voice stronger now.

Ford smiled to himself. She'd do. "Yeah, suck it up, kid. We got a problem here and I can't do everything by myself."

He'd provoked her deliberately and got the expected results. She started slamming things around like women did when they got a mad on, but she *was* doing what he asked. In a hurry, too, even if she was noisy about it.

He exposed Perry's side again. Then he turned him a little and found the exit wound. It was messy, but looked as though the bullet had gone straight through. Ford was glad it hadn't bounced around inside. He made a compress out of the shirts Mary had handed him and held it firmly against both wounds to stanch the bleeding. His own arm was giving him fits.

Mary tugged off Perry's jacket and shirt while Ford continued to apply pressure. Her actions were hasty and none too gentle.

Perry had passed out the minute they'd moved him. Ford regretted they were going to have to bring him around pretty soon, if they could. Blevins was coming, he'd said. But when? And why, if he thought Perry was his hit man? It didn't make much sense. But then, none of this did.

What kind of case was Perry on that would require his having a false file distributed to the field offices? Internal crapola, maybe? Strange that Duvek hadn't informed him about who Perry really was, since Ford had laid out the whole story. Maybe Duvek hadn't known about Perry, either. Jeez, could Duvek be involved?

Mary sniffled as she worked, crying. "Aw, honey, he'll be fine. Don't worry."

"D-don't you call m-me *honey!*" she warned. But her next words sounded frightened. "Will they arrest me for— for this? I did it on purpose."

Ford forced a laugh. "No, no! Of course they won't arrest you! I'd have shot him myself if I'd been awake. If he had been trying to kill us, that's the only thing that would have saved our lives. Buck up now, everything's cool."

Damn cold, in fact. His butt was freezing and his feet were numb. Perry lay between him and the fire and Ford was wearing nothing but his birthday suit and a bandage around his arm.

"Here, hold this for me," he ordered Mary. "I need to put on some clothes." She obeyed without comment.

He watched her as he dressed. It took a while since his bad arm didn't work that well. She was holding up okay, all things considered. While she was occupied with Perry, Ford took the time to gather his weapon and Perry's. He knew it would upset Mary if she had to look at them, so he put on the safeties and stowed them beneath the end of the mattress near Perry's feet.

"I'm *so* sorry," Mary said to Perry as he began to stir.

"Good shot," Perry grunted in a pain-filled whisper. "Little low and off...center."

"Perry, I need some answers," Ford said as he knelt closer, edging between Mary and Perry as best he could, without interfering with her pressure on the wound.

"We'll get you some help soon as we can," he said to Perry. "Meantime, what can you tell me about Blevins?"

Perry sucked in air, steeled himself. Ford admired his determination to stay conscious and calm. Most men would be screaming for an ambulance.

"Blevins called me when he got your location. Sent me again...to take you out. Last call...helped me identify who he was. Couldn't before."

It took a minute for Ford to put it together. "He hired you anonymously, then, to do the hit? What about Antonio, the antiques dealer?"

"Did that one...himself," Perry said, speaking a little more easily now. "Brought me in after that. I was waiting for an...expected call...different subject. You were a surprise job. Tried to catch you. Warn you."

"What about that shooting on the road over by Franklin?"

Perry shook his head slightly. "Not me. Lost—lost you at the museum."

"But he told you where we were when I called him from the mansion, didn't he?"

"Yes. You're the…devil to catch. You're his main mark."

"Me? What about Mary?"

Perry blinked hard, his lips firm in a grimace as he fought passing out again. "Her, too. When she gave up the stones."

"Why me?" Ford asked.

"You got too wise, I guess. He didn't get…specific."

Ford suspected there might be more to it than that. Blevins hated his guts, for one thing. "And you think he's coming here? Why, if he hired you to get rid of us?"

"To get rid of me, too. Said stay with…your bodies till morning. He'd help bury you. Ha!" Perry uttered a harsh little grunt supposed to be a laugh. "Bet he'd make me…dig my own hole. Sorry bastard."

"The two politicians. How'd you get credit for them?" Ford asked, wondering just how far the powers-that-be would go to set up Perry's cover as an assassin. And, more to the point, why they would do it.

"They…hired someone else, too. Insurance. Didn't know that till after." He paused and sighed. "I claimed the kills. For my cover."

"Cover for what?" Ford demanded.

Perry smiled, nearly a death-mask rictus, and glanced at Mary. "'Need to know.' Familiar with that term?"

"Well, shoot. You creeps have all the fun, double-0 numbers, too, I bet. Why'd Blevins use you? Sort of overkill, looks like."

"Available. Local at the moment. And he knew you'd go down hard. He set you up, guarding her," Perry said, looking toward Mary.

"So you could do us both at once," Ford guessed. "And

our unknown courier would take the heat while Blevins took the gems. End of investigation.''

Perry didn't answer. He'd dropped off again with perfect timing. Ford could allow him to sleep now and escape the pain.

''The bleeding has slowed, almost stopped,'' Mary said as she lifted the pad on the entry wound and then checked the other one. ''I'm going to try to wrap him.''

Ford helped her as much as his arm would allow. When they had finished, he said, ''I'll take over now. Why don't you go wash your face or something. You look sorta done in.''

She abruptly stood. Then, very quietly, she leaned down and whispered directly in his ear, ''Will he live, Ford? Really?''

''Absolutely.'' He nodded emphatically. ''Hey, you can't kill these guys. They've got orders not to die.''

''How are you?'' she asked softly. Too softly, like she might cry again.

''A damn sight better than I was before this afternoon's delight.''

She cursed him as she whirled around and stalked off into the darkness of the bedroom. Ford grinned. Deviling her and watching those furious little hips wag was going to be one of the great joys of his life, he decided.

But first, they had to make it until morning and then face Blevins. After that, he'd give Mary a rush that would put Casanova to shame. He felt damned inspired.

''She's gonna shoot you, too,'' Perry said, his eyes still closed.

Ford looked down at his fellow spook and laughed. ''Well, why the hell do you think I hid the guns?''

Mary leaned forward against the wall in the small bathroom, her head resting on her folded arms, wondering whether she could get by without throwing up. She had almost killed a man. He might die yet. She might have felt justified in shooting him if he really had been trying to kill them, but he hadn't.

From what she gathered, he had been trying to warn them about Blevins all this time. Now he might die because of her. He was a young man, too. She guessed around thirty to thirty-five. Might even have a family.

Mary's legs trembled and she quickly sat down on the closed lid of the commode. She buried her face in her palms and began to cry in earnest.

The release of tension helped and Mary began to think more clearly. She wiped her eyes with her fingers, sniffled and smelled the residue gunpowder on her hands. It was stupid to sit here in the bathroom and cry, even over spilled blood, she thought. What was done, was done. There was another man out there somewhere, this one truly intent on their deaths. She might have to do this again.

"Come on, Shaw," she muttered to herself, raking her hair back with her fingers and taking a deep, cleansing breath. "Get over it and get out there."

"Good attitude." Ford's voice came out of the darkness.

Mary jumped up. "Good grief! Did you have to do that?" She couldn't see him in the dark, but she knew he must be filling the doorway. "You scared me to death!" The last word rang in her ears. "What about that—Perry? Is he—?"

"He'll make it."

Ford entered the bathroom and stepped close enough to touch her. He ran his hand down her arm and threaded his fingers through hers.

"You okay now? If you are, we need to make a plan."

She nodded, realized he couldn't see, and answered, "Fine."

"That you are, Mary," he said, and brushed his lips across her forehead. "So fine." He trailed his mouth along her brow and cheek and found her lips. She melted into him and let him hold her. When they broke the kiss, Mary rested her head against his chest.

"Ford?"

"Hmm?" He stroked her back with his hand—not a prelude to anything, just a caring gesture.

"I can't do that again."

"What, sweetie? What can't you do? Fire the gun?"

"Have you ever…killed anyone?"

For a long moment he remained still. She could feel the tenseness he tried to conceal from her. Strange how the total darkness revealed things she might have missed had she been looking at him.

Finally he replied. "Yeah."

That one word, so softly and hesitantly spoken, conveyed so much. Mary sensed his regret, sorrow, defensiveness, even a little pride.

"Well, I can't do it," she whispered.

His hand pressed her closer to him. "Okay," he said. "But we need to decide what you will do when it goes down. Blevins is coming. I'll try not to kill him, either, but you gotta understand, I might have to."

"I know."

He stepped away, but kept hold of her hand. "Come on, let's go back to the fire and get you warm. We can talk in there."

Mary went with him, clinging to his strong, capable hand with both of hers, like a child in tow. She promised herself she would be strong in a minute—as soon as they found the light again and began to map out tomorrow morning's probable events. But for now, just for the time it took to cross the cold, dark bedroom, she wanted to forget everything but the steadying comfort of his grip and the feel of his fingers interlaced with hers.

Ford wondered what in the world he would do with Mary. He couldn't send her out in the dead of night to cross the six miles of devastation to Knoblett's place. Assuming she could find it, she wouldn't be safe there anyway. She had just told him that she'd given Blevins directions to Knoblett's house when she thought he was Duvek.

No way could he call for help. His phone was as dead as a mackerel and Perry didn't have one. He couldn't send her back to the Jeep. Even if she made it to the vehicle and got it started, it might die on her before she got somewhere safe.

One thing he did know—he had to get Mary out of here. Perry would be useless, probably out cold, and Ford didn't feel too spry himself.

He had been fighting the dizziness and need for rest since he awoke to the sound of the shots. Alternating chills and urges to go outside and cool off told him his fever was back. If it returned full force, he would be as ineffective as Perry. Mary might find herself on her own against Blevins.

He considered sending her to her grandmother's house. Blevins knew about it, of course. And Ford figured that if he blew it when Blevins arrived, that might be the first place the bastard would look for Mary. However, it still seemed the safest alternative. Blevins would be coming in by way of Knoblett's, and she would be headed in the other direction. Once she got there, she could call for help and then hide in that wine cellar she had told him about.

Hopefully, just before dawn wouldn't be too late to send her. Blevins had no reason to rush in here before morning. Anybody who planned to approach Perry in the dark, no matter what the reason, would have to be crazy. Blevins wasn't crazy, just greedy as hell.

Looking down at Mary where she sat on the edge of the stone hearth, he spoke decisively. "Okay, here's what we'll do. Just before first light, you're going to take off for your grandma's place. Soon as you get there, call somebody who lives close by to come right away and take you somewhere else. Anybody but Knoblett. Blevins might be there. The minute you're safely away, call Duvek to come and get you. Tell him to send a few troops in here, too, while you're at it."

He reached for her tote bag, which she had laid near the hearth, and tossed it onto her lap. "Find me a pen in that jumble of stuff and I'll write his number on your hand."

Mary set her lips and raised that stubborn little chin. "No. I'm not leaving without you."

Ford snatched the bag away and found the pen for himself. He crouched down beside her and grabbed her hand.

She tried to snatch it back, but he held on. She fumed. "I'm not going anywhere, Ford! You got that?"

He squeezed the hand he held, rubbing his thumb into her palm as he met her determined gaze. He kept his voice low and tried to sound reasonable. "Mary, there *will* be shooting."

"I'm not a fool, Ford! I know that. You'll give me one of the guns."

"You told me not ten minutes ago that you couldn't do it again," he reminded her, hoping to rekindle her fear, or guilt, or whatever it took to get her to agree to go.

"Anybody can get rattled for a minute. Give me a break here, will you? Maybe I don't do this for a living, but I *can* do it!" she declared. "Didn't I prove that I can? Didn't I shoot *him?*" Mary nodded once at the unconscious Perry.

Ford saw her wince and then regain her resolve.

"Well, that's mighty brave of you, honey, but you'll hesitate next time. That split second could be fatal. I don't want you to die." Ford realized he was scaring himself with that warning worse than he was her.

"I won't," she promised, pulling her hand from his. "I'll fire the minute he opens that door. You'll see!"

Ford started shaking his head, but she stopped that in a heartbeat. She had snaked one hand under the edge of the mattress and pulled out his Glock.

"I'm not going," she said as she ejected the clip, visually checked the load and replaced it with a snap of her palm. "And you can't make me."

With eyebrows raised and hopes lowered, Ford blew out

a breath of frustration. She was right. He was in no shape to enforce anything at the moment. "It's your neck, then."

"Yours, too," she replied with a lift of her chin.

Ford got up and headed toward the kitchen area. "How did you make that witch's brew of yours?" he asked, effectively changing the subject. "If it won't make me sleepy, I think I need another shot of the stuff."

Mary immediately abandoned the weapon and hurried after him. First she felt his forehead and neck, her cool hands more gentle than his mother's had ever been. No matter how bad he felt, his mom was a no-nonsense kind of woman when it came to coddling. Ford appreciated the fact that Mary was still prone to a little nonsense now and then.

"You do feel really warm," she said, looking worried.

Ford watched while she found the substance she had stored in an old jar and returned to the fire for the hot water.

She worked quietly and efficiently, pouring the steaming liquid over the flaky bits she had placed in one of the heavy ceramic coffee mugs they had found in the cabinet when they'd first come here.

"What is that, anyway?" he asked.

"White willow bark," she informed him. "We'll let it steep for a little while before you drink it, since it's a tea," Mary said.

"An expert in folk remedies, are you?" he asked, even though he didn't want an honest answer—not when he was about to become a test animal again. "Convince me."

"The hills around here are a veritable pharmacy," she said, sounding like a tour guide again. At least the conversation was taking her mind off what could happen in a few hours.

"That so? I heard ginseng grows wild. That's an aphrodisiac," he told her with a leer.

"You would know about that one!" she replied, scoffing. "Well, I'll bet you didn't know that a form of birth control's available, too! Since ancient times. The knowl-

edge was lost to medical *men*—they were probably con-
centrating on the ginseng—but midwives knew about it.
Guess what it is.''

"Abstinence!" he said, laughing.

"Nope," she said. "Guess again. It's quite common."

Ford traced his lips with his tongue, wondering if there
might be a message in this somewhere. Had she used whatever it was she was talking about? Was that why she'd been
so accommodating this afternoon? He caught her gaze and
held it, trying to see if this was going anywhere deep. "I
give up."

"Queen Anne's lace!" she announced. "It's true! Isn't
that amazing?"

"Are you afraid you're pregnant, Mary?" The words just
popped out.

She looked shocked. "Of course not. I just used that as
an example of what I know—what I studied about plants.
I didn't mean—"

"It's okay," Ford said gently, trailing his hand down her
arm. "Don't get upset. I just wondered."

She stared at him, eyes wide. "I just didn't want you to
think I'm—well, that I knew nothing about plants and
things, and gave you something dangerous. I do know
some. Enough, anyway."

"You read a book once," he guessed.

Mary broke eye contact. "Well, it was an *excellent*
book," she muttered.

Ford laughed and picked up the mug, flipping off the
makeshift cover. He drank it down to the flaky dregs.
"There you go, Doc. How's that for trust?"

She smiled up at him and took the mug from his hand.
"I'm sorry I don't know more, but I did the best I could."

He laid his hands on her shoulders and squeezed gently.
"Yes, and you've done that every step of the way. Thank
you for that." He kissed her on the cheek. "But now you're
going to have to leave things to me. Tomorrow morning,

you *will* go back to your grandmother's house. You'll take one of the guns for protection, and you will leave.''

"No," she said. "I won't."

Ford pushed her away and turned, running a hand through his hair and down the back of his neck. "Damn it, Mary!"

Just then the door crashed open and banged against the wall.

Chapter 16

"Well, well, how's it going, Devereaux?" Blevins said, laughing. "And Ms. Shaw! At last." He glanced quickly at Perry, who lay completely still. "Dead?"

"Looks like it, doesn't he?" Ford replied, inching closer.

"Oh, I'd stop right there, Dev," Blevins warned. "And toss your weapon."

Mary sucked in a shuddering breath. Ford didn't have a weapon to toss. What would the man do to him? To them? Shoot them, of course. He had no choice now.

Blevins didn't look the way she thought a murderer would. He might have been an insurance salesman, a clerk at Sears, or a CPA. Blevins looked like Mr. Everyman— pushing forty, with slightly thinning hair, neat mustache. Not handsome, yet not ugly, either. Even his casual clothing looked ordinary, though a little worse for wear from his trip through the woods. There was nothing remarkable about him at all except the deadly weapon he held.

"In the bedroom. I'm not armed," Ford said, turning

around so Blevins could see his back. "Guns make the lady nervous."

Blevins *tchhed* and shook his head. "My, my, such a gentleman, aren't you? Didn't they teach you anything at the Farm, you idiot? Where's Perry's piece?"

Ford pointed to his own Glock. It lay on top of the mattress at Perry's feet where Mary had left it. "Right there."

"Well, let's get that out of the way," he said. "Just on the off chance you might try something suicidal. Ms. Shaw, go very slowly. Right hand over your head. Pick it up by the barrel with your left, two fingers only. Then bring it here and toss it out the door."

"I—I can't," Mary said, wringing her hands. "I can't touch it! Please don't make me." She couldn't wait to get her hands on that gun.

"Go ahead, Mary," Ford encouraged her. "The safety's on. I promise it won't hurt you. Do *exactly* as he says."

Mary did as he said, and she didn't risk trying to use it. She knew she couldn't get the safety off and fire quickly enough to save both herself and Ford. But Perry's gun still lay under the edge of the mattress. If only Ford would distract him so she could get to that one, she might take Blevins by surprise.

Ford seemed to sense the need. "Want to tell me why you turned?" he asked Blevins.

Blevins laughed again as he stepped to one side and reached behind him to close the door. He aimed the pistol directly at Mary. "Ah, you want revelations?" He shrugged slightly. "I never turned, actually. I joined the Bureau because it's an excellent information source if you're on the inside. The talent I discovered listed in our computer files would amaze you. The best in the business. Perry, for example. But I do believe I overestimated his potential. It's easy to subvert investigations if one is in charge, too. It has been a profitable career."

"You were in league with Nelson McEvan all along," Ford said, nodding. "The appraiser."

"Oh, yes, an excellent partner these past twelve years," Blevins replied. "But I decided not to share this time. Retirement, you understand. I've merely been tying up loose ends."

"That explains Antonio. But why have Mary killed?"

"Now, now, Dev, don't be dense. The fool gave her the diamonds before I could intercept them. She's our famous courier."

Ford stared at her as though she had betrayed him.

Blevins chuckled. "Only for the last two jobs, of course. Antonio did give them to her concealed in the dolls. She was to auction them off at one of her little society galas, just as she did the others. That top bidder got a real steal, so to speak. Actual treasure that sailed right through customs with a bill of sale and provenance. That was always the difficult part—getting them out of the country."

Mary gasped. "*Jim* set it up! He was the one who notified potential buyers. All in the name of love and Christian charity."

"Well, he did have a good cause other than that. If he hadn't participated so enthusiastically, someone might have revealed the cons he ran before he was so wonderfully 'saved.'"

Mary had drifted slowly backward away from Blevins while he talked. She had only a few feet to go before she would pretend to faint on the mattress, slide one hand under and—

"You may join your valiant protector now," Blevins said, smiling, his eyes watchful and trained on Ford. "Stand over there with him." He waggled the pistol slightly.

Mary tried not to show her frustration. She had to get to that gun.

He shifted his gaze to Mary. "I'll take those diamonds now. I don't have a lot of time to waste here."

"Less than you think," Ford advised him. "Duvek knows."

"I gathered that from the phone conversation. More reason for me to hurry and hit the road, huh?" His wide, evil smile bared slightly crooked teeth and his eyebrows slanted à la Jack Nicholson. The man looked insane, but Mary knew he wasn't. Blevins might be greedy and amoral, but he was not crazy. "I'll have the diamonds now and we'll get this over with," he said.

"I don't have them," Mary told him.

"Did you forget I was on surveillance that night? I heard Antonio give them to you. I'd have found you after I shot him if you hadn't made that damned call. Now, get them." He shifted the gun so that it pointed at her.

"They're gone," she said. "I left the dolls in my purse and somebody took them. We thought it might have been you."

He fired. The bullet struck the cabinet door just behind Mary. "Quit jerking me around, you little bitch!" he shouted.

"I'm not!" Mary cried, her hands clamped over her ears. "I swear I'm not!"

"Settle down," Ford said calmly. "Let's talk about this."

"Don't you play buddy-buddy with me. I'll kill you right where you stand. I don't need you to find those gems and I don't like you worth a damn, anyway!"

"That's pretty obvious," Ford retorted, his words clipped with anger. "Maybe we could cut a deal here, though. Mary doesn't have your damned diamonds. *I* do."

Blevins quirked his mouth and raised one dark brow. "Then how 'bout I just shoot her now? Let you watch her die. That'll give you some incentive to cooperate, huh?" He pointed the pistol at Mary.

"Do and you'll never see them," Ford warned. "You know how stubborn I can be. Let her go. Give her half an hour to get out of here and I'll give you the gems."

"Like hell. Nobody's going anywhere but me."

Mary couldn't imagine what good Ford thought his blatant lie about the diamonds would do, but he kept it going, almost convincing her that he did have them.

"Look, Blevins, you've already been made. There's no need to kill the woman. It'll take hours for her to make it out of the woods in any direction. Hell, she'll probably get lost anyway. Don't *do* this."

"You're a dead man, Dev, but I might be persuaded to tie her up and leave her alive, *if* you play nice. Now give me the stones," Blevins ordered. "Now!"

Mary stared down the small round hole in the end of the pistol, not six feet away. The man was going to kill her, too. She didn't believe for a minute that he'd leave her alive, no matter what they did or didn't do.

Ford neatly stepped in front of her, shielding her for the moment. "Just take it easy, man. I'll get 'em. Okay?"

Blevins laughed. "Tell you what. Let *her* get them. Tell her where," he ordered. "Just in case you're planning to surprise me with something the way you did Perry."

Ford slumped a little and looked over his shoulder at her. The firelight flickered over his face, bright enough that Mary could discern his every feature. She didn't see the resignation she'd expected to find there. Instead, she read confidence and encouragement in the ghost of a smile.

"Look under the foot of the sleeping bag, Mary. Be *quick* about it. Give the man what he needs. Go on."

"No funny stuff, sweetheart, or I'll blow him away right now," Blevins said.

He was going to blow them both away in a few minutes anyway—Perry, as well, once he found out he was still alive.

This was it. Their one chance.

She edged away from Ford, taking cautious side steps toward the hearth, keeping her eyes on Blevins.

Ford tried to keep him busy talking. "McEvan's dead, isn't he? You killed him, too."

Blevins grunted. "Everybody's gotta die sometime. Now it's your turn." He waved the gun menacingly. "Such a hotshot, aren't you? Commendations up the kazoo. I hate you career-jumping punks who snatch up promotions without paying your dues. Bad for morale.''

Mary could tell that Blevins was agitated now, or maybe just eager, working himself up for what he meant to do. He hated Ford and looked forward to killing him.

She quietly sank to her knees beside the hearth and lifted the corner of the sleeping bag. There it was. Perry's gun. Different from Ford's. Larger and, she imagined, heavier. Was the safety on or off? She wouldn't get a second chance to find out once she picked it up and pulled the trigger. Would it fire as easily as Ford's had or would it take more pressure?

Mary gambled that Ford would automatically put a weapon's safety on to store it. She slowly turned her body to face Blevins and clicked the switch with her finger. *Please let that be the Off position,* she prayed.

I can do this. Did it before. Can do it again. Her hand closed around the unfamiliar grip and she slid her forefinger into the trigger guard. She ran her other palm beneath the grip for support.

''Promotion?'' Ford said with a wry laugh. ''What are you talking about?''

''You were up for one, cowboy. Don't tell me you didn't know about it!'' Blevins said with a menacing chuckle. ''Well, you can kiss that goodbye!'' He raised his weapon and aimed.

Mary hefted the gun up level with her shoulders, and fired.

Blevins jerked toward her as Ford rushed him, wrecking his aim. The bullet dinged off the stones of the fireplace behind her. Another lodged in the ceiling.

Ford's head connected with the man's midsection. Blevins's next shot exploded with the impact of their bodies.

Had she hit Blevins? She didn't think so.

The two grappled for the gun. Suddenly, Ford reared up

off Blevins, drew back with his right hand and shoved it up and into the man's nose. Both men fell limp.

Mary's ears still rang from the deafening reports, and her equilibrium felt scrambled. She watched Ford reach over, scoop up Blevins's pistol and crawl away from him.

She shook off her shock and ran to Ford. "Is he—?"

"Dead," Ford affirmed. "It's over." He held his injured arm close to his chest. Mary felt him trembling all over. When she touched his face, it felt hot—too hot to be due to exertion.

"Were you hit?" she asked, running her hands over his torso and then wrapping her arms around him.

He shook his head slightly as if to clear it. "No, but I think I'm gonna fall down anyway."

Leaning on her, he staggered toward the fireplace. Together they sank down on the edge of the mattress where Perry lay unconscious.

"Check his pulse," Ford rasped, still trying to steady his breathing. "If he's dead, too, we have a large problem."

Mary grabbed Perry's arm and pressed her fingertips to his wrist, then his neck. "Steady," she reported, "but weak."

"Gotta get him some help," Ford said. He sounded really worried and he looked that way, too. "If Perry dies, there's nobody to corroborate our story. We could both be up for murder. You for Perry. And me, for my own team leader!"

"But you told Duvek!" she insisted. "He knows everything. And there's me! I can tell them what happened. Self-defense. He was trying to kill all of us!"

Ford shook his head and let out a deep breath. "Duvek knows only that I said I suspected Blevins. There's no proof. Think about it," he said. "Duvek may believe, like everybody else did, that you have the diamonds. And that I'm in cahoots with you. Stands to reason, if that were so, I'd try to throw the blame on Blevins."

He was right. "What do we do?"

"Go for help," he said decisively, "and hope to God Perry makes it. He's the only one who can clear us."

"You can't go anywhere," Mary pointed out.

"I know. You're it."

Mary hated to leave him, but she knew he was right. "To Gran's house?" she asked.

"Knoblett's is closer." He looked away from her, worry written all over him. Worry for her. "I just wish you had daylight for this."

Mary knew she had to put on a brave face, even if she was scared to death. "That's okay, I'll have Westy! He'll guide me."

"I wouldn't count on that if I were you. He takes off after a squirrel, and you could be wandering in circles till the cows come home. Bundle yourself up and get the flashlight."

After she had pulled on her warmest clothing, he struggled to his feet and ushered her to the back door. Blevins's body blocked the front. Ford hadn't the strength to move him and neither did she.

Once they were outside, Ford looked up at the sky. "There you go," he said, and pointed. "North star. Keep it directly behind you."

"You are kidding, right?"

"Yeah," he said with a short laugh, and reached into his pocket for his keychain. "Here's the compass."

The moon afforded enough light that she could almost see his features. She stepped closer. "Ford, will you be all right?"

"Just dandy," he answered softly, "but only if you give me a little mouth-to-mouth before you go."

Mary rose up on tiptoe as he bent down to settle his lips over hers. His heat frightened her more than it excited her at the moment. She wondered what percentage was fever and how much was passion.

Surely the fight with Blevins had depleted too much of

Ford's energy for him to feel anything but exhaustion and pain. She wondered how he could still stand.

"Better go," she said breathlessly as she broke the kiss. "Get back inside and lie down now. I'll be back with help before you know it."

"Mary?" he said, his voice husky. "We left a lot unsaid. I want you to know that—"

"You love me," she interrupted softly, touching his face, brushing back the hair that tumbled across his brow. "I know you do." She had no doubts left after having watched him jump between her and a bullet. A man, even one like Ford, wouldn't do that for just anyone. "I love you, too." There was no doubt about that, either.

But she still wondered how long these feelings they had for each other would last—feelings that could very well have been prompted by the danger and proximity she and Ford had shared over the past week. She and Ford were as different as two people could be, in their hopes, priorities, life-styles. How could all of that translate into anything permanent?

She no longer believed that Ford took risks unnecessarily—not the way her parents had, at any rate. He didn't thoughtlessly tempt fate just for the hell of it. He made instantaneous decisions and acted on them. Good decisions that had kept them alive these past few days. Ford was the soul of courage, and she admired him as much as she loved him. But she couldn't be enough like Ford to share a life with him. Could she?

He held her close now, leaning against her and resting his head on top of hers. His body swayed as he spoke, his voice gruff. "Glad we got that love stuff straight. Guess you know we'll have to do something about it."

"You bet," she said, trying to disengage without seeming too abrupt. "But now's not the time." She had to persuade him to go back inside before he collapsed on the cold ground. No way could she pick him up or even drag him. "Let me go now, Ford. All that's just happened might sink in in a minute if I stand still and don't do something."

He released her and raised his hand to cup her face. "Be safe, Mary," he whispered. "Please, be careful."

"Always! You know me, caution personified. See you in the morning, Ford," she replied, and hurried across the small yard and into the trees. She stopped there for a moment and turned to watch him walk haltingly back to the door of the cabin.

Leaving him when he needed her made her ill, but the sooner she got to Knoblett's and called for help, the sooner he and Perry could get to a hospital.

Mary switched on the flashlight and began the arduous trek through the tumble of downed limbs and the wet slush of melting ice and snow.

"We'll lower a body basket and a medic," the rescue pilot said to Duvek. He had to shout to be heard over the loud thumping of the blades. "Thanks for the directions, ma'am." He tipped his cap and hurried back to the med-evac helicopter.

Michael Duvek started to follow him.

"Wait for me!" Mary cried, rushing to catch up.

"No!" Duvek shouted as he came to a stop beside her. "Not enough room. They're stretching the load rule to take me."

Wind from the blades whipped their hair and buffeted their bodies. She had trouble standing firm. "But I have to—"

"Stay here!" he ordered. "That's final!"

Reluctantly Mary nodded and began wringing her hands, watching as Duvek bent over to dodge the blades and climb inside. The helicopter immediately lifted from the pasture beside Mr. Knoblett's house and veered sharply toward the pine forest where Ford and Perry would be waiting.

She said a fervent prayer that they would both recover—

Ford, because she loved him more than life, and Perry, because she couldn't bear to be responsible for his death.

She tried not to think about Ford, strapped into a cabled basket and swinging like a pendulum beneath the hovering chopper.

Mr. Knobblet approached and laid his arm across her shoulders, turning her toward his house. "Come on, Marybud, let's get you cleaned up a little."

"Which hospital? Did he say which one?" she demanded frantically, kicking herself for forgetting to ask Agent Duvek.

"Didn't say," he admitted. "But we'll sure call and find out. I'll take you into town when we do."

In the next few hours, they called every hospital in the area. And learned nothing.

Ford, Perry and the rescue squad had vanished without a trace that Monday morning. That afternoon, agents arrived, escorted her to her father's house in Nashville. And stayed.

The following Thursday, just before noon, Mary finally had the house to herself. Two agents had held her there in what they officially called "protective custody." She knew it was a ruse, and they knew she knew it. "House arrest" was more like it. Southern hospitality had worn exceedingly thin over the past few days.

Their endless questions about the past week's events and the diamonds, repeated again and again, ran around in her head like a tuneless song she couldn't banish. A very irritating song.

At least they hadn't formally arrested her, but that wasn't out of the realm of possibility even now.

She was exhausted, but more than that, she was worried. Where was Ford and *how* was he? The two agents—one of them female—who had arrived at Mr. Knoblett's less than an hour after Duvek had left, had refused to tell her a thing.

They had taken her straight to her father's house and kept her there.

Every moment they were not firing questions that sounded like accusations, they spent searching the place. On Tuesday afternoon, all of her dolls disappeared. The whole precious collection—her childhood memories in solid form, already torn apart by the first invader who had ransacked her room last week—was now gone.

Mary grieved for them, but nothing like the way she suffered over not knowing the fate of the two men she had left in the hunting cabin. She had no idea whether Perry still lived or had died of the wound she'd inflicted. He was probably alive, since they hadn't charged her with his death yet.

She didn't believe Ford's injury was life-threatening, but she kept waking from horrible nightmares about him missing his right arm. Had the doctors been forced to amputate because of her incompetence? God, she would never forgive herself—the man she loved beyond anything, handicapped because of her.

She had called the museum, found out his sister's married name and tried to phone her at home. No answer. Information gave her the number of the Memphis FBI office. Michael Duvek either wasn't there or refused to talk to her. She knew her phone was monitored. Otherwise, she wouldn't have been allowed to use it. But Mary didn't care about that. She only wanted assurance from somebody that Ford was all right and Perry was alive.

That Thursday, just before lunch, the agents had informed her that they were leaving. They also warned her that they would probably be back with more questions.

Mary had tried every way she could think of to contact Ford. Surely he would have called her by now if he had been able. He must have gotten much worse after she'd left him. Or maybe he had decided it would be best if they never saw each other again.

The doorbell rang. Mary flew to the door, hoping against hope that it would be Ford, or somebody with word of him.

"Hey, Mary," said Molly. "Want a ride to Memphis?"

Mary just stared, shocked by something going right for a change. Ford's sister had come. *Memphis.* They had taken him to Memphis.

The tall, jeans-clad redhead shifted from one sneakered foot to the other, wearing the feminine version of Ford's grin. "The bulldozer wants to see you. Rolled right over three nurses last night before a big old orderly stomped on his brakes. He was coming after you."

"You're taking me to Ford," Mary said, her relief so great, she had to lean against the doorjamb.

"Who else? Unless you've got a new fix on that delicious Perry guy. He is a hunk, isn't he? Um!"

"Is he all right?"

"Damn straight, he's all right," Molly said, waggling her brows. "A real looker. And so po-*lite!*" she said, dragging out the last word.

"Not *him!* Ford!"

Molly laughed out loud, sounding so like her brother, Mary couldn't help but join in.

"I didn't mean it that way. Ford's handsome. And he *is* polite!" Mary declared.

Molly turned around as if to leave, glancing over her shoulder and grinning. "Well, you're obviously talking about a Ford I never met." She started down the steps.

"Wait for me," Mary called. "I'll get my bag and lock up."

Ford was fine, just fine. He *must* be or Molly wouldn't be so happy. And if Damien Perry was being a "polite hunk" and impressing the daylights out of Molly, he couldn't very well be dead. Mary snatched up her purse and keys and ran. She had to see for herself.

Nurse Toney removed the blood-pressure cuff and patted Ford's arm. "Lookin' real good today, baby," she said.

Ford grimaced and pushed himself higher up in the bed. "Get me my clothes, *Mommy,* or you're gonna have a raving maniac on your hands."

"Got plenty of straitjackets," she warned with a twitch of her full red lips. "Better behave yourself."

"Come on, Toney, I've got company coming. Be a sport, huh?"

She raised one jet-black brow and picked up his chart. "I do that and you'd be outta this place next time the elevator dinged."

"I promise I won't," he pleaded. It galled him to beg, but he couldn't greet Mary wearing this half-assed hospital gown. You could read a newspaper through the front of it and there was no back. "How am I supposed to get up and hug my lady with my butt hanging out the back of this getup?"

The nurse grunted her amusement. "Hey, you got a nice butt! She won't mind. Besides, you got them cute little briefs your sister brought you." With a deep-throated giggle, she spun around on her crepe soles and departed.

"Damn!" Ford knocked his head back against the pillow. Here he was, all ready to propose to Mary when she got here, and he looked like an escapee from the mental ward. Molly had promised to have her here by four o'clock. It was a quarter to.

He ran a hand through his hair, trying to smooth it down. He had shaved early that morning and he already had stubble. How was he going to convince an uptown lady like Mary that he could be slick when he wanted to be, when he looked as if he lived under a bridge?

"Where'd I put that comb?" he mumbled, sliding off the side of the mattress to his feet.

"Under the bed where you dropped it," Perry said, drawing back the curtain between their beds and pointing.

"Thanks," Ford replied, and crouched down. He saw it. Leaning over, he reached out with his good arm.

"Hey, bro! Showing out again, I see," Molly chirped.

Ford glanced up and there she stood. *Mary.* Beautiful as ever, though she looked tired. She was also biting her lip to keep from laughing. He knew why. He looked ridiculous.

"You're looking…well," she said finally, clearing her throat. Ford quickly rose to his feet and held out his arm.

She came to him smiling, those green eyes shining. Her arms slid around his neck where they belonged, and that sweet mouth lifted to his. He acquired a new appreciation for thin hospital apparel when he felt her body nestle against his.

"Should we be taping this, Agent Perry?" Ford heard Molly ask the man in the other bed. "Duvek would love it."

"We shouldn't even be *seeing* this, Ms. Jensen. Shall we take a stroll down the hall?"

"Great. I'll buy you coffee."

Perry grunted. "Don't dissuade me before I get started."

Ford continued kissing Mary, purposefully ignoring the rustle of Perry's sheets and his slow progress to the door. The moment he heard it close, he broke the kiss with an exaggerated sigh. "I thought they'd never leave! Will you marry me?"

Mary backed up a step. She looked away from him. "An affair, maybe. And you can live with me at Gran's since you like the place so much—"

"That's a yes!" he declared, and kissed her again. "I am serious, Mary," he said sincerely, grasping her chin in his hand and urging her to look into his eyes. She had to believe him this time. "I love you. I *do.* I want to marry you, have babies, get gray, the whole nine yards."

"I love you, too, but—"

Oh, Lord, she was going to cry. He'd always hated it when women did that. But anything Mary did was fine by him. If anything made her cry, he would just change, destroy or fix it.

"A bad word, *but.* Mom used to spank me when I said

it. Are those happy tears?'' He wiped one away with his thumb.

"I wish,'' she said, and pulled away from him completely. He watched her cross her arms over her chest, hugging herself. She shouldn't have to do that when he wanted nothing more than to hold her for the rest of his life.

She leaned back against the side of Perry's bed and held up a hand when he would have approached her. "Molly says your arm will be okay,'' she said, distancing herself. But why?

This was not going well, Ford decided. "The arm's fine. The doc said that bark tea might have helped. The fever, anyway.''

"Why didn't you let me know something, Ford?'' she asked. "I tried everything I could think of to find out how you were! How Perry was. Nobody would tell me anything. Those agents kept—''

"Duvek ordered me not to call you. He was checking our stories to see if they coincided, still trying to locate the diamonds, picking up your erstwhile fiancé, and generally making me miserable.''

"What about Perry?'' she asked.

"He had a little surgery and was pretty much out of it until yesterday morning when they finally debriefed him. Soon as I got the green light for outside contact, I phoned Molly to get you here as fast as she could. I would have called you then, but—''

She looked up at him, not smiling now. "You were afraid I wouldn't come.''

He nodded. Mary had just said she loved him and was willing to live with him. She might even marry him eventually, if he kept insisting, but she wasn't all that happy with the idea.

Suddenly Ford realized what the problem must be. She had gotten an up-close-and-personal view of what his job was like. It hadn't been a pretty picture, either. Nan had left him with less cause. She had only *heard* about the danger involved when he was a military intelligence agent, and even that had been a severely edited version. He couldn't afford to change careers again. But he would, if that was what it took. "Mary, what's the holdup? Is it my work?"

She sniffed. "No. I know every case isn't like what we went through. It's not that at all."

Relieved by that, he stepped closer, brushed his hand down her arm and laced his fingers through hers. "Then tell me."

"What if it doesn't last? What if you only love me now because of what we went through together? We stayed so keyed up for that whole week!" She threw up her hands and shook her head. "What happens when it's just day-to-day living? Buying groceries, shopping for towels, that sort of thing? Can we survive it?"

"Don't you worry about that," Ford said, tapping her nose with one finger. "You and I can make a happening out of just about *anything*."

"That's just it, Ford," she told him, her voice growing bolder, louder. "Maybe I don't always crave just thrills."

"Couldn't prove that from all I've heard," said a deep voice from the doorway. *Duvek.*

Ford turned and stood tall. "Sir!"

Duvek strolled into the room and braced his fists against the footrail of Ford's bed.

The man looked like a huge cat built for hunting, Ford thought. The laid-back attitude deceived some people. That lazy growl of his could jump to a roar in a heartbeat. But Duvek almost never lost his cool.

He had taken Ford's report. Didn't like it, but he hadn't said much so far. It looked as though that was what he had come for now. Analysis was over. Time for the evaluation. As desperately as he'd wanted her here, Ford now wished Mary were somewhere else.

"The doctor says you can go home. I've authorized four

weeks' medical leave. After that, you're on suspension for a month.''

Ford nodded once. He clenched his jaw and remained silent.

"And just why is that?" Mary demanded, irate, and on his behalf. Ford barely stifled his smile of satisfaction. A reprimand was nothing. This was worth getting fired.

"You, of all people, should know why!" Duvek accused, turning his glare on her. "You might not be familiar with the regulations governing our agents, Ms. Shaw, but I would bet my badge you knew that you two weren't supposed to get...personally involved."

Mary drew up to her full height. Not a great height, Ford admitted, but the effect was very impressive.

"That is none of your business!" She glanced at Ford and added a belated and pretty sarcastic, *"Sir!"*

Duvek straightened, fists clenched as he propped them on his hips. Then came his roar. "The fool broke every rule in the book! What do you expect me to do? Let my agents throw women over their shoulders and haul them out of their places of employment like...like sacks of meal? And then, to top it all off—"

"He was only doing his job!" Mary shouted. Boy, she could make a racket when she wanted to. Ford silently urged her on, looking back and forth between her and Duvek while he wore what he hoped was his "innocent" face. He wouldn't jump in there and break this up if he never worked another day in his life. *Go, Mary!*

Duvek looked livid. "Well, he won't be doing that job for the next two months! And you're no better than he is. You both took chances that set my teeth on edge, just hearing about them! Yes, he told me. And Perry added his two cents' worth, as well. Thought he was out cold, didn't you? That man has sense. When he knew *he* couldn't help, he stayed out of the way. That's exactly what you should have done instead of playing Annie Oakley. Civilians should not—''

Mary marched forward and poked Duvek right in the chest with her finger. "You might be Ford's supervisor, Mr. High-and-Mighty, but you're definitely not mine! Whatever I decide to do is no—"

Ford quickly abandoned neutrality in favor of prudence. He grasped her around the waist and hauled her backward, surprising her into silence.

Duvek blew out a pained breath and rolled his eyes. "Will you just get dressed and get out of here, Devereaux?" He threw up one hand. "Take her to…Hawaii or someplace!"

"Hawaii, sir?" Ford relaxed his grip on Mary and stepped around her. "What in the world for?"

"Hell, I don't know. It's a good place for R&R," Duvek said, making a dismissive motion with his hand as he turned to leave. "If you can't stand to take it easy and get well there, then climb a damned volcano or something. I'm sure she'd *love* that!"

He reached into his inside pocket, retrieved an envelope and slapped it down on the bed. "Your bonus. Promotion's effective in January."

Then he inclined his head toward Mary while looking at Ford. "Somebody ought to marry that woman. She needs a keeper."

"Yes, sir," Ford agreed, staring down at the envelope. "Thank you." But Duvek had already gone.

Ford's smile grew as he looked down at Mary. "You heard that. Orders from headquarters! Marriage, it is."

Mary was holding her head between her hands as though she couldn't believe what she had done. "He just said 'somebody.'"

Ford shrugged. "Well, he meant *me*."

"Okay." She looked up at him, her eyes wide with anticipation. There was maybe a little fear there, too, but he'd fix that.

He reached out and pulled her close for a simple kiss

that turned wild and left them both gasping. "Will you take a chance with me, then?"

She nodded, grinned and peeped over his shoulder. "Does that door have a lock?"

His eyebrows flew up. "Why, Mary, Mary, are we about to have us an adventure?"

"Right here in River City," she said, reaching for the hem of his gown. "This can tide me over until we get to the volcano."

Epilogue

"This has been the longest two weeks of my life," Ford grumbled. "We could have been lying on a beach in Maui all this time, already married." He waltzed her around the ballroom at Gran's house in their first dance together as man and wife.

Mary tilted her head and smiled. He'd certainly appreciate her eagerness more if he knew how hard she had worked to plan a wedding in so short a time.

She wore her mother's elaborate wedding gown that Gran had carefully packed away all those years ago. Thelma Knoblett had helped make the cake, Lucy was taking wedding photos with a borrowed camera, and Molly operated the stereo system. Mary figured she must have bought up every potted poinsettia within a hundred-mile radius. This wedding might not qualify as the event of the season by society's standards, but at least their friends, family, and her students were sharing their joy.

"We still have Hawaii to look forward to," she told Ford. "Surely you don't begrudge me a little tradition?"

"I would never begrudge you anything," he said, brushing a kiss on her cheek. "I'm just impatient, and I *hate* wearing a monkey suit. You look fantastic, by the way," he added.

"You do, too." He did. But she was just as eager as he was to get him out of that tuxedo. "Oh, look, Mr. Knoblett's dancing with your mom. She is so sweet, Ford."

Ford laughed. "'Sweet'? Mom would love hearing *that*."

Mary watched others join the dance. But one man stood alone and unsmiling, cradling a flute of champagne. "Duvek looks more surly than usual. What's his problem?"

Ford's smile faltered. "Lives for his job, that's all. The mess with Blevins left two of his pet projects dangling. Somebody was running an employment agency using our suspects files for reference. You know—the way Blevins found safe crackers for the thefts, the couriers, and Perry for the hit on us. Could have been Blevins's brainchild from the get-go. Probably was, but Duvek can't be sure of that, now that Blevins is dead.

"And, of course, there are the missing diamonds," Ford continued as he pressed her closer for an intricate turn. "Duvek feels responsible that they disappeared while we were using them in the investigation."

"Ah. Will they take it out of his paycheck?" Mary asked, faking a hopeful look. Her anger at Duvek hadn't abated yet.

"He should live so long! Do you have any idea what we public servants make?"

"More than preschool teachers, I'll bet. I *hope*."

"Don't you worry, hon. You and I are the richest people in the world. What we have is priceless." He kissed her soundly and released her as the music stopped.

The mother of Sarah, one of her students, approached them as they arrived at the punch table. "You two look so happy," she said. "Such a beautiful wedding. And very Christmassy!"

"Thank you, Mrs. Claire," Mary responded, noticing the three-year-old standing by, clutching her ever-present blanket.

"Yours," Sarah said, shoving the wadded bundle into Mary's hands.

"But you already gave us a gift, Sarah," Mary told her. "A pretty vase. I love it."

Michelle Claire smiled down at her daughter as she spoke to Mary. "Sarah brought a couple of your dolls home with her on the Monday after the Friday you left. They were wrapped in her blanket and I didn't notice them until bedtime. They're so old, I knew they must be part of your collection. I tried to call you."

And she had been gone. Mary felt the small, solid forms within the fuzzy bundle. She knelt beside the little girl and unwrapped them. "You took these out of my purse, Sarah?"

"You missed share time 'cause *he* made you go with him." Sarah shot Ford a dark look of reprimand. "So Libby and me got 'em. We showed and told for you 'cause Miss Lucy was too busy. You didn't come back," she said.

The dolls *had* been there at the school that night, in Sarah's cubby, safely wrapped. Mary could imagine her two little helpers taking over after she had left. They eagerly awaited the surprises she brought each day in her tote bag. "Thank you, Sarah," she said to the child.

Ford crouched down beside Mary and took the dolls, handing them back to Sarah. "Take these and give them to that ol' frowny-faced man by the punch bowl. Tell him where you got 'em, and I'll bet you a cookie you can make him smile."

Mary laughed and nodded encouragement to the little curly-top.

"Which reminds me…" Ford added, taking Mary's arm to help her stand. "Come upstairs, and I'll bet you a cookie I can make *you* smile."

Ignoring her laughing protests about leaving the reception early, Ford rushed Mary up the stairs to her old room.

"A treasure for my treasure," he quipped as he gave her a beautifully wrapped gift about the size of a shoe box. "I thought about waiting until Christmas, but— Well, go ahead, open it!"

Mary tore the wrappings away and lifted the lid. "Ruthie!" she exclaimed. "Oh, Ford, you fixed Ruthie!" She laid the box aside and threw her arms around his neck, kissing his face all over until she landed on his mouth. "Oh, you are *so* wonderful. It's the best, the greatest gift I could imagine!"

He grinned. "Well, Mom knew about this doll hospital. Ruthie's little friends are still recuperating."

"All of them?" Mary asked in a hushed voice.

"Mom said most of them will make it. Now it's your turn."

Mary sighed. "I couldn't top this present, no matter how hard I tried."

"Bet you can. Never one to be subtle, I'll drop a very large hint. Okay?"

She snuggled against him, loving the way they fit together. "Fine. What would you like? Anything at all, because I love you more than chocolate."

"I want a doll, too. A Betsy Wetsy. One around, oh, say, twenty inches long. Dark hair, please. A costume's not necessary. I'll dress her myself. Next year's model. I don't care for antiques." He pressed his palm against her middle and patted.

Mary nudged him, laughing. "I was saving that for a surprise! How did you guess?"

He slid his hands up to cup her breasts, which had filled out considerably in the past month. "Brilliant investigative techniques."

*　*　*　*　*

SILHOUETTE® SENSATION™

AVAILABLE FROM 17TH JANUARY 2003

SMOOTH-TALKING TEXAN Candace Camp

Lawyer Lisa Mendoza didn't plan to get involved with infuriatingly irresistible Sheriff Quinn Sutton. But was the biggest case of her career enough to distract her from this strong, sexy lawman?

THE PRINCESS AND THE MERCENARY
Marilyn Pappano

Romancing the Crown

Tyler Ramsey thought his mission was to find Montebello's missing crown prince, not guard Princess Anna Sebastiani. But then he realised his biggest challenge would be fighting the explosive passion between them…

MIRANDA'S VIKING Maggie Shayne

Viking warrior Rolf Magnusson had been frozen for centuries when scientist Miranda O'Shea found him in a glacial cave and revived him. His body was hot to the touch, but could she thaw his ice-cold heart?

SMALL-TOWN SECRETS Linda Randall Wisdom

Detective Bree Fitzpatrick was unprepared for the dark mystery in the town where she wanted to raise her children. But handsome reporter Cole Becker was determined to help her find the truth—and a second chance at love…

TO WED AND PROTECT Carla Cassidy

The Delaney Heirs

Sexy Luke Delaney was coming to terms with his past—until he met single mother Abby Graham running for her life. Luke wanted to wed and protect her, but could she ask him to put his life on the line?

THE VALENTINE TWO-STEP RaeAnne Thayne

Outlaw Hartes

City vet Ellie Webster didn't care if rugged rancher Matt was reluctant to plan the Valentine's Day dance with her. It wasn't as though she *wanted* to keep imagining what it would be like to be his partner—for real…

AVAILABLE FROM 17TH JANUARY 2003

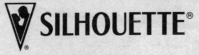

SILHOUETTE®

Intrigue™

Danger, deception and suspense

FROM THE SHADOWS Rebecca York
BEHIND THE VEIL Joanna Wayne
SULLIVAN'S LAST STAND Harper Allen
HIS WITNESS, HER CHILD Ann Voss Peterson

Special Edition™

Vivid, satisfying romances full of family, life and love

LILY AND THE LAWMAN Marie Ferrarella
WRANGLING THE REDHEAD Sherryl Woods
MARKED FOR MARRIAGE Jackie Merritt
HANDPRINTS Myrna Temte
MATCH MADE IN WYOMING Patricia McLinn
HER SISTER'S SECRET SON Lisette Belisle

Superromance™

*Enjoy the drama, explore the emotions,
experience the relationship*

MAN WITH A MISSION Muriel Jensen
THE DAUGHTER MERGER Janice Kay Johnson
MATT'S FAMILY Lynnette Kent
A RANGER'S WIFE Lyn Ellis

Desire™ 2 in 1

Two intense, sensual love stories in one volume

TALL DARK & ROYAL Leanne Banks
MATERNALLY YOURS Kathie DeNosky

MR TEMPTATION Cait London
PLAIN JANE'S TEXAN Jan Hudson

SINGLE FATHER SEEKS... Amy J Fetzer
ONE WEDDING NIGHT Shirley Rogers

0103/18b

Cordina's Royal Family

NORA ROBERTS

New York Times bestselling author of
Night Tales and *Night Moves*

Available from 21st February 2003

Available at most branches of WH Smith,
Tesco, Martins, Borders, Eason, Sainsbury's
and most good paperback bookshops.

books and a surprise gift!

We would like to take this opportunity to thank you for reading this Silhouette® book by offering you the chance to take TWO more specially selected titles from the Sensation™ series absolutely FREE! We're also making this offer to introduce you to the benefits of the Reader Service™—

- ★ FREE home delivery
- ★ FREE gifts and competitions
- ★ FREE monthly Newsletter
- ★ Exclusive Reader Service discount
- ★ Books available before they're in the shops

Accepting these FREE books and gift places you under no obligation to buy, you may cancel at any time, even after receiving your free shipment. Simply complete your details below and return the entire page to the address below. ***You don't even need a stamp!***

YES! Please send me 2 free Sensation books and a surprise gift. I understand that unless you hear from me, I will receive 4 superb new titles every month for just £2.85 each, postage and packing free. I am under no obligation to purchase any books and may cancel my subscription at any time. The free books and gift will be mine to keep in any case.

S3ZEA

Ms/Mrs/Miss/Mr ....Initials...................................
BLOCK CAPITALS PLEASE

Surname ....

Address ....

....

....Postcode...............................

Send this whole page to:
UK: FREEPOST CN81, Croydon, CR9 3WZ
EIRE: PO Box 4546, Kilcock, County Kildare (stamp required)